Warship

Book One of the Black Fleet Trilogy

Joshua Dalzelle

*****

Edited by Monique Happy Editorial Services

www.moniquehappy.com

Chapter 1

Year: 2423

"Captain Wolfe, the admiral will see you now, sir."

Jackson Wolfe nodded politely to the NCO manning the desk in the reception area, stood up and smoothed out his dress blacks, and strode purposefully towards the open door that led to Admiral Winters' office. He walked in and stopped three paces in front of the desk, coming to attention as Alyson Winters pointedly ignored him.

Nonplussed, Jackson held his rigid stance as the admiral made a show of fishing around on her desk for a stylus as she continued to work on her tablet computer, a device colloquially called a "tile" by everyone in the Fleet due to the branding of an electronics company that no longer even existed. Three minutes later and he knew this was not the usual games higher-ranking officers played with those of lower rank to remind them of their place. This was a deliberate insult. He took it doubly so since Admiral Winters obviously thought him so dense that he needed nearly five minutes for the lesson to sink in. She set the tile down with a clatter and looked up at him, seeming to notice him for the first time, and held him with an icy stare for another half a minute.

"At ease, Captain," she said. Jackson shifted to a loose parade rest, his eyes flicking momentarily to one of the two chairs in front of her desk. But he hadn't been offered a seat, so he remained standing. "Do you know why I called you here today?"

"I would not presume to know, Admiral," Jackson said. He offered nothing more as he was more than used to these little games. At first he had thought it due to petty jealousy over the manner in which he had attained his rank. In recent years he had come to realize that it was something much more vile.

"The *Blue Jacket* has passed her inspections—*barely*—and I've called you here because I've narrowed the list of potential executive officers down for you," Admiral Winters said. "I thought it would be a good idea to discuss them with you in person."

"Potential execs?" Jackson asked, clearly confused. "I'm afraid I don't understand, Admiral."

"Didn't Commander Stevenson tell you?" Winters asked, taking obvious pleasure in the moment. "I approved his transfer to Fourth Fleet yesterday. He will be departing with a supply convoy to his new assignment."

Jackson was seething. It was all he could do to not let his countenance crack in front of the admiral. "The commander must have been too busy to come inform me personally," he said neutrally. "I'm certain there's a message in my inbox I've yet to read."

"Of course," Winters said with disappointment. She'd been watching him closely and obviously hoping for some sort of outburst. "The short list is down to three candidates. Honestly, Captain, you're lucky to even get that many. Not too many qualified execs wanting destroyer duty and fewer want to take an assignment in Seventh Fleet."

"Understandable, Admiral," Jackson said, unflappable. "We are away from ports of call for many months and cruises last over a year. It can be tough on those spacers who aren't mentally tough enough for it."

"Yes," Winters said in a deadpan voice. "I'm sure that must be it. Anyway, please take the seat to your right, Captain, and we'll review these personnel records. Let's try to move this along as quickly as we can, I have a reception down on the surface in two hours."

It took less than thirty minutes to realize that the list really only contained one name. One candidate that Admiral Winters had handpicked out of a list and was adamant about putting on his ship. Reading through the fitness reports in the personnel file, Jackson couldn't figure out why. He was used to getting stuck with less than stellar performing officers and enlisted spacers, but this person didn't seem to fit that description. If he didn't know any better, he would think he was finally catching a break and that his ship would have a motivated, competent executive officer for their next cruise. After seeing the oily smile Admiral Winters gave him when he agreed to her recommendation, however, he told himself that he was being wildly optimistic.

****

After leaving Admiral Winters' office, Jackson walked aimlessly along the curved, outer walkway of Central Command's orbiting fortress: Jericho Station. The complex was the central hub for all fleet operations and was a dizzying array of access tubes, docks for starships, and compartments that housed all the people of CENTCOM who made the day-to-day decisions that affected the lives of people like Jackson. He paused on the walkway, leaning against the railing and looking though the curved acrylic of the access tube at the spinning planet below. Haven, located in the Alpha Centauri system, was one of the first planets colonized by humans once they'd begun to leave Earth and still where most of the real power in human space was concentrated.

The planet below him blurred as he shifted his focus on his own reflection, looking at the features that seemed to so disgust his fellow officers. He was of average height and build, a little on the lean side from a poor diet and an obsession with running, among other things. His olive skin, dark eyes, and jet black hair made it fairly obvious that he was from Earth, however. The muted racial traits, typical of someone who had been born on Earth, also made it difficult to determine his age at first glance, as he looked at least ten years younger than his forty-one years.

For generations the upper ten percent of humanity had been skimmed off the top of Earth's population and sent into space, the best and brightest loaded up on starships and sent to colonize all the newly discovered worlds. They gladly left behind an overcrowded, polluted, and largely dysfunctional Earth. After a couple hundred years of this exodus, Earth became little more than a slum in the eyes of most people. Those that were born there faced an uphill battle for recognition. It was a battle most did not win.

Jackson sighed and continued on his walk. It wasn't often he was consciously aware of the enormous chip on his shoulder, but his meeting with Admiral Winters had brought a lot of the bitterness and anger to the forefront. Even as he walked he felt like he could hear the unspoken thoughts of those he passed.

"Charity case."

"Token."

"Earther."

He aborted his plan to speak with the dock master about the status of his ship and took the next transfer tube that led back to billeting. All he wanted to do was make it back to his quarters without speaking to anyone. He also knew that his escape was tucked safely in his spacebag, waiting for him. Although he had managed to stay away from it while his destroyer was in dock for maintenance and inspections, the events of the day had crumbled his resolve.

Chapter 2

The next morning Jackson walked along the access tube that led down to the docking complex, instantly picking his ship out of the other dozen moored there. The *Blue Jacket* had been moved from the fully enclosed maintenance dock to the open anchor point sometime during the previous day. He would take the tender out later and do a full inspection of the hull once he made a thorough inspection of the engineering spaces and anywhere else the CENTCOM crews had been during their work.

He paused along the walkway and took in the rare sight. It wasn't very often he could gaze at his ship from stem to stern, as he was usually either inside her hull or in a cramped shuttle craft. The *Raptor*-class destroyers were similar in construction to most of the other warships humans fielded. The hull was roughly cigar-shaped, though flattened to provide a narrower side profile and a wider top and bottom to mount the super structure and the mag-cannon turrets. The main engines, four third-generation magneto-plasma drive pods (commonly called MPDs), were mounted near the aft of the ship. They were oriented so that their pylons made an "X" when viewing the ship head-on. Even though the ship was a destroyer class vessel it dwarfed the largest aircraft carriers from twenty-first century Earth's ocean-going navies, displacing seven hundred thousand tons and having a length of just under six hundred meters.

Jackson glanced at his comlink to check the local time and continued down the walkway to the security check point that would lead him out to the docking arms. After a perfunctory check of his ID and bioscan he was cleared through the gate with a sloppy salute from the bored looking Marine sentry. He let the mildly disrespectful gesture slide and made his way over to the moving walkway that would take him the remaining two kilometers to his ship. He stepped on the blinking circle and waited as the walkway calculated his weight and his destination before accelerating away. The material on the floor was able to move passengers at various speeds and accelerations simultaneously. Jackson gave a short chuckle as he realized that the system was one of the more advanced bits of technology on Jericho Station.

The circle he was standing in began to slow and drift over to the left side of the walkway, eventually stopping near the large archway which had a digital banner over it that said "*TCS Blue Jacket*, DS-701." He stepped off the walkway and towards the gangway arch, waiting for the sentries to notice him.

"Captain Wolfe," the Marine said crisply, coming to attention and saluting. Jackson returned the salute and hefted his spacebag up on the table so it could go through the scanner. Even an admiral on a fleet carrier had to submit to the same security procedures before boarding a starship as a lowly spacer apprentice. He stepped through the scanning portal, waiting for the sentry to give him the go-ahead before walking though.

"All clear, Captain," the Marine said. "I'll have your bag taken to your quarters, sir."

"Thanks, Marine," Jackson said with a nod. He walked up the main gangway slowly, looking at the hull of his ship through the transparent tube walls. This close he could see the deep pits and scarring in the alloy from years of micrometeor impacts while gliding though the void. As he approached the main hatch he could also see that the skeleton crew still aboard were maneuvering the pallets of material they'd taken on.

"*Blue Jacket*, arriving," the ship's computer automatically called over the shipwide intercom as Jackson stepped over the threshold of the hatch and into the port cargo bay. At the announcement several of the spacers working in the hold stopped and turned to him, rendering honors.

"As you were," Jackson called out, returning their salute as he walked to the hatch on the aft bulkhead that would take him to the lifts. He fully intended to make a complete inspection of the ship as soon as he could, but he would rather his chief engineer accompany him when he did. Instead, he decided to go to the bridge and look over the diagnostic data from there. He preferred to look over the reports in peace while the *Blue Jacket* was still running with a skeleton crew. The rest of his spacers weren't due to board for another five hours.

He keyed the lift and rode the magnetically powered car up to deck fifteen, the last deck within the main hull of the ship. From there he had to walk another twenty meters to a different set of lifts that would take him up into the superstructure, the tower affixed to the dorsal surface of the hull that contained the main bridge and a handful of other critical departments. Jackson had never understood why the bridge wasn't buried deeper in the ship, but even after a dozen generations of starships human builders still seemed to draw a direct line of comparison between ancient seagoing vessels and those that would spend their entire lives in a vacuum.

"Captain on the bridge!" the Marine sentry called out from the large archway that led onto the main bridge. Jackson heard the commotion of people clambering out of seats and snapping to attention before he cleared the threshold of the arch.

"As you were," he said. "Officer of the watch, has Jericho released the maintenance files for the *Blue Jacket*?"

"Yes, sir," the young ensign standing at the operations station said.

"Send them to my office," Jackson said. "I'll be expecting my new exec within the hour. Send them directly to me."

"Aye, sir," the ensign said hesitantly. "What happened to Commander Stevenson?"

"Greener pastures, Ensign, greener pastures," Jackson said. "Carry on. Don't forget to send the new XO to my office."

He walked off the bridge and down the curving passageway to the hatch marked with his name and rank. His office was just off the bridge and within sight of the Marines who were on sentry duty. The office was a sanctuary where he could try and keep on top of the unholy amount of administrative work that went along with commanding a starship. The sad truth was that because of a series of somewhat unreliable, or unwilling, executive officers there were some cruises when he only slept in his quarters a handful of times. Instead, he would end up sleeping on the sofa in his office as he tried to keep on top of the workload. Procrastination wasn't an option since when the ship came back into port CENTCOM wanted the logs and files from the cruise before the ship was even towed back into her berth.

Jackson was skimming through the reports on the work done to his ship when there was a single knock on his hatch.

"Enter!"

The hatch slid open at his command and a petite brunette woman in pristine dress blacks walked into the office. She stopped right in front of his desk and snapped a crisp salute, staring at a spot just over his head.

"Commander Celesta Wright, reporting as ordered," she said sharply, holding her salute.

Jackson had no tolerance for the silly games officers played such as making subordinates stand at attention while being stared down. He paused long enough to look the officer over, noting her impeccable military bearing and impressive rack of service ribbons over her left breast.

"At ease, Commander," Jackson said. "Have a seat."

"Thank you, sir," she said, sliding gracefully into one of the chairs in front of his desk, her back still ramrod straight.

"Britannia?"

"Excuse me, sir?" she asked, confused.

"From your accent I'm assuming you're from Britannia," Jackson clarified. He already knew almost everything about her from the personnel file Admiral Winters had provided, but getting to know a new second in command just before a cruise was more than just learning a list of facts impersonally entered into a file.

"Yes, sir," she said. "Daven, to be specific."

"I've heard it's a lovely planet," Jackson said perfunctorily. "So rather than tiptoe around the obvious here I'll get right to it ... why aren't you flying with First Fleet anymore?"

Commander Wright squirmed uncomfortably at the direct question, her polished façade cracking just a bit. "Permission to speak freely, sir?"

"By all means," Jackson said, gesturing with his hand for her to continue.

"First Fleet is a top notch organization," she said, "the best of the best. But making rank is exceedingly difficult. The average age for a captain is sixty-five and the entire fleet is rank heavy. As a commander I was still only fifth in line for command on the cruiser I last served on. If I wanted a shot at a ship of my own someday I knew I needed to transfer."

"Why not Fourth Fleet?" Jackson asked. "Or even the Fifth?"

"I applied to Fourth Fleet," she admitted. "I did not bother with Fifth Fleet since the New European Commonwealth has a notorious dislike of anyone from Britannia. Even if I had been accepted I do not think I would have enjoyed my time there. It seemed Bla—Seventh Fleet was the only logical choice. Sir."

"You can say it, Commander," Jackson said with a humorless chuckle. "Black Fleet wasn't always a pejorative term. I'm assuming you know the full history of the Terran Confederate Starfleet?"

"Of course, sir," she said.

"Indulge me."

"When the Republic was first reorganized as the Terran Confederacy it still fielded a fleet that was based entirely out of Haven," she began, looking slightly annoyed at being made to recite ancient history she'd learned before even applying to the Academy. "The fleet was originally divided into taskforces, but it became too large to realistically manage and was then divided into numbered fleets similar to what we have today. Some decades later the logistics of supporting all the fleets while they served all the individual Terran enclaves became too much and they were formally assigned to their patrol areas permanently and the responsibility for maintaining each fleet fell to each enclave rather than the Confederacy."

"A fairly straightforward answer I would expect on a first year cadet's entrance exam," Jackson said, watching Commander Wright bristle. "You failed to mention that the Seventh Fleet stayed assigned to Haven and was tasked with patrolling the deep space lanes between all the human worlds, often being sent on cruises longer than a year, isolated and cut-off. The nickname Black Fleet came about because of those deep space missions, not for what it's become. It used to be a name that the spacers of Seventh Fleet wore with pride."

"Sir, I didn't mean to imply that Black Fleet was an undesirable assignment," Commander Wright said, suddenly understanding what her mistake had been.

"I am not stupid, Commander," Jackson said, perhaps more harshly than he intended. "For the last thirty years Black Fleet has been where CENTCOM has allowed the other fleets to dump their discipline problems and otherwise undesirable officers and enlisted spacers until their contracts run out. Even the fleet itself isn't exactly on the leading edge. Take this ship, for example. This destroyer was state of the art ... forty-five years ago. While we're here on Jericho trying to patch new sensors into a forty-year-old MUX, New America is getting ready to deploy a destroyer into the Fourth Fleet that is faster, better armed, and better armored than the single remaining Black Fleet battleship."

"Sir," Celesta began slowly, "I'm not sure I understand where you're going with this."

"My point is this, Commander," Jackson said. "While I appreciate ambition and I respect drive, do not think that Black Fleet is a place where you will walk in and step on the heads of all the scrubs on your way to commanding your own ship. I expect you to perform the job of Executive Officer to the best of your ability. I expect you to carry out your duty without the distraction of you looking for the opportunity to leapfrog into a ship of your own. Am I clear?"

"Crystal clear, sir," she said stiffly. "If I may be so bold, sir, isn't just such a scenario how you came to be in command of this ship?"

"I am well aware of the rumors regarding my promotion, Commander," Jackson said, his face flushing as he fought to control the momentary flash of anger. "Whatever did, or did not, happen during that mission does not change the current situation. I can only imagine the things that are said of the uppity Earther who lucked into command of a worn-out destroyer in a squadron that eats officers and craps out dead careers. To be honest, I couldn't care less. I hope for your sake that you haven't taken an assignment on this ship because you think that my chair is up for grabs."

"Of course not, sir," Celesta said quickly, looking as if she regretted her last comment. "I meant no disrespect, sir."

"I'm sure you didn't," Jackson said calmly. "I would just prefer us to start our working relationship with no misunderstandings. I've read your fitness reports and, to be honest, I'm fairly impressed. You'll be a great asset to this ship if you can fully dedicate yourself to her. This is a good crew. They're a little rough around the edges but a solid group of spacers nonetheless. Get to know them, earn their respect, and I promise you you'll get your shot at a command of your own ... but you have to earn it. Do you have any questions for me?"

"Just one, sir," she said. "I tried to research this myself but the public net on Daven had conflicting information on the reference. Why is this ship called the *Blue Jacket*?"

Jackson leaned back, considering her question.

"The fact I command this particular ship is a bit of serendipity," he said with a genuine smile. "All the destroyers in Ninth Squadron were named after Native American war chiefs. *Blue Jacket* was the war chief of the Shawnee, an ancient tribe that used to inhabit the area where I grew up."

"So you weren't just born on Earth," she said. "You grew up there as well?"

"Yes," Jackson said. "I was born in the North American Union in a smog-choked city on the Ohio River and lived there until earning a slot to the Academy. Anyway, there are four ships in total in this squadron: *Blue Jacket*, *Crazy Horse*, *Pontiac*, and *Black Hawk*. There were two others but they were decommissioned years ago and never replaced."

"Fascinating," Celesta said, seeming to genuinely mean it. "Is there any information I could read on the subject?"

"I have some books that I will send to your comlink," Jackson said. "In the meantime, we'll come up with a duty schedule to maximize our coverage and effectiveness. I don't expect you to simply fill the space Commander Stevenson previously occupied, I want you to figure out how you'll be most effective. The crew won't begin showing up for another few hours and we're not scheduled to depart for another week or so after that. I'd like you to accompany me and the chief engineer on our walk-through."

"Of course, sir," she said. "It would be an excellent opportunity to meet much of the crew."

"That's the idea," Jackson said. "Go ahead and get settled in your quarters and I'll contact you when we're ready to begin. Welcome aboard." At his last statement he reached across his desk and offered her his hand. She rose out of her seat to shake it before standing up and offering another salute.

"I'm happy to be here, sir," she said.

"Dismissed, Commander," Jackson said, picking up his tile as she opened the hatch and walked out of his office. He stared at the hatch for a moment after it closed, still unsure how he felt about his new exec. Despite her qualifications he couldn't help but feel there was a bull's-eye on his back. The fact that Admiral Winters, not one of his biggest fans, had enthusiastically pushed her candidacy didn't do much to dispel the feeling.

Chapter 3

"Captain on the bridge!"

"As you were," Jackson said with a dismissive wave. He climbed up into the raised command chair and began navigating through menus on the display attached to the left armrest. "Ensign Davis, what is the crew status?"

"All crew accounted for, seven still not aboard," the short, shapely operations officer reported, consulting her display. "Those seven are being brought to the ship by local law enforcement. A ship's officer will need to meet them at the gangway to secure their release."

"XO to the bridge," Jackson said loudly. The computer would automatically ping Commander Wright's comlink and inform her she needed to report to the captain on the bridge. "OPS, tell the Marines at the main gangway that the new exec will be down shortly to deal with the locals."

"Aye, sir," Ensign Davis said, speaking into her headset.

It was a few minutes later when an only slightly winded Celesta Wright strode onto the bridge. "You needed to see me, Captain?"

Jackson looked over and noticed that she was still in her dress blacks, and obviously not the same set that she had reported onto the ship in as evident by the razor-sharp creases.

"Yes," he said. "We have seven crewmembers who had a little too much fun on their shore leave down on Haven. Local LEOs are escorting them to the gangway now. I want you to meet them there, secure their release, and then review the case files to determine punishment."

"You want me to do that, sir?" she asked after a moment of hesitation.

"Is there some problem, Commander?" Jackson asked, his voice neutral.

"No, sir. I just assumed you'd have wanted to review the case files yourself as I am unfamiliar with ship's personnel."

"Commander, you are in charge of junior personnel matters, including the enlisted ranks," Jackson said softly, not wanting to dress his new exec down in front of the crew. "You'll need to figure out how best to integrate yourself into the crew. Either way, it looks like you'll be meeting these seven first."

"Yes, sir," she said quietly, but strongly. "Is there anything else, sir?"

"Just one," Jackson said. "Uniform of the day is utilities unless otherwise stated. This is still a combat ship despite the fact that there hasn't been a war in over two hundred and fifty years."

"Yes, sir."

"Go get our people," he said as a dismissal. "Don't let the locals give you any shit either. Other than apprehension and detention they have no authority over Fleet personnel."

He watched her leave the bridge, glad to pawn some of the administrative actions off on her. His former exec had become so chummy with all the crew that it became almost impossible for him to enforce discipline. It fell to Jackson to come down hard on all the department heads to keep their people in line, a move that made him even less popular among the other officers ... if that was even possible.

"Captain," Ensign Davis said, snapping him out of his reverie.

"Go ahead, Ensign," he said.

"Boarding hatch sentries are telling me there is a group from CENTCOM on their way up," she said apologetically. "They had all the proper authorization to board the ship."

"Very well," Jackson sighed. He hadn't even gotten everyone back on the ship and resumed normal watch schedules and some desk jockey from CENTCOM was no doubt on their way up to make some absurd request that would do nothing but slow him down in trying to get the ship through her shakedown and underway. He also had no doubt which admiral's signature he would find at the bottom of the orders.

It was twenty minutes later when he heard some discussion at the bridge entrance as the group of visitors negotiated with the Marine posted there. He made no move to get up and ease the process along, still rankling at the delay they would inevitably cause.

"Captain Wolfe," a young, fresh-faced lieutenant said, approaching the command chair. "I'm Lieutenant McCord, I'll be your docking pilot today. My team is ready to go and the tugs will be here within the hour."

"Docking pilot?" Jackson said, dumbfounded. "Lieutenant, we are not scheduled to decouple from Jericho Station for another six days."

"Change of plan, Captain," a well-dressed civilian said, walking up behind McCord.

"And just who the hell are you?" Jackson demanded, feeling control of the situation slipping away from him. The oily smile that had been pasted on the man's face began to slide at Jackson's abrupt tone.

"My name is Aston Lynch," he said. "I am an aide to Senator Augustus Wellington, Chairmen of Fleet Operations Committee. You will be departing immediately for Tau Ceti, and I will be accompanying you. Here are your orders." He handed Jackson a sealed hardcopy which the captain grabbed and stuffed into the gap between the seat and the armrest, making no move to open or even look at them.

"Well that will be a bit tough, Mr. Lynch, as we have yet to even fire the engines for the first time since coming out of a major depot level overhaul of half a dozen systems," Jackson said through clenched teeth. "We have weeks, probably months of trials and testing within this star system before returning to normal duty."

"As I said, plans have changed," Lynch said with a bored shrug. "The issue is non-negotiable, Captain. While I understand this is somewhat unusual, orders are orders. The senator wants this ship on its way to Tau Ceti as quickly as possible and Admiral Winters not only agreed but signed the orders personally."

Jackson felt completely impotent, and it was manifesting itself in a rage that burned in his chest. He looked around and could see his bridge crew trying to pretend they were engrossed in their duties and not hearing their captain being dressed down by an arrogant civilian. He reached around as calmly as he could and popped the seal on his orders. Sliding out the synthetic sheet he quickly read the overview on the first page.

Sure enough, the admiral had decided to force him to skip his planned series of tests on the *Blue Jacket's* new systems and depart as soon as they could. Her justification was that navigation and warp drive systems hadn't been touched during the overhaul and were technically still within their calibration window. There was a scancode at the bottom of the page that would link him to a secure server on Jericho to download the complete set of mission parameters. Just above that was the signature of Admiral Winters, unmistakable with the obnoxiously flamboyant "W."

"Putting aside the fact that the admiral hasn't actually ever commanded a starship," Jackson began in a controlled tone, "I hope that you are aware that these orders place the ship, and my crew, at significant risk. Just because the warp drive or the navigational sensors weren't supposed to be touched doesn't mean that something connected to those systems wasn't. My orders specifically state that I will be underway *as soon as possible*. I see no problem in complying." Lynch looked surprised and suspicious at the same time at Jackson's sudden acquiescence.

"Very well, Captain," he said slowly, looking around the bridge in that uncomfortable manner one adopted when their argument has been completely deflated just before they were about to launch a full-voiced counterattack. "If there is nothing else, I will leave you to your work."

"Of course," Jackson said pleasantly. "Your escort will show you to your guest quarters."

Once Aston Lynch left the bridge Jackson grabbed the orders and stepped down off the command dais. "I'll be in my office. Notify me when the tugs show up. Do not allow them to grapple onto the hull without me being present."

"Aye, sir," Ensign Davis said to his departing back.

****

Jackson sat at his desk and read over the details of his orders for the second time, no less confused than he had been after the first. None of it made any sense. The Confederacy had access to an entire fleet of courier ships that could carry a senator's aide to Tau Ceti, some of them faster than an aging destroyer could. There were no details as to why Aston Lynch was being ferried to a New America planet by a Black Fleet ship or what his purpose was. The sentries had reported that Lynch had only brought on a single bag, so there wasn't any special cargo he was ferrying.

He sat back and rubbed his temples, the aftereffects of his previous night's self-medicating still lingering. If Senator Wellington needed to talk with someone in Tau Ceti the simplest, and cheapest, way would be just to send an encrypted message via the long-haul com drone network that crisscrossed through human space. Instantaneous communication was still the stuff of imagination, but the high-warp com drones that transported digital content from system to system at least made back and forth conversations possible, if somewhat slow.

For now he would play along with the politicians, a group in which he included Admiral Winters. He didn't have much of a choice while they were still docked. If he refused to comply with his orders Winters would gleefully have him removed from command and someone else would take the *Blue Jacket* to Tau Ceti. But once they were underway he would no longer be so constrained. He would have the authority to lock down coms and execute his orders how he saw fit and there would be nothing the arrogant young staffer could do about it.

He jumped slightly at the single knock on his hatch. "Enter!"

"Captain," Commander Wright said as she walked in, now dressed in her dark gray utilities. "All crew are aboard and accounted for. I've sent a summary of the non-judicial punishment I gave our seven troublemakers to your command inbox."

"Have a seat, Commander," Jackson said distractedly. "Did those Haven Internal Security assholes give you any trouble?"

"Only a little, sir," she said as she slid into the chair. "Six were simple public intoxication incidents, but the seventh was a drunk and disorderly with a physical assault tossed in for good measure."

"I'm guessing they wanted to keep that one for a trial here on Haven?"

"Yes, sir," Celesta confirmed. "They blustered a bit about their right to try him locally, but they weren't very serious about it."

"I wouldn't think so if they bothered to bring him all the way up to the station," Jackson said. "Are you aware the docking pilot and his team are already aboard waiting on the tugs to pull us out of port?"

"I thought we weren't even decoupling from dock power for another six days according to the schedule you gave me," she said with a frown.

"The schedule has apparently changed," Jackson said, looking at her intently. "Senator Wellington himself has taken an interest in this ship, apparently, and wants us underway to ferry one of his aides to Tau Ceti immediately."

"While I'm new to the Seventh, this seems highly unusual," she said.

"Try unheard of," Jackson confirmed, sliding the orders brief across his desk to her. She picked it up and skimmed through it, one eyebrow arching as she did.

"Does the Senate task Black Fleet with covert operations often?" she asked, tossing the sheet back onto the desk.

"Explain," Jackson said with a frown.

"This reeks of CENTCOM Intel Section," she said. "I've had a few interactions with them and they like to play games like this: put an operative on a ship that won't draw unnecessary attention to itself and give the captain vague orders. To be honest, sir, it looks to me like we may be glorified couriers for Senator Wellington and our cargo is something he'd rather not have going through normal channels."

"I hope you're wrong," Jackson said. "I'd hate to think Admiral Winters is risking the safety of my ship and crew over some political wrangling. To answer your question, no ... Black Fleet does not have any normal interaction with Intel Section. They don't really trust us with anything like that."

"That's a shame," Celesta said diplomatically. "A contact within Intel can be a good resource to have."

"Oh I never said I had no contacts," Jackson said with a half-smile. "I just said we have no normal interaction. Go ahead and take the rest of this watch on the bridge. Call me when the tugs show up to pull us out of dock."

"Yes, sir," she said, rising and twisting out of her chair gracefully before leaving his office. He leaned back in his seat and closed his eyes, enjoying just one more moment of peace and quiet while the *Blue Jacket's* engines were silent in the dock.

****

"Captain Wolfe to the bridge," the computer's dispassionate voice said over the intercom. The ship knew where he was at any given time and would only activate the speakers near him. He'd been walking back to his office after a quick shower and change in his quarters. It had been a choice between getting cleaned up or grabbing a much needed meal in the wardroom, but he knew that he'd been sweating. Anyone on the bridge with a sharp nose would likely catch a whiff of sour sweat as well as the previous night's bottle.

"Report," he said, interrupting the announcement that he had arrived as he strode onto the bridge.

"Tugs are in place two hundred meters off the prow," Ensign Davis reported. "Jericho Station is standing by to disconnect all umbilicals and moorings."

"What is our status?"

"Propellant tanks are full, consumables are full, fuel tanks are topped off," Ensign Davis said, reading off the checklist she'd already had up on her station. "All hatches are clear, all personnel are accounted for, and all departments are signaling ready for flight."

"Very well," Jackson said loudly, getting everyone's attention. "Prepare the *Blue Jacket* for departure. Close all external hatches and prep reactors one and three for startup."

"Aye, sir," Davis said. "Preparing the ship for departure." She pulled her headset around and began giving commands to the various departments in accordance with a new checklist that she had brought up onto one of her screens. Jackson pulled her status screen up on his armrest display so that he could see how efficiently his crew prepared the ship. After a moment of watching he switched it off. Apparently the sense of urgency that his orders had imparted in him wasn't felt by the rest of the crew, as the status percentages showed a fairly lackadaisical approach to their work. He suppressed the sigh he felt coming up and motioned for his XO.

"Yes, sir?" she asked softly. She'd been pacing the bridge, looking over the shoulders of the crewmen as they went about their tasks.

"Don't hover, you're making them uncomfortable," he said to her, barely moving his lips. "If you want to see what they're doing, pull the displays up on your station." He motioned to the chair that was to his right and slightly lower. It also had a pair of large interactive displays, one on each armrest. Celesta looked chagrined as he showed her how to switch through the various bridge station displays.

"Of course, sir," she said. "My apologies for not being familiar with my station."

"No apology needed," Jackson said. "Just don't make the same mistake more than twice and we'll get along just fine."

"Engineering is reporting they are ready for startup on reactors one and three," Ensign Davis said from her station, not looking up.

"Inform Lieutenant Commander Singh that he is clear to begin reactor startup," Jackson said. "Let him know he is responsible for coordinating with Jericho Station."

"Aye, sir," Davis said.

If was a quiet fifteen minutes later when the lights dimmed on the bridge, then blinked off altogether. The soft red emergency lighting came up and the hiss of the air handlers went away, making the rest of the ambient noises on the bridge seem overly loud. Jackson watched his power management display and saw that reactor one's magnetic constrictor rings were fully charged and massive amounts of power from Jericho Station were being fed in through the umbilical cable. That power would be used to kickstart the reaction and during that process the rest of the ship was put on emergency power.

The reactor started up without a hitch and began spooling up into its operating range. With at least one reactor started, the power from the umbilical connecting them to Jericho Station was fed back into the power MUX, the multiplexing system that managed power distribution shipwide, and the bridge lights came back up and the air handlers began blowing cool, dry air from the vents again.

"Reactor one has successfully started," Davis said. "Lieutenant Commander Singh says it will be providing power to the ship within fifteen minutes."

"Very good," Jackson said. "Tell him to wait until number one is providing stable power before moving on to number three."

"How long until we're ready to depart, Captain Wolfe?" Aston Lynch asked from an observation chair along the rear bulkhead.

"How many starships have you been on, Mr. Lynch?" Jackson asked.

"Enough," the aide said defensively. "I travel extensively in Senator Wellington's service."

"I'm sure you do. But this is not a brand new courier ship that was already in orbit. This is a forty-year-old destroyer that was completely shut down. The short answer is, Mr. Lynch, that we will not be departing this system until sometime well after tomorrow."

"Tomorrow?!"

"I said *after* tomorrow. Probably closer to a week," Jackson said, struggling to maintain his calm. "We have a single reactor started, one out of four. The *Blue Jacket* will need to be pulled out of dock, put into transfer orbits until reaching departure altitude, and pushed out of Haven's local gravity. After that the reactors will be run up and the mains will be fired. They haven't been running for over a month so it will be a cold start. Then, once they are capable of providing thrust … do I really need to go on?"

"No," Lynch said sullenly. "If there's no need for me to be up here I will return to my quarters, Captain."

"That would probably be best, Mr. Lynch," Jackson agreed pleasantly.

The political operative stood, smoothed his jacket out, and walked off the bridge, but not before taking a moment to admire Commander Wright's side profile while he thought she wasn't looking.

"This is going to be a pleasant cruise," Celesta said quietly.

"Orders are orders, Commander," Jackson said, not taking his eyes off his display. She gave him a confused frown before turning back to her own displays. Jackson completely agreed with her, but he didn't see any use in pissing and moaning in front of the crew. It set a bad precedent and punctured holes in the illusion that a ship's captain was master of his domain.

"Engineering reports that reactor three is now running," Ensign Davis said, breaking into the quiet conversation.

"Lieutenant McCord, you may begin," Jackson said to the docking pilot who had been standing patiently off to the side of the bridge.

"Thank you, Captain," the pilot said. He sat at the secondary helm station and configured the station to his liking before nodding to the spacer second class, who was sitting at the primary helm station, to indicate he was taking control of the ship. The young enlisted man just nodded and put his hands down in his lap.

McCord slipped on his headset and patched himself into the com panel, allowing him access to the *Blue Jacket's* short-range radios. Jackson could see him talking to the small armada of tugs that had assembled just in front of their docking berth, ordering them around and watching their progress through video feeds piped in from the destroyer's external cameras and feeds from Jericho Station.

Jackson watched semi-interestedly as the small, powerful tugs attached themselves to the hull in half a dozen places with their magnetic grapples. After some more back and forth with McCord it looked like they were ready to depart.

"Captain, we are in position and ready to proceed on your order," Lieutenant McCord said.

"Proceed," Jackson said before keying on the shipwide intercom. "All hands, prepare for microgravity conditions. Secure all loose items and ensure anyone not strapped into a seat is wearing mag-boots. That is all."

"Jericho Control, this is *Blue Jacket* requesting permission to depart," McCord said over the open com channel that controlled the space directly around the massive station.

"*Permission granted, Blue Jacket,*" the controller replied after a few seconds. "*Retracting moorings and disengaging feed umbilicals now. You are clear to push out of dock, thrusters only, and follow standard insertion vector for your first transfer orbit. Safe travels, Blue Jacket.*"

"Thrusting out now," McCord reported. Jackson saw the two tugs anchored between the MPD pylons, one on each side of the ship, flare softly as a minimal amount of thrust was applied to gently nudge the destroyer out into open space. While in dock the ship was not able to engage its own artificial gravity field, not needing to while within the sphere of influence of Jericho's generators. But in the time it would take them to fully move away from the station and out of Haven's orbit they would keep their own generators powered down, forcing the crew to operate in weightless conditions.

Jackson and Celesta watched the common monitor near the command dais as it showed split views of the *Blue Jacket* easing out of the scaffolding-like external dock. McCord had a focused, yet relaxed look on his face as he coordinated all the smaller ships to ensure the big warship would make it out into open space without damaging herself or the station. Once the MPD nacelles cleared the opening there seemed to be a chorus of relieved sighs on the bridge as the part of the ship that protruded the most was out of harm's way. The ship was now navigating freely in open space, flying over Haven sideways at just under fifty-five thousand kilometers per hour as she kept pace with Jericho Station.

"Turning into the spin," McCord reported. "We'll begin accelerating to our first transfer momentarily." Jackson watched as the prow of the ship turned so that they were flying straight ahead in relation to their orbital path. Once McCord had executed his turn the bridge crew was pressed back into their seats gently as the tugs at the aft throttled up and the ship began to accelerate away from Jericho Station.

The process was maddeningly slow, but there was no avoiding it under normal conditions. While the main engines of the *Blue Jacket* were more than powerful enough for them to easily break orbit without the help of the tugs, there were some claimed environmental concerns about the amount of ionized gas released by the current generation of starship engine at such a low altitude. Jackson didn't buy it since the new engines had next to zero harmful emissions compared to the older, nuclear-pulse-powered ships that blasted raw deuterium reaction byproducts from their exhaust. Even so, other than an emergency on the station or an attack of the planet itself, ships were not routinely authorized to depart under their own power. It was just as well … at the acceleration the MPDs were capable of they wouldn't survive the trip without their gravitational field active and stabilized to null the effects of inertia.

"We'll be accelerating at a steady 1G before breaking away from the planet," McCord reported. "There is almost no traffic in the higher orbits so I don't foresee any delays."

"Thank you, Lieutenant," Jackson said. With the acceleration he felt like he was lying on his back as he was pressed into his seat. It was quite disorienting when his vestibular system was telling his brain something his eyes didn't agree with. Even veteran spacers could still be made ill from the effect.

It was just under an hour later when McCord announced they were at departure altitude and swung the ship away from the planet, accelerating out of the system. Once they were four hundred thousand kilometers away from Haven, Jackson ordered reactors two and four started.

"Tell Lieutenant Commander Singh that once he has reactor four stabilized he can go ahead and start prepping the main engines," Jackson ordered. "I want the MPDs ready to provide thrust within the hour. Helm, what is the status of directional thrusters?"

"Thrusters online and operational, Captain," the helmsman answered. "The ship is answering commands from the helm."

"Thank you," Jackson said. "You may depart at your convenience, Lieutenant McCord. Feel free to remain until we have our gravitational field stabilized."

"If it's all the same we'll get moving now, Captain," McCord said, maneuvering himself around in the microgravity like the seasoned professional he was. Now that the tugs were no longer accelerating everyone was experiencing the gut-flipping sensation of freefall. "My crew has two more departures and an arrival scheduled today. I can make it down to the airlock without the gravity active."

"Suit yourself," Jackson said. "Thank you for the smooth flight."

"Our pleasure, Captain," McCord said. "Stay safe out there, sir." Jackson simply nodded to him as he walked off the bridge.

"How much longer until gravity is up?" he asked once the docking pilot had gone.

"Reactor four is now providing power, gravimetric generator is coming online," Ensign Davis said. "Engineering is telling me another ten minutes and we'll start feeling it. The plasma generators have been started in all four main engine nacelles; another forty minutes and they should be providing thrust."

"So all this time to cold-start all our systems while gliding out to the edge," Celesta said. "By the time the mains are up we'll be ready to shut them down and bring the warp drive online. It would have made more sense to let us stay in dock and prep for departure there."

"As I said, our orders were fairly specific," Jackson said. "We operate in situations that are often less than ideal. This is no great obstacle."

"Of course, sir," she agreed, leaning back in her seat. Jackson made a mental note to speak to her about her demeanor on the bridge later when they were alone. His ship already had a reputation for discipline problems, deserved or not, and that was among a squadron known for a certain lack of professionalism that concerned the brass at CENTCOM greatly. Not enough for them to allow Jackson to start weeding out the troublemakers on his crew, but enough that he never seemed to get a very good score during his review boards. Either way, he'd prefer she kept her complaining about orders and procedures to herself as it did nothing but give the junior crewmembers an opening to do the same.

He sat patiently, beginning to feel the pull of gravity as the machinery in the belly of the ship created a localized gravitational field that pulled everything on the ship down at a steady, stable 1G. It was a dynamic field that also nulled out the effects of inertia on the crew when they were underway, but it wasn't perfect. During hard acceleration or violent combat maneuvers there would occasionally be a noticeable lag from when the accelerometers detected the change to when the generated field could adjust and compensate for it.

“Magnetic constrictors are active and plasma pressure is building in the mains,” Davis said as she watched the status reports from half a dozen sections stream across her display.

“Just let me know when we can begin to accelerate,” Jackson said as he felt the gravity stabilize. He took the opportunity to get up and stretch his legs. Looking at the status of the engines over his operations officer’s shoulder he decided he had enough time to head down to the wardroom and grab a coffee.

The ship felt alive under his feet, seeming to wake up after being dragged out away from Haven with barely enough power to run life support systems and start the rest of the powerplant. Now there was an ever present thrum of machinery and the hiss of blowing air from the environmental system ducts.

Walking into the wardroom he grabbed one of the lidded, spill-proof mugs that were secured to the wall and went over to the coffee machine. He had to fiddle with the spout since it had locked down automatically when the gravity had been removed. Eventually he was able to fill the mug up, taking an appreciative sniff before locking the lid down. Though it might seem counterintuitive given the lack of many common comforts aboard the ship, CENTCOM made sure that the coffee, and most other rations, that made it onto Fleet ships was as good as anything you’d find planetside.

“Captain on the bridge!” the sentry announced loudly. Since they were now underway nobody leapt out of their seats to snap to attention. It was standing policy on his ship that once out of orbit or out of dock nobody on the command deck would render courtesies at the expense of taking their attention away from their station. In fact, the Marine shouldn't have even announced it.

"Report, Ensign Davis," he said, sitting back in his chair and slipping the mug into the holder, feeling the magnet grab it with a *click*.

"Magnetic containment is stable and the plasma chambers are fully charged on the mains," the operations officer said. "Engineering reports we have full thrust available."

"Let's take it easy until we've had a bit more shakedown time," Jackson said with a smile. "Set course for the Tau Ceti jump point, ahead one quarter."

"Ahead one quarter, aye," the helmsman said, grabbing the throttles on his left. Immediately there was a deep rumble as the main engines throttled up and the *Blue Jacket* surged ahead under her own power. There was a gentle tug of inertia before it was nulled out by the gravimetric generators.

The main engines were basically enormous, electric rocket motors. Inert argon gas, the propellant, was ionized and then converted into superheated plasma through radio frequency excitation. The plasma was magnetically confined and directed out the nozzle to produce thrust. The advantage of a magneto-plasma engine is that the propellant is nonvolatile and it is capable of impressive amounts of thrust. The downside is that it takes a prodigious amount of electrical power to operate, but electrical power was something the *Blue Jacket* had plenty of. Four deuterium fusion reactors sat in a row in the belly of the destroyer, capable of running the engines and weapons simultaneously and able to provide enough power to the warp drive to achieve long-duration, sustained faster-than-light travel.

"At current acceleration, how long until we reach our jump point?" Jackson asked.

"Fifty-nine hours, sir," Ensign Davis answered.

"Go to standard watch schedule," Jackson ordered. "I want all department heads in the conference room in forty-eight hours. That gives them two days to make a complete inspection of their areas and personnel before we even attempt to power up the warp drive."

"Standard watch, aye," the communications officer said, sending the appropriate orders through the com system.

"XO, you have the ship. I'll have my comlink if you need me," Jackson said, grabbing his half-full coffee mug and walking off the bridge.

Chapter 3

The next two days were a blur of inspections, problems found, and emergency repairs made while the ship steamed out of the system. Jackson secretly liked the pace, enjoying the frantic activity around him even while his crew grumbled and complained about the "idiots at Jericho fucking up their ship." He also took the opportunity to really lean on Commander Wright and see if he could detect any cracks in her polished surface. She looked exhausted and harried by the end of the second day, as she was the main point of contact to coordinate work between departments. She was the one who had to tell certain groups to stop, start, or listen to them complain bitterly about other people being in their way.

She handled it all with a forced professionalism and didn't let the department heads bully her into getting their way. Jackson was impressed considering that she'd only been on the ship for a few days and had never served in the capacity of Executive Officer, but outwardly he made sure she knew that there was plenty of room for improvement. He wasn't being harsh for no reason; he wanted it perfectly clear in her head that the road to a command slot did *not* go through him. If she was captain material then she would have to earn a spot on her own ship.

"All things considered, I expected the ship to be in much worse shape," Jackson remarked, putting his feet up on the conference table and taking a pull of his coffee mug.

"You can't be serious?" Lieutenant Commander Singh said, slouching down into his seat a bit. The other department heads had all filed out after the status meeting and Jackson, Daya Singh, and

Celesta Wright were the only ones left in the room. Celesta watched the casual interaction between the two with great interest. The pair were obviously friends outside their capacity as captain and chief engineer.

"I am serious," Jackson said. "Those were all very minor problems. A connector pinned wrong here and a check valve installed backwards there, all on redundant or secondary systems. All our primary flight systems look good."

"As good as they always do on this antique," Singh grumbled. "So what are we doing out here, Jack? Is this actually a mission or is Admiral Winters trying to kill us and make it look like an accident?"

Jackson shot an uncomfortable look at Celesta before answering. "You know as much as I do, *Lieutenant Commander*," Jackson said, emphasizing his chief engineer's rank. "I can only hope it's something truly vital for us to be taking so many shortcuts while redeploying the ship."

Singh's next question was cut off before he'd uttered the first syllable as Aston Lynch burst into the conference room, his face red from either anger or exertion.

"Why was I not informed of a staff meeting being called prior to departing this system?" he demanded hotly, indicating it was the former.

"Is there a change in your status I am unaware of?" Jackson asked coolly, planting his feet back on the floor. "My understanding is that you are a passenger, a dignitary if you will, aboard my ship. If you've been assigned to my crew I will need to see those orders."

Lynch turned an even darker shade of red before getting himself under control enough to answer. "I am in operational command of this mission," he finally ground out. "In essence, you report to me."

Jackson had carefully read every word included in his orders and knew the arrogant little prick had zero command authority over his ship and her personnel. Not only that, but Lynch's demeanor—bursting into a room and accosting him in front of his crew—angered him greatly. He sucked in a breath to respond in kind, but Celesta jumped in just before he could.

"It was my fault, Mr. Lynch," she said, managing to sound sincerely apologetic. "Captain Wolfe tasked me with running this status meeting. I assumed you wouldn't be interested in a list of maintenance issues, which was the only topic of discussion, so I excluded you. My apologies."

Lynch stood in the hatchway, mouth opened to deliver another blistering salvo, but Celesta had sucked the wind out of his sails. He straightened back up, adjusted his clothes, and assumed a lofty, bored expression. "Well, Commander," he said after a moment, "please see that you do not make an oversight like that again. I will decide what information I do or do not need for the duration of my stay on this ship."

"Of course, sir," she said calmly, meeting his eyes. Jackson still looked apoplectic as his executive officer apologized for doing nothing wrong. For his part, Singh looked to be thoroughly enjoying the entire spectacle.

"Will there be anything else, Mr. Lynch," Jackson asked through a clenched jaw.

"I believe that will be all, Captain," the aide said, turning to leave.

"We will be transitioning to warp within the next five hours. I'll ensure that you're alerted."

"See that you do, Captain." Lynch was through the hatch and gone before Jackson could respond.

"Pleasant young man," Singh said blandly.

"Lieutenant Commander, would you please give Commander Wright and I some privacy," Jackson said. It wasn't a request.

"Of course," Singh said, raising one eyebrow as he left the conference room, keying the hatch shut as he did. Jackson waited a moment longer before turning to Celesta.

"Explain yourself, Commander," he said.

"Excuse me, sir?" she said, clearly startled.

"There was no misunderstanding as to the attendees of this meeting," Jackson said. "Why did you claim otherwise?"

"Sir," she floundered, off balance from the question. "I was simply trying to get Lynch off your back. I apologize if I overstepped my bounds."

"Commander, if the day comes when I can't handle some senator's self-important toady then I will resign my commission as I would be clearly unfit for command," Jackson said. "Until then, I would prefer to speak for myself. Clear?"

"Clear, sir," Celesta said stiffly. "Is that all, sir?"

"That is all," Jackson said, leaning back. "Please report to the bridge and check our speed and heading. We'll be increasing velocity soon and deploying the warp drive. I want you to be there for that to familiarize yourself with the procedure on a *Raptor*-class vessel."

"Aye aye, sir," she said, still biting off each word. Once she had left Jackson was able to chuckle out loud about how she'd yanked Lynch up short before it had really turned into a pissing contest. He believed he was still right to correct her, however. While he appreciated her instincts to deflect irritants away from him at the expense of bringing heat upon herself, they hadn't served long enough for her to know when it was appropriate and when she needed to simply sit and keep her mouth shut.

****

"Helmsman, steady as she goes … ahead full," Jackson ordered. "OPS, start the clock … mark."

"Ahead full, aye," the helmsman said, running the throttles all the way up to the stops.

"Yes, sir," Lieutenant Peters, the second watch OPS officer said. Instantly there was a clock that appeared up on the long, narrow display that ran the length of the bridge, just over the forward "window" (that was in reality a ultra-high resolution display which wrapped around the bridge.) It began ticking with elapsed time, the ship rumbling and shaking as the main engines came to full power.

"Hold this course and acceleration for fifteen minutes," Jackson ordered, re-checking his data on his own display. "At mark plus fifteen go to zero thrust and begin shutdown of the main engines. Navigation! Where are my calculations for warp transition?"

"Coming, sir," the chief spacer standing by the navigation station said. He was a burly man with a salt and pepper crew cut and was currently looking over the shoulder of a nervous spacer third class who looked like he could have been the man's grandson, so great was the age difference. "Warp data for transition from Alpha Centauri to Tau Ceti going to your station now."

Jackson began breaking down the data for the different course profiles in his head and compared it with the telemetry coming from the OPS station. The *Blue Jacket* would be carrying some extra velocity when they engaged the warp drive, but better too much than too little. After a moment's consideration he decided to stick to his original course and speed.

"Navigation, you're approved for transition course Bravo," Jackson said after looking over the rest of the data. "Finalize your calculations and disseminate the data to the appropriate departments. Let's make sure Engineering gets the correct power requirements. I'd prefer not to have a repeat of the Asteria incident."

"Of course, Captain," the chief said gruffly, apparently not appreciating the reference.

"The Asteria incident?" Celesta said quietly, leaning in towards Jackson.

"We were leaving the planet Asteria, that colony the New European Commonwealth has been propping up, and the power requirement data Engineering received was ... off ... from what it should have been," Jackson said uncomfortably. "When we transitioned to warp we only made it a little over four light-seconds before getting dumped back into real-space."

"Oh," Celesta said.

"Yeah," Jackson said. "As if that wasn't enough, there were two Fifth Fleet frigates in the system. They asked repeatedly, on the open channel, if we needed assistance since we only went half a million kilometers. Not our finest hour."

"I—" Celesta floundered, completely unsure as to what she could say to a story like that. It was a screw up of such magnitude that she was surprised she hadn't heard about it when she came over from First Fleet.

"You should probably call Lynch up here," Jackson said, rescuing her. "I'm sure he'll want to strut around the bridge and get in everyone's way while we're trying to transition out of here."

"Yes, sir," she said, relieved. "I'll have one of the Marine sentries escort him up."

"No escort," Jackson said. "Just send a message to his comlink."

"Thirty seconds until zero-thrust," OPS reported, cutting off any reply Celesta was about to make.

"Confirmed," the helmsman said. "Standing by."

Jackson watched the elapsed time on the display march towards fifteen minutes. He remained silent, letting his crew execute his orders without badgering them.

"Mark!" Lieutenant Peters said. "Zero thrust. Secure main engines and prepare for shutdown."

"Zero thrust, aye," the helmsman said, pulling the throttles all the way back. Immediately the harsh vibration and rumble that had been present for the previous couple of days vanished, replaced by an eerie silence.

"Engineering reports main engines secured," Lieutenant Peters said. "They're purging the plasma chambers and thrust nozzles."

"Prepare to deploy warp drive emitters," Jackson ordered. "Open hatches, fore and aft, and begin high resolution scans ahead of the *Blue Jacket*. I want all debris from here to our jump point mapped." After a chorus of confirmations from the bridge crew he leaned back, taking a long drink off his coffee mug before motioning Celesta closer.

"It's not always this clunky," he said quietly. "We're stepping through the procedure slowly right now for your benefit and for the junior bridge crew we're training up. Normally I trust them to know how to execute the more general commands I give."

"I was wondering about that, sir," she admitted. "I'm not used to actions being broken out into so many commands."

"It's not the norm," Jackson said. "Although, between you and me, most of this is completely unnecessary. Under normal operating conditions you're not going to do anything the computers aren't in full agreement with."

"True," she said. "But in the event the automation fails it's always good to have a well-trained bridge crew."

"That's why we do these drills when we can," Jackson confirmed.

"Forty-five minutes from jump point at current velocity," the chief at Navigation called out.

"How does our flight path look?" Jackson asked OPS.

"Long-range data is still being verified, sir," Lieutenant Peters said. "We have a clean sky for over half the remaining distance. I'll have the complete picture in a few minutes."

"Good enough," Jackson said. "Deploy warp drive emitters and begin charging drive capacitors."

Eight onyx cylinders, each roughly ten meters long and three meters in diameter, began to extend out of the open hatches on the *Blue Jacket's* hull on spindly telescoping arms until each emitter was two hundred and fifty meters away from its opposite. Due to the ship's oblong shape the arms on the flanks were shorter than the arms on the dorsal and ventral surface. The emitters divided the ship into thirds, four forward, four aft, each trailing a thick shielded power cable.

"Emitters deployed," Lieutenant Peters said. "Capacitors are at sixty percent and climbing, seven minutes until completely charged."

"Navigation?"

"Fifteen minutes until jump point, sir."

"Let's close her up," Jackson said. "Deploy all shields and close all heat exchanger hatches. Go ahead and start charging the emitters off the main bus."

"Deploying external shields," OPS reported. An instant later there was the uncomfortable sound of metal on metal grinding as large alloy covers moved to protect any sensitive electronics and the few actual windows in the ship. The external heat exchangers were retracted and covered as well. They were mostly for auxiliary use as the ship was completely capable of cooling all four reactors and the engines on internal, closed-loop coolant systems.

"Navigation, you have command authority for the warp transition," Jackson said. "You may engage at your discretion."

"Aye, sir, we have command authority," the chief said while pointing emphatically at something on the screen and nudging the junior spacer's head with his elbow.

"Emitters are charged and ready, Captain," Lieutenant Peters said.

"Good, good," Jackson said absently as he watched the timer count down to the five-minute mark. The emitters for the warp drive, an apparatus in its fifth iteration on human ships, were able to charge in a remarkably short time. Jackson liked to wait until the last minute to begin applying power so that there was less chance of a variance developing between the fore and aft arrays before they were slammed with power from the drive's capacitor banks. If for some reason they didn't charge in time the ship would simply overfly the jump point and either come back around or move off-course to begin diagnostics. It wasn't Fleet procedure, but neither were about two dozen other standing orders Jackson had on the *Blue Jacket*.

"Go ahead and spin the gravity down to one half G," he ordered when the clock showed three minutes to go. OPS entered the appropriate orders and he could immediately feel the pull of gravity lessen.

"Gravity set to one half G," Peters confirmed.

Since the warp drive worked on the principle of gravimetric wave manipulation, standard procedure was to reduce power to the primary gravimetric field generator. It eliminated the risk of the two systems interfering with each other. While in warp, most of the ship would feel a nominal one-half G while the compartments at the fore and aft would experience around one-fifth G. If the crew ever forgot to reduce the field the ship would do it for them or it would not allow them to initiate a warp transition.

"Stand by for warp transition!" the salty chief at Navigation bellowed, causing everyone else on the bridge to start slightly. Jackson grinned to himself as he knew the chief's exuberant announcement was carried shipwide by the computer. There was a sharp klaxon alarm that blasted once and then Jackson could see the forward emitters begin to glow bright blue as the capacitors dumped an incredible amount of energy into them. The main display automatically began to dim the areas around the three visible emitters as the glow quickly increased from blue to brilliant white and visible distortions could be seen arcing between them, creating a ring of gravimetric energy around the prow of the ship that was inverse to the one happening at the stern.

In less than a second the main display dimmed completely and there was a violent shudder as the warp field stabilized and the *Blue Jacket* simply disappeared from the Alpha Centauri system in a brilliant flash of light from the residual protons left by the warp transition.

Chapter 4

The next four days passed quickly as Jackson, Celesta, and Daya Singh made a thorough inspection of the ship to verify the remaining depot checklist items from the work Jericho Station did and to give the new XO a chance to tour the ship and meet the crew. By the end of the fourth day Jackson was sure she wouldn't remember the names of even a tenth of the crew since she'd probably shaken the hands of over eleven hundred spacers during her tour.

She'd impressed Jackson with the fact she had obviously been studying the *Raptor*-class specs in her downtime and was willing to crawl into the dingiest access hatch without a moment's hesitation. She was attentive and remembered even the most mundane detail she was told by the ship's technical staff. Jackson allowed himself just a sliver of hope that he'd finally been assigned a decent exec. It was only the way in which she'd been placed on his ship that gave him pause. Stevenson may have been a slovenly, lazy, piss-poor excuse for an officer, but he was loyal to a fault and didn't balk at Jackson's more ... unconventional ... approach to commanding a starship. In fact, the more he thought about it the more he doubted that Stevenson had actually asked to be transferred. The man simply had no ambition and a transfer to Fourth Fleet meant he would need to start living up to Fleet standards. Like bathing every day.

"Fucking bitch," he muttered under his breath.

"Excuse me?" Celesta asked, a look of shock on her face as she looked up from the report she was reading.

"No!" Jackson said quickly. "Sorry, Commander. I was talking to myself."

"I see," she said, obviously not convinced.

"So what do you think of the *Blue Jacket* and her crew?" he asked, wanting to change the subject.

She maintained her icy silence for a moment before answering. "At roughly six hundred meters long and over a hundred meters at the beam, I'm honestly a little surprised at how cramped everything is on the lower decks," she said.

"Well, the outer hull is nearly two meters of solid alloy," Jackson said. "Then you have another ten meters of layered protection before even getting to the inner hull. All the machinery and storage areas take up most of the space, which means the crew has to live in some fairly cramped quarters."

"I understand that, sir," she said. "It was just an observation. The last cruiser I was on had much more room and we weren't tasked with cruises even half as long as this ship sees."

"I've read about the ship you were on, Commander," Jackson said with a chuckle. "It was only commissioned five years ago. A lot of advancements in ship design since this destroyer was built, not to mention a shift in focus."

"How do you mean that, sir?" she asked.

"Your cruiser was contracted, designed, and built by companies on planets within Britannia," he said. "While it may give an obligatory nod to CENTCOM and Haven, it was built with the intent that it would never leave Britannic space. This ship was designed at a time when there was still the outside chance it would actually have to fight, not just carry the flag."

"I would disagree with you on principle, but I think I see where you're coming from," she said with a frown. "Most newer First Fleet ships are beautiful to look at, impressive in their size and technology, but I don't see the hardened systems or multiple layers of redundancy I've seen on the *Blue Jacket*."

"I don't necessarily disagree with the new approach," Jackson said with a shrug. "With all the planets and resources out there for the taking, humans haven't fought with each other for centuries. We've never seen any evidence of another potentially hostile species and the expansion of the com drone network means less and less trips out for manned ships. I think we may see CENTCOM dissolved in our lifetimes and Fleet operations turned over to private contractors."

Celesta shuddered at that. "I certainly hope not, sir," she said. "I would hate to see Fleet be broken up and sold to the highest bidder."

"As would I," Jackson agreed. "The signs are there, however. Each year it gets harder and harder for the Senate to agree on the operational budget, never mind anything remotely resembling weapons R&D. But I suppose that's well above my paygrade."

"It's interesting speculation nonetheless, sir," Celesta said. "If you have nothing else for me, I think I'll turn in before my watch starts."

"Of course, Commander," Jackson said with a nod. "Dismissed." She nodded to him and walked out of the office. He hit the control to lock the hatch and to extinguish the illuminated indicator that let people know if he was in or not. He made the pretense of pulling up some overdue fitness reports and going through them.

Absently he keyed open a locked drawer at the bottom of his desk, reached past the antique sidearm sitting in its holster, and wrapped his fingers around the neck of a squat, heavy bottle. He pulled it out and set it on the corner of his desk without actually looking at it, continually shuffling around words in the report statements, all the while watching the clock closely out of the corner of his eye.

When First Watch officially ended he leaned back in his chair and stretched, yawning hugely. Shrugging to himself, he grabbed a short plastic cup off the shelf by his desk and poured a generous two fingers from the bottle into it. He swirled it around in the bottom, bringing it to his nose, giving a little shudder as he did. This was genuine Kentucky bourbon from his home planet, not the rotgut he suspected his engineering staff was making in stills down in the lower decks. Alcohol was strictly forbidden on Fleet starships for obvious reasons, but there never seemed to be a shortage of it once a cruise started.

Jackson took the first tentative sip, letting the amber liquid play across his tongue before tilting his head up and letting it burn all the way down to his stomach. He followed that with another, more generous sip before setting the glass back on his desk. There were only four bottles left in the case in his quarters so he would need to conserve what he had until he could figure out a way to get another shipment, or at least get some of the acceptable commercial spirits available on any civilized planet they came across.

He continued pecking at the keyboard for the better part of an hour, draining two-thirds of the bottle away without being consciously aware of it. When he finally grew bored of pretending he was working he shut off the interface to the ship's personnel server and brought up a playlist of soft jazz, piping it into the speakers in the ceiling at a low volume. He grabbed the bottle and, with teeth set, screwed the cap back on before replacing it in the locked drawer. As the soothing music washed over him, the familiar self-loathing rose up in him at his inability to control himself. Sighing heavily, he killed the music, pulled a pillow out of a wall locker, and stretched out on the sofa that ran along the bulkhead. It wouldn't do at all to have his crew see him stumbling bleary-eyed back to his quarters.

****

"These are your new mission parameters," Aston Lynch said, handing Jackson another sealed envelope with hardcopy orders enclosed.

"You couldn't have given me these before we left Alpha Centauri?" Jackson asked as he plucked at the seal on the envelope's flap.

"Operational security, Captain," Lynch said in a condescending voice that earned him a hostile glare from Jackson. "If these had been available while still within range of the com drone network the mission could have been compromised."

"Mr. Lynch, I have a hard time believing anybody would really be that concerned that you are traveling to Tau Ceti," Jackson said, his head pounding as he tried to read the small print on the sheet in front of him. "These are just navigational updates. What could possibly be so secret about these?"

"Look closer, Captain," Lynch said. "There are also emission security protocols and very specific com instructions for once we arrive."

Jackson just rolled his eyes and passed the sheet over to Celesta. "Sort it out, Commander," he told her. "If anything appears to be too far out of the ordinary please inform me."

"At once, sir," she said and began reading through the document.

"Is there any particular reason we're deviating course and stopping outside of the system instead of flying the normal route?" Jackson asked.

"That is sensitive information, Captain," Lynch said.

"I understand that," Jackson said, rubbing his temples with his left hand. "But the bridge is a secure location and they're going to find out sooner or later ... unless you planned to confine them to quarters and fly the ship in yourself."

"Just follow the orders given to you, Captain," Lynch sneered. "Everything you need to know is in them and nothing more."

"Your course correction has us transitioning into real space outside the system, but not so deep in space that there aren't navigational hazards," Jackson said with more patience in his voice than he felt. "That's why we have pre-determined routes into, and out of, star systems. If I feel like you are putting this ship at unnecessary risk I will ignore these orders and stick to our original course. That is, of course, unless you can give me some assurances otherwise."

"The spot in which we will transition is clear," Lynch said quietly, still seeming unaware that every ear on the bridge was straining to hear what he was saying. "It's an area that's been used for these types of handoffs before. The data Commander Wright has in her hand will confirm the details of that."

"Very well," Jackson said, not feeling like dragging out the conversation any longer than it had already gone. "I will review the orders and make the necessary adjustments. If I have any other concerns I will contact you, otherwise be prepared to arrive in approximately thirty-six hours."

"Thank you," Lynch said, stepping over and whispering something in Celesta's ear before continuing off the bridge. Despite a burning curiosity, Jackson didn't ask what he had said and she didn't offer to tell him.

"While these orders are a bit unusual I don't see anything in here to be overly concerned about, Captain," she said, handing the orders back to him. "We'll be rendezvousing with another ship in that area so I think we can assume it's clear of any hazards."

"Maybe," he said, unconvinced, before raising his voice. "OPS! Scan these orders in and ensure they're properly disseminated."

"Yes, sir," Ensign Davis said, grabbing the sheet from Jackson and heading back to her station. The scancode on the orders would access the data all the different departments would need to execute them from the secure server that had been loaded at Jericho Station. The hardcopy orders were an archaic method to ensure the server couldn't easily be accessed until it was necessary.

"If it's as simple as the orders seem to indicate, once we deliver Lynch we'll be on our way to our next port of call," Celesta said quietly, leaning in towards Jackson a bit so she didn't have to raise her voice. He self-consciously leaned away from her and simply nodded at her assessment, not wanting to breathe on her.

"Provide me a synopsis of the order updates and send it to my inbox," he said, standing up. "See if you can dig out who we're supposed to be meeting up with in all that cloak and dagger nonsense I was reading in there. I'll be in my office."

"Aye, sir," she said, the narrowing of her eyes barely perceptible as he walked quickly off the bridge.

Chapter 5

"Navigation, confirm our position and time until transition," Jackson said as he settled himself into his seat, securing his coffee mug carefully.

"Position is confirmed. We're ten minutes away from transition into real space," the spacer second class reported from the Nav station. He looked a little too old to still be a second class, but the telltale silhouette on his sleeve indicated that he'd been busted down in rank recently. Two stripes by the looks of it. Jackson made a mental note to ask Commander Wright why someone with such a disciplinary record was manning a station on First Watch during sensitive operations like a transition.

"OPS?" he asked.

"Confirmed, Captain," Ensign Davis said crisply. As a courtesy she began putting up the countdown timer and relative position of the ship on the main display. "Nav data has passed redundancy checks. We should come out where we're supposed to."

The bridge remained silent as everyone tensed up for the coming transition. Even Aston Lynch, secured in an observation seat, kept his mouth shut, though he looked at the display pensively.

"Five seconds!" Ensign Davis called out loudly and a sharp klaxon sounded twice throughout the entire ship. A few seconds later the ship shuddered violently and there was a slight dip in power on non-essential systems that caused the ambient lighting to dim slightly.

As soon as the shuddering subsided the main display cleared and became a window once again, allowing the crew to see that beyond the glowing warp drive emitters there was a clear star field, letting them know that they had reemerged safely into real space.

"All departments have checked in," Davis reported. "Waiting for confirmation of position." Jackson waited patiently as the spacer at the Nav station determined their position by taking star captures and measuring local gravitational anomalies.

"We're fifteen thousand kilometers from our expected transition point," he reported. "I'm sending the data to OPS and Engineering."

Jackson frowned. Even though this was still within the limits for the length of the previous flight, he'd hoped to emerge much closer to their target. When the ship was in warp it was literally flying blind, relying on internal instruments to make sure they emerged where they were supposed to. The *Blue Jacket's* crew routinely hit targets of less than five thousand kilometers on longer flights so he was inclined to believe it was something that Jericho Station had done to his equipment rather than an error on his crew's part.

"I expect that to be tightened up on the next jump," he said, giving fair warning to everyone that they needed to find out why the internal navigation systems were off by so much. "Plot a course to our rendezvous coordinates and send them to the helm. OPS, retract the warp drive emitters and close the external hatches. Once they're stowed, start the main engines and let me know when we're clear to begin maneuvering."

"Aye, sir," Ensign Davis said, the emitters beginning to slowly retract into the hull even before Jackson had finished issuing orders. He watched as the delicate devices were carefully nestled back into their storage nooks and the heavy external hatches were swung over and locked into place, protecting them from debris hits or potential enemy weapons-fire. Early generations of Terran starships had two enormous rings, one fore and one aft, that made up the warp drive and were permanently affixed around the hull. Jackson had always been idly curious how many of those ships were lost because they became stranded between jumps due to a micrometeor impact damaging an emitter ring.

"I don't like the fact we're not permitted to take an active scan of the area," Jackson said quietly to Celesta. "I'd like to you to go down to the CIC and begin a passive scan of surrounding space, full spectrum."

"Aye, Captain," she said, popping the latches on her restraints and hustling off the bridge.

The Combat Operations Center was the heart and soul of the ship when it came to flying, tracking, and shooting. It was a room located near the middle of the main hull and was crewed by fifteen specialists at all times manning every instrument on the *Blue Jacket*, ready to feed information to the bridge whenever needed. There was even a command station in the room where the captain could run the ship from there if needed. The Operations Center used to be referred to as the Combat Information Center back before human vessels were capable of travelling between the stars, but the term "CIC" was an anachronism that had survived to the modern age of starships. Jackson was semi-certain it was because the acronym COC led to a phonetic pronunciation that Fleet deemed to be inappropriate.

The passive scan wasn't the only reason he wanted Commander Wright in the CIC. He wasn't entirely sure what was going on with regards to his orders and having her in the ship's nerve center was one more direct channel of information. So far Lynch seemed calm and unconcerned and he wasn't sure if he took that as a good sign or not.

****

Commander Wright quickly made her way to the CIC and relayed Captain Wolfe's orders. As luck would have it, the second watch OPS officer, Lieutenant Peters, was in charge of the CIC during the transition back to real space. Having served on the *Blue Jacket* for three full cruises, he immediately understood what the captain wanted without Celesta having to spell it out for him.

He offered her the command seat and quickly went to each station and got the operators moving in the right direction. A lot of the task would simply be data processing since the ship's passive sensors were recording at all times. The operators would need to go back from the time the ship emerged into real space and look for any anomalies. While the computers were good at picking out patterns and sudden shifts, they often overlooked subtle changes that a human was able to intuitively pick up on.

As Celesta sat patiently waiting for them to sift through the data she felt a deep rumble resonate through the ship. The main engines starting up caused quite a bit more vibration down in the CIC than they did on the bridge. She felt the change in intensity and pitch and surmised that Captain Wolfe was moving the ship to the rendezvous coordinates listed in their orders. She assumed they were simply delivering their political operative to a ship in Fourth Fleet so that he could discreetly make contact with the New American government on behalf of Senator Wellington without raising any flags, and she really didn't understand Jackson Wolfe's increasing paranoia about the mission. While she would be glad to be rid of Aston Lynch, especially given the number of unwelcome advances he'd made since coming aboard, she had to admit to herself she was more than a little concerned about some perceived erratic behavior from her new commanding officer.

"We have something, Commander," Lieutenant Peters reported. "Thermal anomaly, two hundred thousand kilometers off the port bow, twenty-two degrees elevation."

"Show me," Celesta said, rising from her chair and walking over to the sensor station.

"These two points of light, completely in the IR band, exactly seventy-three meters away from each other," Peters said. "They were there when our sensors came back up after transition and disappeared shortly afterwards."

"You have an idea what they were?" Celesta asked.

"Yes, ma'am. Those are the reverse thrust nozzles of a *Descendant*-class destroyer, flown exclusively by Fourth Fleet. That newer class only has two main engines instead of our four," Peters answered. "If you'll give us a moment we can tell you which ship it is."

"The contact was that strong?" Celesta asked, surprised.

"It was enough for us to get an engine profile for the ship, ma'am," the sensor operator spoke up. He was a young specialist first class and had a scar running down the length of his left cheek. Celesta read the name on the front of his utility top.

"Get me that ship name as quickly as you can, Specialist Jacobs," she said. "The captain will want this information immediately." She waited patiently behind the operator while he ran the brief thermal flash against the ship's database of engine profiles for that class of ship.

"Got it," Jacobs said. "She's the *Oscar Marks*, registry DS-8101."

"Good work, Specialist," Celesta said. "Begin scanning real time data again and see if you can reacquire her."

"Aye, ma'am."

"They must have been out there, waiting for us, and closed off their reverse nozzles as soon as we transitioned in," Peters said.

"That's what I'm thinking," Celesta said. "Since they were also using passive sensors, by the time they received the data of our arrival we were already recording their engine heat." She moved to the command seat, pulled the terminal over to her, and began to type a message that would go directly to Captain Wolfe.

****

"Fourth Fleet destroyer Oscar Marks standing off our port bow at a range of two hundred thousand KM when Blue Jacket transitioned in. She's gone dark. CIC working to reacquire. Will advise. Cmdr. Wright."

Jackson read the message twice before replying to Celesta to keep at it. He looked over at Lynch and tried to get a read on the man's demeanor. He still just sat there with the same bored, slightly irritated look that he seemed to always have.

"Mr. Lynch," he said loudly. "So here we are. What happens next?"

"You'll know soon enough, Captain," Lynch said, looking at ship's time again. "In the meantime, maintain emission security protocols."

"The thermal bloom from our engines will be visible to anyone looking," Jackson reminded him. "We're not completely dark out here."

"By the time anyone will be in a position to investigate we'll all be long gone," Lynch said, giving Jackson an annoyed glare. "The mission is to wait until we're contacted. Until that time—"

"Contact," Ensign Davis said. "Tight beam com laser has just been detected on the forward array, running decryption routines now."

"See, Captain?" Lynch said. "Nothing to worry about."

"Do not mistake impatience to resume our actual mission with worry," Jackson said, growing weary of the other man's smugness.

"Encryption codes on their side were valid, Captain," Davis said, cutting off Lynch's response. "Receiving the message in its entirety."

"Send it to me."

"Aye, sir."

Jackson watched as the text began scrolling across his display. The message was short and to the point:

Civilian passenger Aston Lynch to be brought by shuttle to pre-arranged coordinates. Will receive in one hour from receipt of this message. Send no reply.

Regards,

Capt. Asiri, CO, TCS Oscar Marks

"I assume you have yet another set of secret coordinates in your possession, Mr. Lynch," Jackson said.

"I do."

"Then follow the bridge sentry down to the shuttle hangar and prepare to depart. Ensign Davis, alert Commander Juarez that a shuttle will need to be prepped and a pilot ready to take our passenger over to another ship," Jackson said, still not happy with how he seemed to have little control over the events taking place on his ship.

"Aye, sir," Davis said. "Alerting Commander Juarez now."

"It looks like we may be here for a while," Jackson remarked to the crew once Lynch had left the bridge. "Go ahead and return gravity to normal and stand down from Transition Alert; normal watches until further notice."

"Aye, sir," came a chorus of confirmations as the crew sent his orders to all the departments in the ship.

****

"You still think this is just some political wrangling between Haven and New America?" Jackson asked Celesta when she walked into the wardroom to find him in front of the coffee machine.

"I've already admitted that this is a bit unusual," she conceded as she grabbed a clean mug. "But I'm not ready to call it anything more nefarious yet. Besides, we should be underway soon enough."

"Have you ever had any clandestine operations like this in your time in First Fleet, Commander?" Ensign Davis spoke up from a table where she was reading from an oversized comlink the younger officers tended to prefer and eating a pastry.

"Nothing this dramatic," Celesta said, turning to the younger officer. While the bridge was a formal place, officers tended to be a bit more relaxed and approachable in the wardroom. "We had our fair share of secret passengers and bizarre orders, but I've never transitioned this far outside a star system. I'll admit that it is a bit unnerving."

"I sometimes think the politicians miss the old days when nation states were constantly fighting with each other," Jackson said with a snort. "We haven't had so much as a mild cold war in centuries."

"Why do you think that is, Captain?" Davis asked. Celesta noticed that the young ensign, while respectful, wasn't nearly as aloof around Captain Wolfe as the majority of the crew she'd observed.

"Distance coupled with nobody wanting for anything," Jackson said, leaning back against the counter and sipping his coffee. "All the major enclaves have more resources and space than their populations could consume in a millennia, and despite the newest generation of warp drive from Tsuyo Corporation, the idea of trying to invade seems ludicrous."

"There's also that," Celesta offered, taking a seat at another table. "Tsuyo corporate office controls the flow of technology to all the worlds, and Haven has a firm hand on their board. Anybody that doesn't play nice risks being cut off."

"You may have that backwards, Commander," Jackson said with a mirthless chuckle. "I believe Tsuyo's chairman has a firm hand on Haven's representatives, and by proxy most of the Senate."

"Maybe," Celesta said, "but you'll never hear me admit that out loud where the wrong person can hear it."

Jackson just shrugged. "It's not exactly a secret," he said, pushing himself off the counter. "The system has worked for so long it's more or less an institution and nobody seems to have any real interest in changing it. Tsuyo has controlled all aspects of spaceflight since before the first colony ships were sent to Alpha Centauri. They mete out technology at a rate that can be absorbed by the population to ensure maximum profitability and we dutifully allow them to maintain control over it. Did you know there are systems on this ship that Fleet personnel are not allowed to work on or even access?" When Celesta shook her head, he continued. "Not many people do. As XO you'll want to get with Lieutenant Commander Singh and familiarize yourself with those. Per the agreement with CENTCOM those systems are leased to the Confederacy and can only be worked on by Tsuyo technicians except in the case of an extreme emergency."

"That's certainly something I would like to be sure about," Celesta said, furiously making notes on her comlink to remind herself to talk to Chief Engineer Singh.

"It's not such a big deal on a ship this old," Jackson said with a shrug as he walked to the hatch. "But on a newer vessel any tampering could land you in front of a board of inquiry." He stepped through into the corridor and made his way back towards the bridge.

Nodding to the Marine sentry, he slipped into his seat and began checking over statuses on his display as all the departments sent their post-transition reports to the bridge. As he'd expected, the relatively short flight was uneventful and there were no concerns that he needed to address.

"Captain, Shuttle Three is on its way back with Mr. Lynch aboard," the com officer said. "They'll be docking in approximately fifteen minutes."

"Did the shuttle report in or was it another tight beam from the *Oscar Marks*?"

"Tight beam com, sir,"

"OPS, tell Commander Juarez to debrief the pilot and send the last known coordinates of the *Oscar Marks* to my station," Jackson said. He thought about having Lynch brought up to the bridge to report to him directly, but he knew the political operative wouldn't be pinned down so easily. It was almost certain that the little weasel had an order in his possession that was a catch-all to make sure he didn't have to answer any questions he didn't want to. "Also, keep me apprised of Mr. Lynch's movements once he's back on the *Blue Jacket*," he ordered instead.

It was nearly half an hour later when his terminal pinged with a message from his flight operations officer, Commander Javier Juarez. The *Oscar Marks* was sitting eighty thousand kilometers off their bow, twelve degrees declination. Captain Asiri was still running dark and had deployed stealth countermeasures that completely obscured the large ship from the *Blue Jacket's* passive sensors as well as completely confusing Jackson. Why bother to keep hiding when they'd already identified themselves in the previous communications?

He was mulling over the possibilities when a specialist he recognized as being one of Juarez's spacers walked onto the bridge and handed him yet another official packet, this one bearing Admiral Winters' signature.

"Mr. Lynch asked me to bring this to you, sir," the young man stammered. Not serving on the bridge, or anywhere near Officer Country, he was clearly intimidated standing before the captain.

"Thank you," Jackson said simply, reaching out and taking the packet. "You're dismissed." The spacer spun on his heel in an honest to God facing movement, something nobody did after basic training, and marched off the bridge with his eyes fixed on the exit. Jackson would have almost laughed had it not been for the bundle of almost certain unhappiness he held in his hand.

"Ensign Davis, you have the bridge until Commander Wright returns," he said as he climbed out of his seat.

"Aye, sir," Davis said.

****

"Captain Wolfe," Admiral Winters began on the video that was playing on Jackson's terminal screen. "This message is to accompany your official change of orders, which will have been in the packet Mr. Lynch handed you containing this recording.

"The need for the utmost security should be apparent by this point, so I won't waste time explaining to you why it was necessary. Honestly, all you need to do is follow orders and you don't need to understand the big picture to do that. Now ... the reason for this message has nothing to do with your new routing orders.

"While I would have ... enjoyed ... telling you this in person, this will have to suffice. This will be the last cruise for the *Blue Jacket*. In fact, the entire Ninth is being stood down. The *Pontiac* and the *Crazy Horse* are already steaming for the Sierra Shipyards to be decommissioned and dismantled. The destroyers from the Ninth will not be replaced. Black Fleet is paring down operations in the face of no threats, immediate or potential. CENTCOM feels the funding can be better allocated and, frankly, I couldn't agree more. With the implementation of the second generation Tsuyo com network the need for Black Fleet at all is coming to an end. But, I digress.

"I think we both know that given your fitness scores and background that the chances of you being assigned a new command are quite slim. I've taken the liberty of drafting your retirement orders and will have them waiting for you on Jericho when you come back through. I'd like you to take the time you have left on this cruise to give Commander Wright as much time as possible in command. I don't necessarily want you mentoring her, I'd just like her to have as much seat time on a starship bridge as possible." She stopped talking and stared into the camera, her face contorting as she tried to keep her expression neutral and not allow her smugness to be a part of the official record. Apparently not having a graceful way to end the message, the video simply ended.

"Fucking bitch," Jackson said, the curse coming out as an exhausted sigh as he leaned back in his chair. So that was it. His entire life cut off at the knees in one short, dispassionate video message. The fight was officially over. All the hard fought battles for acceptance and recognition were for naught as someone sitting behind a desk decided four aging warships, in an era of peace and prosperity, were no longer worth keeping around.

He wasn't sure how long he'd been staring off into space when a chiming sound let him know someone was outside the hatch. It also let him know that person was a civilian as his crew would give the customary single knock. "Come in, Mr. Lynch," he said with all the enthusiasm of someone being led to the gallows.

"How did you know it was me?" Lynch asked as he strolled in. "It was the chime, right? Every damn ship is different. Some stick to the old traditions and others don't."

Jackson was staring at the man in slack-jawed confusion, not completely sure it was the same person he'd been ferrying from Jericho Station.

"You seem ... different, Mr. Lynch," he said carefully, eyeing the worn, casual attire and the changed demeanor. Lynch's facial expression, normally scrunched up into a pretentious sneer, was relaxed and affixed with a lopsided grin.

"And?" Lynch said, seeming to be thoroughly enjoying the moment.

"You're a damn CIS spook," Jackson said, things suddenly snapping into focus.

"Not bad, Captain! First guess and a quick one at that," Lynch said, smiling broadly. "Agent Pike, CENTCOM Intelligence Section, at your service."

"Can this day get any more bizarre?" Jackson asked to nobody in particular.

"Ah ... you saw the admiral's little love letter I take it," Pike said, slouching into one of the seats in front of the desk.

"You knew about it?"

"Spook, remember? I went through all your orders and whatnot before I resealed them and had them delivered," Pike said. "Tough break, Captain."

"Yeah," Jackson said noncommittally. "That's how it goes, I guess. So why drop the act now?"

"You mean besides the fact that it was exhausting playing a preening, pretentious dick that worked for a pompous, arrogant ass?"

"Besides that, yes."

"There was no longer a need for it," Pike said with a shrug. "The deception was for Captain Asiri and the New America representatives that were aboard the *Oscar Marks*. I also think I'll have a better shot with Commander Wright being myself."

"Are you certain about that?" Jackson asked, raising one eyebrow. Pike let out a genuine, hearty laugh at his own expense.

"I like you, Captain," he said. "And what the hell? It certainly couldn't hurt. She was rather unimpressed with Mr. Aston Lynch."

"The fact she shot you down as Lynch makes me respect her a bit more," Jackson said.

"Me too," Pike said distractedly. "Anyway, the real reason I came up here, Captain, is to give you a bit of advice." Jackson noticed the serious expression on the man's face and leaned in a bit despite the fact they were the only two in the office.

"Your new orders are going to take you out to the frontier, right up to the rim. I'm talking beyond the official boundaries of the Asianic Union and out to the newest colony worlds and newly opened warp lanes. You'll be asked to simply conduct survey scans, check atmospheric condition, the usual ... but there is also the directive to monitor local media and communications."

"What possible purpose could that serve?" Jackson asked.

"There's something happening along the frontier, specifically along the Asianic Union, Warsaw Alliance corridor," Pike said carefully. "Just so you know, I could get in a lot of trouble for telling you this, but I want you to know that you need to fly into this with your eyes wide open."

"When you say 'something' you mean what, exactly?" Jackson said, skeptical of anything a CIS agent would tell him.

"That's just it," Pike said, leaning back again. "We have no idea. There's conclusive evidence that we've had two ships disappear under suspicious circumstances, but there's no concrete evidence to tell us who did it, why, or even where the ships are."

"I hadn't heard anything about that," Jackson said, suddenly very interested.

"Classified," Pike said. "One was an automated exploration vessel verifying a safe course to a new system with three habitable planets. The other was a merchant fleet cruiser that went to see what happened to the unmanned ship. CIS and the Senate Committee on Exploration have clamped a lid down tight on this one."

"What's the most popular theory?"

"The Asianic Union is preparing to make a move on Haven," Pike said without preamble.

"What?!" Jackson said, almost laughing. "That's fucking absurd."

"Is it?" Pike pressed. "Why? Third Fleet is well equipped and loyal to the AU's Parliament. They know Black Fleet is being whittled away at an increasing rate so CENTCOM bean counters can make their numbers look good to Haven. Don't let centuries of peace by lack of proximity fool you, Captain. We're all still very human and thus lustful of what our neighbors have."

"Okay, I'll play along. What would the AU gain by making a move on Haven? That's tantamount to declaring war on the Terran Confederacy. The other enclaves wouldn't stand for that."

"Not a war, a raid," Pike said. "What is on Haven?"

"The Confederate Senate, CENTCOM Operations Center, and Tsuyo corporate headquarters," Jackson said.

"You missed one," Pike said. "Tsuyo R&D is also on Haven. It's not something that's widely publicized, but it's there. A raid on that facility would garner the AU a technological edge that would be hard to surmount. Couple that with their superior population numbers and manufacturing base ... you see where I'm going with this."

"I suppose it's plausible," Jackson admitted, the words seeming to cause him physical pain to say. "But why attack a frontier drone and a freight hauler?"

"Obviously to keep a secret hidden," Pike said with a shrug. "Like I said ... that's one of the more popular theories. Not to mention the least exotic."

"Oh yeah?"

"Oh yeah," Pike confirmed. "It does sort of make sense in a way. Given Tsuyo's Japanese heritage from when the company was on Earth, the AU may feel they're entitled to it anyway. Other theories range from conspiracies to keep the new planets uninhabited all the way to attack from aliens."

"Aliens?" Jackson laughed. "Digging deep for that one, aren't they?"

"We've discovered at least one race of intelligent aliens," Pike said, holding up a finger.

"Yeah, a species of methane breathers on a world that would kill us within seconds," Jackson said. "We can't even communicate with them. Has anybody even been back to that planet in the last hundred years?"

"Just the occasional scientific expedition." Pike shook his head.

"So, I suppose I should thank you for the warning," Jackson said. "What happens next? Are you coming along?"

"No," Pike said. "I'm not much of a crew person myself. The *Oscar Marks* should be departing soon; we'll wait a bit after that and then we'll fly under normal power a short distance and then you'll drop me off. After that you're clear to warp to your first waypoint."

"So we just wait?" Jackson asked, not bothering to ask the operative what was waiting only a short distance away.

"Well, we could pass the time more quickly if you'd be so kind as to offer a weary traveler a drink out of that bottle in your lower left drawer," Pike said with a grin.

"I'm not even going to ask you how you know about that," Jackson said sourly, not bothering to deny the charge. He reached down, keyed the drawer open, and pulled out a still-sealed bottle of his precious Kentucky bourbon. "Grab some glasses from that shelf and lock the hatch."

Chapter 6

"The *Oscar Marks* is pulling away," Ensign Davis reported, giving Pike a long sideways glance as she did. His changed appearance and demeanor had caused a hush to fall on the bridge when he and Jackson had walked back in. For his part, Jackson didn't bother explaining the change to his crew.

"Not even so much as a tight beamed 'safe voyage,'" Pike remarked from the observer's seat. "Asiri really is an arrogant ass." The last comment caused jaws to drop and stay open. Jackson just rolled his eyes, but said nothing.

"New coordinates?" he said instead.

"Here you go," Pike said, handing his comlink to the operator at Navigation.

"We're fifteen minutes away from there at half-thrust, Captain," she said after inputting the coordinates from the display.

"Also, I'll need you to transmit a standard Fleet hail on this frequency," Pike said, walking over to the Com station and bringing up another screen on his comlink. Jackson nodded to the ensign manning the station when he looked over for confirmation. The response to the hail was immediate.

"New contact!" Ensign Davis said sharply. "It's ... sitting one hundred meters from our new target coordinates."

"That's my ride," Pike said, returning to the observer's seat. "She's been sitting stealthed for the last four months. Glad the computer brought her to the right place."

"A Broadhead," Jackson said as he looked over the sensor data on his display. "I've never seen one up close. Hell, I thought they might actually just be a rumor."

"A Broadhead?" Celesta spoke up from her station. "What is a Senator's aide doing with a ship like that?"

"Things aren't always what they appear to be, are they?" Pike answered with a wink and a smile that sent Celesta to fuming. The Broadhead was a small ship, five crewmembers at most, that was technologically generations ahead of anything else in Starfleet. Rumor had it that the ship could not only enter an atmosphere but could create a warp transition without having any actual emitters creating the distortion rings. It was something that wasn't expected to appear on Fleet starships for at least another twenty-five years. The ship was a gift from the Tsuyo Corporation to the CIS. They also were rumored to sell them to anyone else with deep enough pockets to operate one. It was a short list.

"Nav, plot a course that will bring up us alongside the new contact and send it over to the helm," Jackson ordered.

"Aye, sir. Course plotted and entered."

"Ahead one-quarter," Jackson said. "We're in no particular hurry. Tell Engineering to begin charging the warp drive capacitor banks."

****

The procedure to dock the massive warship with the comparatively minuscule Broadhead had been absurdly simple. The *Blue Jacket* had been brought to a full stop a few hundred meters away and, once Pike sent the coded command signal, the Broadhead fired her thrusters and the computer guided the ship in for a flawless soft lock against the *Blue Jacket's* starboard boarding hatch.

"So where are you off to?" Jackson asked as he, Celesta, and Pike walked up to the still-closed hatch.

"That's highly classified," Pike said with an impish smile. "To be honest, I won't know until the next com drone flies through the system and updates my orders. If I were to take a guess it will be back out to the New European Commonwealth to keep an eye on this group or that."

"Well ... it's been interesting," Jackson said, holding out his hand as the Marine at the hatch keyed in the security code and popped it open.

"You want to take a peek inside her?" Pike suggested, indicating the flexible gangway that led down into the Broadhead. Jackson nearly said no out of habit, but something in Pike's tone gave him pause.

"Maybe a quick look," he agreed after a moment. "Commander Wright, you have the ship." Before she could protest, Pike moved to cut her off and wrapped an arm around her waist.

"It's too bad we can't continue our budding friendship, Commander," he said conspiratorially. "Perhaps we'll bump into each other again." Celesta was so taken aback by his sudden proximity and contact that Jackson was able to walk through the hatch before she could cite some obscure regulation about him leaving the ship without a security detail.

"*Blue Jacket*, departing," the computer announced the moment he disappeared through the hatch.

"Don't worry, I'm not shanghaiing you, Captain," Pike said as Jackson stepped through the hatch onto the smaller ship.

"You can't shanghai me. I'm already in Starfleet," Jackson said as he looked around. "This would be a simple abduction."

"Ah," Pike said. "I guess I've never really understood that expression."

"So why am I here? Or did you just want to show off your shiny toy?"

"As impressive as she is, no," Pike said. "I wanted to give you this away from prying eyes." He pulled a data card from a slot in the forward console and handed it to Jackson. "That is a set of secondary protocols for the com drone network. A layer underneath the normal com traffic. There are some interesting back channel intel codes on there, but the reason I'm giving it to you is that you'll be able to get in touch with me no matter where I'm at."

"This is highly irregular," Jackson said, turning the card over in his hand. He was vaguely aware of how CIS had built a secure com infrastructure embedded within the normal system. He also knew knowledge of the network was fiercely guarded. "I have a feeling I could be brought up on charges for even taking possession of this thing."

"When did you become so squeamish?" Pike asked. "It's not as if you have to worry about your career at this point, and access to that information could be vital out where you're going."

"You still think there's something that serious going on?" Jackson asked.

"I don't know for certain, but I suspect," Pike said. "The fact Winters was so insistent that the *Blue Jacket* be sent to gather intel means that CENTCOM is equally suspicious and equally clueless. If they had any firm intel on what was going on they would dispatch someone like me to find out for sure or they would mobilize Black Fleet's two remaining battle groups to deal with it."

"Thanks," Jackson said. "But I still have a hard time believing that the AU is planning something as bold as you seem to think."

"Maybe not. Hopefully not," Pike shrugged. "Anyway, it's time for us to part ways, Captain. It's been ... educational. Safe voyage."

"You as well," Jackson said.

"*Blue Jacket*, arriving," the computer announced as he walked back through the hatch and nodded for the sentry to close and lock it. As soon as the indicator showed a hard seal there was a soft bump as the Broadhead retracted its flexible gangway.

"Commander, have our first waypoint laid in and ready by the time I get to the bridge," he said, walking off and leaving her still looking like she wanted to say something about him leaving the ship.

He quickly made his way to the lifts and then rushed to his office after stepping out of the last car. Once he locked the hatch he went to the bulkhead behind his desk and keyed open a hidden panel. Behind it was a formidable looking safe door with redundant biometric locks. He pressed his hand against the panel so it could read his prints, heart rate, and calculate his stress levels before it performed a retinal scan and, finally, opened the door with a solid *thunk.*

Inside was a stack of data cards, an ancient sidearm identical to the one in his desk drawer, and a few file folders with hardcopy documents. He reached under these and pulled out an small, metallic box with an intricate clasp on the front. He quickly stuck the card Pike had given him inside the box and replaced in it the safe. After a quick inventory of the safe's remaining contents he slammed the door shut and waited as it locked itself back up. The small box was a shielded container that would hide the illicit card from even an active scan in the office. While it was true he didn't have a career to worry about anymore, he'd rather not retire just to be put into a CENTCOM detention facility for having the CIS code card.

****

"Course is laid in and ready, Captain," Celesta said as soon as he walked back onto the bridge.

"All ahead full," Jackson ordered as he took his seat. "When we reach transition velocity, secure from standard flight mode and deploy the warp drive."

"Aye, sir, all ahead full," the helmsman said, pushing the throttles all the way up. There was a deep rumble through the ship as the main engines quickly built to full power and the *Blue Jacket* began to race away from Tau Ceti on her way to the transition point. Jackson leaned back in his seat and silently watched their progress on his own display, ignoring the glances Celesta kept sending his way.

It was a short thirty-minute flight later when the rumble of the mains died away and the warp drive emitters were extended out of the hull. Ten minutes after that the *Blue Jacket*, unnoticed, vanished from the space far outside the Tau Ceti star system.

****

"Lieutenant Commander Singh," Celesta greeted the chief engineer as she walked into the room containing reactor one. "Are you busy?"

"No more so than usual, Commander," he said. "What can I do for you?"

"I'd like a word in private, if you wouldn't mind," she said, her voice calm and steady despite how frayed her nerves were. It had been three days since the ship had transitioned to warp and she felt her concerns couldn't wait any longer, but she wanted to make sure she was on solid ground before doing something that would ensure she never rose above the rank of commander.

"My office is one deck up," Singh said, nodding to the ensign beside him to take over at the console he'd been working at. "We're just doing simulation training for the most part. It's too risky to do any real maintenance while the ship is traveling FTL." They walked up the stairs to the next deck and into the chief engineer's office without a word, Singh closing the hatch behind him after he motioned her through.

"So what's the trouble, ma'am?" he asked, sliding down into his chair.

"How long have you known Captain Wolfe?" she began without preamble.

"We've served together for nearly nine years now," he answered uncomfortably. "What's this about?"

"Nothing official," she assured him quickly. "I'm just trying to get a handle on his expectations and his command style. With our rapid departure from Haven I didn't get the break-in period I thought I would during our shakedown."

"You and me both," Singh snorted. "I've got half a dozen new officers and I'm having to pull double watches to make sure they don't do something catastrophic. As to your questions ... from what I can tell you're not doing anything obviously wrong. Between you and me you'd have to try quite hard to be as useless an officer as Commander Stevenson was."

"Is Captain Wolfe always so guarded? Or will he open up eventually?" she asked. "I'm unaccustomed to being so far out of the loop and he shows no inclination to include me in the process."

"You know where he's from, don't you?" Singh asked, seeming suddenly uncomfortable.

"I know he's from Earth," she said. "Somewhere on the North American continent."

"Right," Singh said, looking at her oddly. "You're not aware of the usual stigma applied to people from Earth?"

"I'm from one of the oldest colony worlds in Britannia," she said with a shrug. "I've heard all the tasteless jokes and stereotypes, but I've never thought much of it."

"Well, believe me when I tell you that it's not been a pleasant journey up the ranks for someone born and raised on Earth," Singh said. "Jack has had to fight and claw for everything he's achieved, and even then there are those in CENTCOM just waiting for him to trip so they can be the one to bust him. Surely you've had to notice that even some on this ship's crew have to struggle to hide their disdain."

"I had no idea it was actually that bad," she said. "How can this be allowed to go on so overtly?"

"Officially it's not," Singh said with a humorless laugh. "But since when has a regulation or law stood in the way of human prejudice? If he were to report it, all it would accomplish is to make him a target. So he formed a tough outer shell and is slow to trust those around him."

"It sounds rather lonely," she said, thinking back to her conversations with Admiral Winters prior to taking the post on the *Blue Jacket*. Daya Singh was unknowingly filling in a lot of context that had escaped her during the initial interviews.

"That sums up the man's life as well as anything else I've heard," Singh said sadly. "Commander, while I appreciate what appears to be a genuine attempt to understand the captain in order to be a more effective XO ... I would appreciate a certain amount of discretion with the information I've given you. He is an intensely private man."

"Of course, Lieutenant Commander Singh," Celesta said, standing up. "I would hope that discretion is reciprocated as I doubt he would appreciate what would undoubtedly be seen as an intrusion."

"He'll never even know you were down here," Singh said, also rising.

"Thank you, Mr. Singh"

"My pleasure, ma'am."

Celesta had walked down with the intention of confronting Singh about Wolfe's disregard for procedure and to ask about what she suspected was a drinking problem severe enough that he'd been borderline unfit for duty on one occasion. However, after initiating the conversation and getting a glimpse at what made Captain Wolfe tick, she'd lost her nerve. She resolved to keep him under close observation, but she didn't feel justified in approaching him just yet.

Chapter 7

The *Blue Jacket* shuddered violently as she transitioned back into real space, much harsher than was normal. Jackson ignored the clatter of coffee mugs on the deck and half-stifled curses from his bridge crew.

"Engineering," he said, pressing the intercom key on his armrest. "What happened?"

"*We're investigating now, Captain*," Daya Singh's voice came back. "*There are no damage reports coming in so I'm clearing the ship for normal flight. I'll get back to you when I know something.*"

"Quickly, Lieutenant Commander," Jackson said before closing the intercom channel. "OPS, have all departments check in with non-critical damage or injuries."

"Shall I retract the warp drive emitters, sir?" Ensign Davis asked even as she sent out the query to all the department heads.

"Negative, Ensign," Jackson said. "Let's give the chief engineer a bit before we start changing the drive configuration."

It was two hours of drifting in space near the edge of the Xi'an system, a frontier colony of the Asianic Union, when the com officer finally spoke up. "Captain, I'm getting no transmissions from Xi'an, the com node platform, or any ship traffic."

"So the entire com array is down?" Jackson asked in disbelief.

"All my internal diagnostics are showing a green array," the officer said. "I can perform loop back checks all the way out to the antennas." Jackson climbed out of his seat and walked over to the com station. The officer was a lieutenant J.G. (Junior Grade) that Jackson recognized as the com officer for second watch.

"Show me your diagnostic data, Lieutenant Keller," Jackson said. Keller wordlessly pulled up the logs of the extensive testing he'd been doing since he first suspected that his equipment was malfunctioning. Jackson had to admit that the young officer had been very thorough and logical in his approach. "Good work trying to isolate the problem," he told Keller. "But when there's a systemwide failure like this make sure you at least alert me before you start troubleshooting. Go ahead and pass this down to your section and have them begin inspecting the com array. I refuse to believe we lost all radios, all bands simultaneously."

"Aye, sir."

"Com array failure *and* an inter-warp nagivation malfunction?" Celesta asked once Jackson had sat down again.

"An unlikely and unfortunate scenario," Jackson agreed. His terminal chirped for his attention before he could continue his thought. He read the message from Daya Singh and breathed a sigh of relief. The warp drive had a minor variance between the fore and aft distortion rings that Engineering had managed to isolate and correct. Minor variances were rough; major variances would tear the ship in half. "OPS, retract and stow the warp drive emitters and start the mains. Engineering has fully cleared the ship for normal flight. Tactical ... Tactical!"

"Yes, Captain," a surprised tactical officer, used to having nothing to do on the ship, sat up and nearly fell out of his chair as he tried to turn and face the command dais.

"You don't need to turn around, son, but you do need to listen to what's happening around you," Jackson admonished him. "While OPS is busy reconfiguring the ship I want you to begin active scans of the system and surrounding space. Just use the navigation array for now."

"Aye, sir," the tactical officer said, tentatively manipulating his displays to bring up the appropriate control menu, having to backtrack more than once. Jackson looked at Celesta, who nodded and walked over behind the struggling officer.

"Captain, com section reports no faults detected within the individual systems," Lieutenant Keller reported. "They even went so far as to use each radio to talk to one of the shuttles. All receive and transmit functions appear to be intact."

"Interesting," Jackson said. "Nav, we *are* at Xi'an, are we not?"

"Yes, sir," the spacer at Navigation said instantly. "I took three star shots when we transitioned in and confirmed our position. We're just within the orbit of the ninth planet of the Xi'an system, twenty-eight kilometers from our target jump-in point."

"Very well," Jackson said loudly. "We appear to have a bit of a mystery on our hands. Until Tactical verifies what we have around us we will maintain our position and continue monitoring coms. Lieutenant Keller, please initiate a standard Fleet hail and loop it." He looked over and saw that Celesta was animatedly informing his tactical officer that his underwhelming performance and lack of attentiveness was not appreciated.

Eventually, the returns from the long-range radar scans began to come in and the main display began to populate with objects and identifiers. The data that was being displayed, however, only confused them even more.

"None of this looks right according to our records," Celesta was saying, consulting the scan logs of the last Black Fleet ship to fly through the system. "There's a lot of localized debris, but we can't resolve any of the known constructs or satellites. There appears to be zero ship traffic in orbit over Xi'an as well."

"We know that's not possible," Jackson said. "Do we have another system acting up or are these returns legitimate?"

"They appear to be genuine, Captain," she said.

"Bring the high-res tactical array online," Jackson ordered. "I want the clearest possible picture before we move the ship." The high-res array was a system of high-power radar, lidar, and optical imagers that wasn't used during normal operations. The radar was so powerful it could interfere with other ships so the *Blue Jacket* would normally fly with the comparatively low-power navigation radar.

"Aye, sir," Celesta said, still chastising and directing the hapless tactical officer.

"Commander Wright, relieve your tactical officer and call someone up who is more familiar with the station," Jackson said. He was becoming increasingly uneasy with the situation and Tactical wasn't a station he wanted such an amateur at. He knew the station was normally manned with a "space filler" since the tactical officer was rarely called upon to do anything but assist the other stations, so he had no plans to reprimand his operator. The other spacers in that section would most likely take care of that for him.

While the shamefaced junior officer slunk off the bridge, Celesta slid into the seat and began bringing the tactical array online while they waited for an actual tactical officer from the bullpen. Despite the higher power, physics were physics and they would not have any new data on the system for several hours. The radio waves from the radars would take hours to reach the far side of the system, bounce back to be collected by the receiver, and interpreted by the computer so that it could be displayed on the bridge.

"Let's all take a deep breath and relax, everyone," Jackson said. "We're just going to sit here at the edge of the system and gather as much data as we can before charging in blind. I don't want any rumors or jumping to conclusions. Commander Wright, you have the bridge. Maintain normal watch intervals."

Jackson refilled his coffee mug and then rode the lifts down to the lower decks. Celesta was more than capable of monitoring things on the bridge and he wanted to get a firsthand account from the other departments, specifically Communications and Engineering.

"Captain on deck!" a spacer second class yelled as soon as Jackson entered the hatch to the Com section.

"As you were," he said automatically. "Is Lieutenant Yu in the shop?"

"No, sir," the spacer said. "He's with Specialist Harper in the forward avionics bays. He said he wanted to personally inspect all the transmission lines for the primary com array."

"Good man," Jackson said, looking around the com shop area. It was mildly cluttered, but it seemed to be the result of recent, hectic activity during the recent crisis so he ignored it. "I'll go forward and check in with him myself. Carry on."

The trip forward was slow going. Most of the crew wasn't used to seeing him patrolling the lower decks unattended and unannounced so they were unsure what to do. Some snapped to attention, others froze like prey animals, and more still dove through any open hatch to escape. The *Raptor*-class ship had two main arteries, one port, the other starboard, that gave the crew access fore and aft. The starboard corridor was for moving forward, the port corridor was for moving aft. The need for this distinction became apparent during drills, ports of call in which the crew was allowed to disembark, or when moving heavy equipment around inside the ship.

He could see he needed to have Commander Wright crack down on general cleanliness of the ship, but he had to admit it didn't look as bad as it had in the past when Stevenson would swear he was keeping up on it and the backshops looked like refuse storage. The com shop was located on deck four directly under the superstructure, so it was in the aft half of the ship. Most of the equipment for the primary communications system was located in the forwardmost avionics bay to keep the transmission lines as short as possible. There was so much high-energy equipment towards the prow that most of the forward section of the ship was unmanned due to health hazards.

"Lieutenant Yu," Jackson said as he stepped through the small hatch into the avionics bay. "What can you tell me?"

"The com array is fully functional, Captain," Yu said. He was a short, lean man of obvious Chinese descent. "As far as we've been able to tell, it's never been inactive since we transitioned back to real space. I wish I had a better answer for you."

"It's hardly your fault," Jackson said. "We'll be sitting here for another couple of hours at least. Let me know if anything turns up."

"Of course, Captain," Yu said, turning back to the panel he'd been half inside of when Jackson had walked in.

When he walked out of the avionics bay Jackson nearly collided with a flush-faced master chief petty officer who looked like he'd run the entire length of the access tube.

"Chief Kazenski," Jackson said. "Fancy meeting you here." Kazenski was the senior enlisted spacer on the *Blue Jacket* and was supposed to serve as a conduit between Jackson and the enlisted ranks.

"Captain, I would have appreciated a heads up before you came down and started inspecting the shops," Kazenski said, barely able to hide his dislike for his captain while he still gasped for air.

"I'll bet you would," Jackson said, eyeing the disheveled chief with thinly veiled disgust. "Unfortunately, time was short in our current crisis and I had neither the time nor inclination to hunt you down."

"My comlink is active," Kazenski insisted. "If you're going to be coming down to the lower decks and harassing—"

"This is *my* ship, Kazenski, and I'll damn well go anywhere I please whenever it pleases me," Jackson said, looking around before continuing. "Your connected family has protected you from actually performing your job function up to now, but things are always fluid in Starfleet and they just changed again."

"Meaning?"

"Meaning that starting now if I don't see you in a clean uniform, at your post, and clear headed, I will put you in the brig for the remainder of this cruise," Jackson said, his face inching closer to

Kazenski's. "You've been useless ballast on this vessel for two years. That stops today." The chief's eyes were slowly widening as the captain dressed him down.

"Have you lost your mind?" he asked incredulously.

"You're wasting time, Chief," Jackson said. "You don't have much time to get yourself cleaned up and on the command deck."

He turned and strode away from the gaping Kazenski, his hands still clenched into fists. Ever since the lazy slug had been dumped on his ship he'd been wanting to do that, but the man's family connections made it impossible. His father, Senator Walter Kazenski, Sr., was a powerful, connected politician who could make life miserable for a lowly starship captain with a single message to CENTCOM. The younger Kazenski had been put in Black Fleet as a long-term storage solution for a son that was mostly an embarrassment to an ambitious father.

But now Jackson had nothing to lose. As long as everything he did was in accordance to Fleet policy and procedure, the slovenly chief could lodge any complaints he wanted and it wouldn't affect his career whatsoever. As he walked along the corridor he realized Admiral Winters had given him a great gift. For at least one cruise, he could run his ship how he saw fit without fear of damaging his career by ruffling the wrong political feathers.

****

"This makes even less sense than the nav radar picture did," Jackson said as he paced in front of the main display. "Xi'an had two heavy construction platforms. I'm not seeing enough debris tonnage to account for even one of them, let alone every other satellite and ship that would have been in orbit."

"Two separate computers have compiled the data, so this is accurate," Celesta said, standing beside him. "Still no response to our hails, automated or otherwise."

"OPS, send the debris field data to Nav," Jackson said, walking back to his seat. "Nav, plot us a safe course down the well and put us in orbit over Xi'an. We need to find out what the hell has happened here."

"Aye, sir," the specialist at the nav station reported. "Course plotted and entered. Helm is clear to engage at will."

"Very well," Jackson said. "Helm, ahead one-half and coordinate with OPS and Tactical to make sure the debris doesn't drift onto our course."

"Ahead one-half, aye," the helmsman said, pushing the throttles up to fifty percent, telling the computers to engage the mains at half power. The telltale rumble and surge of inertia told Jackson they were on their way. He still held out the irrational hope that somehow this was all a series of bizarre errors within his own equipment, but he knew that was the least likely scenario.

"We have a flight time of over thirty hours until we reach Xi'an," Jackson told Celesta. "Rotate the watches as you see fit, but I want the first watch bridge crew on duty as we make our approach to the planet. Find an actual tactical officer while you're at it. Unfortunately we only have two onboard. Also, make sure Master Chief Kazenski is presentable and on duty. If he fails to report, notify me immediately." Celesta had to look up Kazenski to even see what position he held on the ship. When she realized he'd been missing the entire time they'd been underway, her eyes widened a bit.

"It's complicated," Jacksons said simply. "Just know that things have changed a bit since we departed Jericho Station. You have free reign to make sure everyone is doing their jobs. I'm going to take the first down time. Feel free to have Ensign Davis take the watch if you need to leave the bridge."

"Yes, sir," she said, sliding into his seat as he moved to leave the bridge. Once he had gone, she pulled up Chief Kazenski's personnel record and began reading. After ten minutes she wondered how many more cases like him were roaming around the ship and, if so, did she really want to know?

****

Jackson sat down at his desk and began pulling up any information on Xi'an the servers had that might begin to explain what had happened to make the system appear deserted. He also requested the latest com logs from the planet's com drone platform, a massive, automated construct that was now apparently gone.

The information was sparse. Xi'an was a fairly unimportant world in the AU save for the fact that it had a naturally stable environment that could support humans. In recent years they had begun to move some ship construction projects to the planet to encourage their citizens to move to the remote world and to take advantage of the slightly lower gravity. There wasn't any sort of political discord as the planet had less than two million people total and most of them were temporary workers setting up the shipbuilding facilities.

The com logs were equally unhelpful as the last drone from the planet had been captured and downloaded only a week ago. Nothing in the package it carried would indicate the planet was suffering some sort of calamity. As best as he could tell, everything on Xi'an was normal as of eight days ago.

On a whim he pulled up a local area star chart and began looking at the corridor that ran between the Asianic Union and the

Warsaw Alliance. There was certainly no love lost between the two enclaves, but an overt and unprovoked act of war seemed almost unthinkable. He saw that Xi'an was close to the accepted border, but still well within AU space. Besides, after centuries of relative peace would the Warsaw Alliance really launch such a devastating attack without even approaching the Confederate Senate first?

Following that line of thought, he pulled up the nearest Alliance planet: Oplotom. Like most Alliance worlds, this one showed evidence of heavy industrialization and resource mining. The CIS synopsis he had on Oplotom said that it was a world that developed most of the weaponry for the Eight Fleet and, more disturbingly, weapons for another fleet of warships that the Alliance had begun to field with no affiliation to the Confederacy or any ties to CENTCOM's command structure. Many of the enclaves had small defense forces for internal security, but the class of ships coming out of the Alliance shipyards would give anyone pause. What in the hell were they arming up for?

Jackson had stretched out on the couch in his office with the intent of only resting his eyes for a few minutes, but the stress of the day caught up with him and the next thing he knew his comlink was chirping to let him know he would be needed back on the bridge in an hour. He stood up with a groan, irritated at himself for falling asleep for hours when the ship was in potentially hostile space. Straightening his uniform, he hustled down to his quarters to get cleaned up and change uniforms so he could make it to the officer's mess before being stuck on the bridge for what would likely be a very long watch.

****

It was six hours after Jackson walked onto the bridge when they began to get their first view of Xi'an on the long-range optics. Unfortunately they couldn't garner any real details from that distance.

There looked to be increased cloud cover, but nothing wildly out of place.

"We're close enough that preliminary sensor sweeps are indicating that the atmosphere is ten degrees above normal on average," Ensign Davis said. "The surface temperature appears to be more uniform than normal, even at the polar regions."

"Whatever it is that's creating that cloud cover could explain that," Jackson said. "Our sensors can't see past that down to the surface. Tactical, begin another series of high-res sweeps. Map out the debris field and then start trying to figure out what it's all from."

"Aye, sir."

"We'll be entering our first transfer orbit in three hours," Celesta said. "Decel burn will begin in ten minutes."

"Understood," Jackson said. "Ensign Davis, you have ten minutes to finish collecting thermal data before the mains reverse thrust and distort your optics."

"Yes, sir," Davis said, seemingly unconcerned.

Each MPD nacelle actually housed two engines, a forward and reverse thrust motor capable of equal amounts of power. While most starships simply spun around and used their aft-mounted main engines to decelerate, a warship had to be able to keep her sensors and weapons on a target no matter their acceleration profile. To accomplish this the designers gave the *Raptor*-class four engines that could direct their thrust fore or aft, the plasma being routed to whichever magnetic constrictor and nozzle that was needed to provide power. One drawback was that when slowing down to make orbit the hot exhaust coming forward from the mains could distort the thermal sensors on the nose if the engines were run up past thirty percent power. Anything above eighty percent would completely wash them out.

"Ten seconds to decel burn," Celesta called over the shipwide intercom. "All crew brace for reverse thrust." Shortly afterwards the rumble of the mains died away for a second before building again, increasing in pitch and intensity as the massive engines began to slow the *Blue Jacket's* descent towards Xi'an. The sensation of being thrown forward was fleeting as the gravimetric generator adjusted to compensate.

They had now gotten close enough to the planet to see that the cloud coverage was actually made of particulate matter, not water droplets. Jackson's mouth formed a thin line as he considered the possibilities. Something had either exploded on the surface with tremendous force, or something had struck the planet from orbit. As he looked through the revised data from Tactical he could almost postulate that maybe both the orbital construction platforms had fallen to the surface simultaneously, but even that astronomically unlikely event didn't explain the disappearance of all the other orbital constructs nor the com drone platform deeper into the system.

"Standard orbital insertion," Jackson ordered. "The debris appears to be sparse enough that we shouldn't have any issues. I want us at an altitude of six hundred and thirty kilometers with an orbital inclination of forty-six degrees. Nav, get the necessary adjustments to the helm."

"Aye, sir."

"OPS, that's going to give us a full orbit approximately every two hours," Jackson said. "I want to be recording the entire time, full spectrum."

"We're still not receiving any transmissions from the surface and we're not detecting any power sources," Celesta said quietly. "Could this possibly have been a natural disaster?"

"No," Jackson said mostly to himself, ignoring the looks from his crew. "Xi'an was attacked. I'm certain of it."

"Attacked? By whom?" Celesta asked. Jackson ignored her and continued looking at the main display as the planet began to grow in size and detail and the horror of the situation began to sink in.

"Sergeant!" he barked without warning. "Lock down the bridge! Ensign Davis, cut all telemetry and sensor data streams to the lower decks, all data comes here and *only* here. I want all the servers locked out and local terminals disabled in the data center. Coms, disconnect all internal links to the bridge and deactivate all bridge personnel comlinks."

"Captain?" Celesta said, seemingly in shock as the heavy blast doors to the bridge entrance slammed shut.

"We are on lockdown until further notice," Jackson said to his stunned crew.

Chapter 8

"Xi'an had four major cities in the northern hemisphere and dozens of smaller support settlements in the south tied to their new manufacturing and production facilities," Ensign Davis said, reading off her screen after the *Blue Jacket* had completed her second orbit.

"Had?" Jackson asked.

"Yes, Captain," Davis said, swallowing hard. "They're gone. There's no trace of them left on the surface."

"That's impossible," Chief Kazenski scoffed. Jackson turned to glare at him, but had to admit he agreed with the man.

"One would think so, Chief," Davis said, still pale and her voice unsteady. "But the images we've captured from orbit don't lie. There is no trace that this planet was ever inhabited."

"Put the images up on the main display," Jackson said, climbing out of his chair and walking towards the front of the bridge. "See here, and here," he said, pointing to two separate images. "Look at the scarring on the surface. This isn't consistent with any type of known weapon. It's as if someone simply scraped the cities from the crust."

"Radiation levels in the atmosphere are normal," Davis said. "We're unable to determine if a biological agent was used from this altitude, but we can say with certainty that nukes weren't the cause of the damage."

"Recommendations?" Jackson asked.

"Send a drone down to the surface," Celesta said without hesitation. "We're carrying ten fully equipped recon drones capable of dropping into the atmosphere from orbit. I think we should collect as much data as we can while we're here."

"Agreed," Jackson said. "OPS, coordinate with Commander Juarez and prepare two recon drones for immediate deployment. Tell him I want them loaded with a full sensor suite. We're still on lockdown protocol. The drone data stream will be encrypted and routed directly to the bridge. We'll bring up additional analysts as we need them. This is a standing order until further notice."

"Aye, sir," Davis said as she slipped her headset back up to talk to the flight operations center that was located just aft of the engine pylons.

Over the next two hours the *Blue Jacket* launched a pair of sensor-laden drones, each on opposite sides of the planet, and waited as the data came scrolling in. The close-up images of the sites where the major cities had stood were horrific. Chunks of what looked like either building concrete or roadbed were sticking haphazardly out of some sort of viscous substance that glistened as if still wet. The oddest thing was that, other than a slight rise in mean temperature and a measurable rise in methane levels in the atmosphere, there wasn't any evidence of a massive bombardment or any type of battle at all, even a hopelessly one-sided one.

"Drones are at bingo fuel," Ensign Davis reported.

"Wipe their onboard memory, disable their sensors, and send the recall command," Jackson said in frustration. "Once they're out of the atmosphere, hand them off to flight ops."

"We're not much closer to finding out what happened here than we were four hours ago, Captain," Celesta said. "What's our next move?"

"Listen up!" Jackson said, not answering her directly. "We're going to continue orbiting Xi'an and collecting data for the foreseeable future. Obviously I have to unlock the bridge so everyone can eat and rest, but the blackout on information is still in place. Until we know what happened here I can't have rumors running rampant on this ship. You will be allowed to take meals in the wardroom and rest in the ready room one deck down, but none of you are to return to your quarters or mingle with your departments. Am I understood?"

A chorus of affirmative responses and head nods met his directive as he moved about the bridge, making eye contact with each one of them.

"Very well," he said. "Sergeant, you may unseal the bridge and resume your post outside. Ensign Davis, you have the hot seat. Maintain our orbit and continue recording. Coms, have Lieutenant Commander Singh report to my office and tell Major Ortiz I want his Marines controlling access to and from the command decks. Commander Wright, you're with me." She turned and followed him off the bridge, nodding to Ensign Davis as she did. Captain Wolfe didn't say a word until they reached his office and he gestured for her to enter before him.

"What a fucking mess!" he exclaimed as soon as the hatch shut, causing her to jump.

"It is indeed, sir,"

"Have a seat, Commander," Jackson said wearily. "We'll need to figure out what the hell to do so don't stand on formality. If you have an idea, even a bad one, toss it out there."

"Do you really think this is an attack?" she asked.

"I'm certain of it," he said. "The problem is, I'm not sure who could have done it." They discussed what little they knew until a Marine from Major Ortiz's detachment escorted the chief engineer in.

"Thank you, Corporal," Jackson said. "That will be all."

"Yes, sir!" the young man said crisply before keying the hatch shut and taking up post just outside.

"They're certainly excited," Singh noted carefully as he took a seat.

"This is the first time they've had anything to do other than ferret out illegal booze stills and break up lower deck fight clubs and gambling rings," Jackson said.

"So what's going on?" Singh asked. "I assume there's a reason the command deck is locked down other than a drill."

"Oh yes, and you're not going to believe it when I tell you," Jackson said.

Over the next forty minutes they brought him up to speed on everything they knew while supplementing the briefing with data from the drones and the *Blue Jacket's* sensors. Singh seemed to accept everything on face value, only stopping them a few times to ask questions but otherwise staying quiet.

"That's what we know," Jackson said, splaying his hands out. "It isn't much. What do you make of all this, Daya?"

"I'm still trying to process the fact that so many civilians are apparently dead. Slaughtered, in fact," Singh said. "I suppose my first question would be why am I here? The ship is running fine and I'm not an investigator nor a tactician."

"Because I'm going to need the ship ready to fight," Jackson said. "Let's be honest ... the old girl's guns haven't been fired in over a decade and even then it was low power laser blasts for marking purposes during that ridiculous exercise with Fourth Fleet."

"*Theoretically*, as per Seventh Fleet and CENTCOM directives, all weapons are ready to be employed in a combat situation in under sixty seconds," Singh said with a straight face.

"And realistically?"

"The expendable munitions haven't been checked in over fifteen years other than to make sure they're accounted for," Singh began, ticking points off on his fingers. "Which is fine, because the loaders that move the missiles to the launch tubes haven't been checked in ten years for functionality. The mag-cannons *might* fire, but I'm certain the accelerator rails are degraded after so many warp transitions without being inspected, and the turret actuators are likely going to cause issues with accuracy.

"The forward lasers were fired in that exercise you mentioned, but at five percent power. I know for a fact the power transmission lines on four of the projectors have deteriorated to the point that it would actually be more dangerous to us than the enemy if we attempted a full power beam. So, other than our nuclear complement, we don't have much that I would be willing to hang my hat on."

"We don't have any nukes," Jackson said quietly.

"What?!" Daya exclaimed. "We most certainly do. They've been sitting in the amidship magazine for decades."

"They were removed and replaced with training units six years ago when we put in at the Sierra Shipyards to have the plasma generators on engines one and four replaced," Jackson said. "CENTCOM has quietly taken all strategic weapons off of Black Fleet ships over the last decade or so. The initiative is highly classified and the dummy weapons will pass inspection when the specialists go to perform maintenance. Even the trace amounts of radiation are there, with no two being identical."

"Why in the hell would they do that?" Celesta asked before remembering whom she was addressing. "Sir."

"Given the nature of the crews assigned to Black Fleet lately, CENTCOM didn't feel comfortable with live nukes aboard the ships given the fact we fly through all the enclaves unimpeded," Jackson shrugged, unconcerned with her outburst. "I was personally happy to see them go. Until now, of course."

"So where does this leave us?" she asked.

"In a mess," Jackson said. "Just from a self-preservation perspective we have no idea if whoever did this is still around or if they're coming back. From a tactical standpoint I'd like something to threaten a potential enemy with that doesn't include harsh words or obscene hand gestures."

"No offense, Jack," Singh said, the familiar use of the captain's first name again causing Celesta to flinch, "but shouldn't we be steaming towards a jump point and transitioning to warp on our way back to Haven?"

"We're not leaving," Jackson said.

"Why not?" Singh demanded.

"Because I said we're not, and that's the only reason you need, Lieutenant Commander," Jackson said, raising his voice and leaning forward. "We have no idea who attacked this world. Or why. Until we have something firm to report we are not running back to Haven with our tails tucked. Now, Chief Engineer, all I need to hear from you is that you have a plan to get the weapons on my ship in at least some semblance of working order. Can you do that?"

"Yes, sir," Singh said, jaw clenched.

"Good," Jackson said, leaning back. "I'd like a report from you within the hour that includes a time table for the necessary inspections and repairs. Dismissed."

Singh opened his mouth to say something, thought better of it, and let himself out of the office.

"Was it a good idea to anger him before asking him to tackle such a daunting task?" Celesta asked carefully.

"Daya?" Jackson asked. "He'll be fine. I needed to break his attention away from wanting to weigh anchor and dash for the nearest jump point. He'll be focused on being insulted and indignant and in the meantime will accomplish everything I asked him to."

"I mean no disrespect when I say this—"

"Commander, as a new standing order, whenever we're alone you have permission to speak freely," Jackson said. "I'm going to need your best in this situation and you can't deliver that if you're tiptoeing around customs and courtesies even when nobody is around."

"Yes, sir," she said. "How is it that Lieutenant Commander Singh was aware of all the problems with our armament yet has not addressed them for what I understand to be over a decade?"

"Budget," Jackson said. "Each ship's expenses are tracked carefully and the *Blue Jacket* is an aging ship. If I turned in requisitions for the raw material or fabricated parts for every single thing on this ship that needed it CENTCOM would recall us to be decommissioned. Ninth Squadron has been running under an informal agreement between the captains to keep essential systems running and to whitewash those that aren't. So, things like power lines to weapons and replacement actuators for mag-cannon turrets take a back seat to drives and life support systems. I'll admit it seems absurd, but when most of our tactical systems haven't been used since the ship was built it appeared to be a viable solution at the time."

"At the time?"

"I'll admit to having some regrets in the last twenty-four hours," he said. "While Daya is flogging his engineering crew to get the ship ready to shoot back if necessary, you're going to have to stay on top of making sure the full scope of what's happened on Xi'an stays need-to-know."

"That will be impossible to do indefinitely," she said. "How much longer do you want to keep this under wraps?"

"Until we're breaking orbit would be ideal," Jackson said sourly. "But I know how fast rumors start and travel on a starship. Eventually we'll have to release the information because otherwise there's sure to be a rumor started that's actually worse than the truth.

"I'm not hiding things from the crew arbitrarily. I need them focused on their jobs and something like this has never happened in any of their lifetimes. Not even a terraforming failure has ever been this devastating. Up until now this ship has simply been a place for them to live and work. The term 'warship' isn't even in their lexicon."

"I think I understand, sir," she said. "Will that be all?"

"No. I need to you to prepare an eyes-only brief for all the section chiefs and department heads," Jackson said. "Keep it fairly vague. You can let on that we suspect Xi'an was attacked, but let's not divulge just how bad it is on the surface right now."

"Yes, sir."

"Dismissed."

Chapter 9

"Drone data confirms that there aren't any biological agents in the air," Ensign Davis said. "The ... slicks ... that are in place where the cities used to be are not out-gassing anything exotic either, just carbon dioxide and methane."

"But thermographic scans and ground-penetrating radar didn't provide any additional data to what we'd already been able to glean from orbit," Jackson stated. "The drones are good, but they're moving too fast to really get any significant detail."

"I'm sorry, Captain," Davis said. "We're only carrying fixed-wing drones. No landers or anything that can hover."

Jackson waved her off. "It's of no importance, Ensign," he said. "I've been suspecting what our next course of action was going to be since we first made orbit. Coms! Have Major Ortiz report to the bridge."

"Aye, sir."

Ten minutes later CENTCOM Marine Major Jeza Ortiz walked onto the bridge, his head up and shoulders back in that strut Marines seemed to adopt around spacers. He was wearing camouflage fatigues that were earth-toned and obviously tailored to highlight his impressive physique honed from hours and hours of time in the gym. Jackson couldn't decide if the major actually thought the browns and greens would help him hide on a ship mostly made of steel or if it was just one more way he and his charges could separate themselves from Fleet personnel.

"Captain!" he said, standing at attention and snapping a crisp salute.

"At ease, Major," Jackson said, returning the salute. "Have you been briefed about the situation on the surface of Xi'an?"

"Yes, sir," Ortiz said with a nod, standing at parade rest. "Commander Wright included me on her initial command personnel brief."

"That brief was necessarily light on details, but all the major points were highlighted," Jackson said. "I asked you to come up here because we've exhausted the amount of data we can collect from orbit."

"We're going to the surface, sir?" Ortiz said with the hint of a smile playing across his lips.

"Affirmative, Major," Jackson said. "I want a ten-man team ready to go in one hour. You'll be accompanied by at least five others: myself and some specialists from Medical and Engineering."

"Aye aye, sir," Ortiz said. "We'll meet you in the shuttle launch bay."

"Very well," Jackson said with a nod. "Dismissed, Major."

"May I have a word with you in private, Captain?" Celesta said from behind his left shoulder so quietly he almost couldn't hear her.

"I was about to refill my coffee," he said, gesturing towards the bridge exit. "You know, we should really think about getting a dispenser installed on the bridge," he said as he popped the lid off his mug.

"I'll make a note of that, sir," Celesta said with a hint of annoyance in her voice. "However, I think right now I'd like to talk about your plan to accompany a group of Marines down to the surface of Xi'an."

"What about it, Commander?"

"Sir, are you really going to make me cite the regulation that strictly forbids your leaving the ship during a crisis?" she asked with mild exasperation.

"No, I already know the reg," he said. "I also know it's not applicable in this case. You're referring to a CENTCOM standing order that limits a captain's movements in a time of war or while actively engaged with the enemy. Neither of those is true in this case. This is more of a battle damage assessment."

"Sir—"

"The matter is not up for debate, Commander," Jackson said. "This is a situation without precedence and I won't take the risk of sending someone else down."

"Yes, sir," she said in a tone that made it obvious she didn't agree and would happily continue the argument if he'd let her.

****

"Captain on deck!"

"As you were!" Jackson shouted across the cavernous staging area of the shuttle launch bay. He had gone down to the Marine detachment's shop area and got himself kitted out in something a little more substantial than his black Fleet utilities. He'd even gone so far as to pull a sidearm from the armory.

The Marines were all there, as were the two specialists from Engineering that Singh had sent. They were still waiting on the two medical technicians. While the specialists looked mildly terrified, the Marines were swaggering around the bay hurling insults at each other and generally looked to be overly excited for what was to be a sightseeing mission.

"Captain," Commander Javier Juarez said as he approached. "The shuttle is fueled and prepped, sir. I've put my best flight crew in it."

"Thank you, Commander," Jackson said. "We'll depart as soon as our other two passengers arrive."

"Of course, sir," Juarez said. "We're ready when you are."

They milled around for another thirty minutes before two specialists with badges identifying them as medical personnel walked into the bay, seemingly against their will.

"Perhaps my orders were unclear when I asked for two med specialists to be here by a certain time?" Jackson asked, mildly annoyed at the delay. If he were honest his nerves were a bit on edge about going down to the surface.

"N-n-no, sir," the senior ranking tech stammered. Jackson turned his back on them and addressed the rest of the team.

"This is it, everyone," he said. "Load up."

The shuttle launching bay was actually outside of the staging area. Instead of moving entire ships through airlocks to load and unload, the *Blue Jacket's* complement of landers, tenders, and ship-to-ship transports were hard-docked to their own individual airlocks and the launch bay was kept at a constant vacuum. All flight ops had to do was open the destroyer's outer hatch and disengage the docking clamps and the shuttle could navigate away from the ship.

As the team moved towards the open airlock hatch the shuttle's crew chief ushered them in and directed them to the crash seats lining either side of the interior. The Marines filed in quickly, found their seats, and were strapped in while the specialists were still floundering about and trying to figure out how the harnesses worked. As they were getting comfortable the pilot walked back and directed the crew chief to secure the main hatch.

"This will be a short flight," the pilot said. "Even so, those of you not accustomed to working in freefall may experience some discomfort as we deorbit and head for the surface. I would take it as a kindness if you would be aware enough to utilize the bags directly under your seat if you find your stomach simply refuses to hang on to lunch. Captain, it's an honor to have you aboard, sir. We'll give you a nice, smooth ride down."

"Looking forward to it, Lieutenant," Jackson said. "Commander Juarez said you're his best." Once the pilot had walked back to the flight deck he addressed his team, "Just a heads up ... anyone who gets sick and makes a mess in the interior of this shuttle will be cleaning it when we return while the crew chief supervises. If you're going to get sick, grab the damn bag. Clear?"

"Clear, sir!" the Marines shouted in unison while the specialists only looked worriedly at each other. The crew chief, however, just smiled at them, nodding his thanks to the captain as he strapped into his own seat near the front of the compartment.

"Stand by," the pilot's voice came over the intercom. "We're undocking from the *Blue Jacket* now."

There was a sharp *clang* with an accompanying bump and then they could hear the hiss of the attitude jets firing, pushing them out of the docking bay and into open space. The shuttle had no windows in the passenger compartment so there was no way to tell for sure when they were clear of the ship other than the sudden loss of artificial gravity.

Jackson felt his stomach do a backflip and his mouth began watering. Out of pride, he began taking slow, steady breaths, forcing his body to calm down from the sudden shock to his vestibular system. He looked around and saw that while the specialists looked a little worse for wear, the Marines actually appeared to be enjoying themselves.

He felt a sharp jolt as the shuttle engines started up and sensed the lateral acceleration as they began their deorbit burn. The *Blue Jacket* had been flying at a much higher velocity than was needed for their orbital altitude so the small shuttle had to run up its exoatmospheric engines hard to slow the craft down enough to begin their descent. The burn seemed to go on forever before the acceleration relented and Jackson could just begin to feel the mild buffeting from the upper atmosphere.

Soon, the shuttle was rocking and bouncing through the increasingly dense air, the friction causing enough heat to tax the climate control system for the passenger compartment. It was another five minutes or so before the ride began to smooth out and they could hear the turbine engines used for atmospheric flight spooling up. There were four engines mounted in nacelles at the ends of the four offset, stubby wings: two front, two aft. The engine nacelles could be pitched down for vertical landing and takeoff, while the thrust nozzles could be articulated a full thirty-three degrees to provide additional control.

Jackson wasn't sure where they'd made entry over the planet so he couldn't be positive how long the flight would be. He waved to get the crew chief's attention and motioned to him for a headset. The crew chief nodded and tossed him a spare set from under his seat. Jackson slipped them over his head and adjusted the microphone before plugging the cord into the receptacle at the base of his own seat.

"This is Captain Wolfe," he said over the intraship channel. "What is our approximate flight time?"

"We've brought you in right over the target, Captain," the pilot's voice came back. "We're descending in a slow, wide arc over the ... affected ... area. We'll be landing one kilometer east of the outer edge of the phenomena on the ground. We'll make landfall in another twenty minutes."

"Copy," Jackson said. He removed the headset and tossed it back to the crew chief. "Twenty minutes," he told the ground team.

The only further excitement during the flight was the flaring of the shuttle as the engines angled down and the air compressing underneath the craft caused a few seconds of bone-jarring vibrations. When the wheels touched the ground the pilot chopped the throttles and angled the engines up so the ground team could exit without being pummeled (or scorched) by the jet exhaust.

The crew chief went back and popped the releases for the rear hatch and hit the control to open the shuttle up. The hatch was actually the entire rear bulkhead that swung down to form a ramp for them to disembark. After a thumbs up from the crew chief they all piled out, the Marines forming up a defensive perimeter while the specialists lugged their equipment behind them.

"Sergeant!" Jackson called to the Marine in charge of the squad. "We need to go west one klick. It's more important we arrive there safely than quickly."

"Understood, sir," the sergeant said. "We'll divide up and put you and the techs between us. If you need to stop, just call for a halt and we'll watch the perimeter."

Jackson waved for him to proceed and then turned to the seemingly bewildered spacers milling around near the ramp. "We're going to be following the first group of Marines. It's a kilometer walk to where the affected area starts; that's where you'll begin running your tests. Any questions?"

"No, sir," a few of them managed to mumble.

"Okay then, let's look alive," Jackson said. "We're not sure what to expect, so stay sharp and call out anything that looks unusual or dangerous."

They were almost two hundred meters away when their objective came into view. The glistening edge of the phenomenon was clearly seen along with the fact that it was moving. Jackson looked on in morbid fascination as the mass undulated and roiled forward like a lava flow.

"It goes without saying, but do not touch the mass ahead of us with anything but your instruments," Jackson said. "Maintain strict quarantine protocols on every sample taken."

"What would you like us to do, sir?" the Marine sergeant asked.

"Stay out of their way," Jackson said, slowing his pace as they approached. "Our previous analysis shows no airborne pathogens, but let's not take the chance of your men accidentally coming into physical contact."

The Marines made no argument about staying away from the viscous substance and formed a loose perimeter twenty meters away.

Jackson looked to his left and right, stunned by the size of the slick. Now that they were close, he was almost gagging on the smell. It was an overpowering mix of sickly sweet and the sharp tang of decay. The technicians were breaking out their equipment and donning protective equipment as they would have to approach quite close to the slick.

"This had to be some sort of biological weapon," Jackson mused to himself.

"Possibly, sir," the Marine sergeant said from his left. "But how do you account for the missing buildings and infrastructure? This was a fairly well-developed city."

"You can see some pieces of building material embedded in the slime," Jackson said, pointing to what looked like a chunk of tarmac. "Maybe they leveled the city and then turned this loose on the survivors."

"That's a hell of an attack," the sergeant said. "It's not normally how you would fight a war ... this is an annihilation. This was personal."

Jackson grunted but didn't respond. He'd been looking at the attack as politically motivated, but if this was something personal as the sergeant had suggested that would open up the list of suspects to ... none. It threw an unwelcome wrench into his investigation because he could no longer look at the closest neighbor as the most likely suspect.

Agent Pike's convoluted musings were still bouncing around in his head about the AU possibly making a move on Haven, further muddying the waters. What if Tsuyo Corporation had caught wind of an impending attack and decided to strike first? Xi'an would be a viable staging area and Tsuyo certainly had the firepower. The company quietly operated one of the largest private militaries in existence, including ships so advanced the technology on them wouldn't be sold to the Confederacy for decades, though they claimed it was strictly for research and their powerful fleet was nothing more than a collection of testbeds. It wasn't outside the realm of possibility that they had some sort of strategic weapon that could level a planet like this.

His contemplation of the situation was cut short by screaming from his technical team. When he snapped his head up he saw the two engineering specialists holding onto one of the medical specialists, who in turn was hanging onto a probe on the end of a telescopic pole. As he ran towards the commotion he could see the med specialist seemed to be getting pulled towards the slick.

"Drop the fucking probe!" he shouted as he ran along, the Marines chasing after him. If they heard him they gave no indication, as the two engineering techs continued to pull futilely on their crewmate. Before Jackson could reach them the strap to the probe let go, which was the handhold one of the other techs was using, causing both rescuers to lose their grip. The tech holding the probe was half-pulled into the slick with a disgusting slurping sound; he began screaming shrilly, his head and shoulders still out of the ooze.

They all looked on in horror as his struggles and screams got weaker and weaker until the latter stopped with a choked-off gurgling sound. It happened so fast they had no time to try to put together a rescue plan or even toss him a line to try and drag him out.

"Everyone GET BACK!" Jackson shouted, snapping everyone out of their shock. They all retreated to what they felt was a safe thirty meters and watched as their crewmate's body was slowly pulled into the slick, the bent pole of the probe sticking up as an obscene marker for his final resting place.

"Captain, what was that?" a shaken technician asked. Jackson looked over and saw it was someone from Singh's department.

"I have no idea," he said. "But I think it's safe to say we know what happened to the population of this planet. What did we get from that thing before it took him?"

"The probes were all transmitting their readings to this box," the remaining med tech said, holding up a non-descript black impact case. "We also were able to secure a few samples before it reached out and took Lott."

"Very well," Jackson said, not sure what to say. He'd never lost anyone under his command, not even to an accident during shore leave. "Let's not waste the data Specialist Lott collected—"

"Sir!" one of the Marines said, pointing back to the slick. Jackson looked up and saw an offshoot of the mass beginning to accelerate towards them, rolling along the ground quickly.

"Back to the shuttle! Double time!" Jackson said. "Sergeant, inform the pilot we'll be departing as soon as we're all aboard."

"Aye aye, sir," the sergeant responded, not having any issue talking conversationally while running fast enough to keep up with him.

Jackson felt a pang of annoyance at that as he was already feeling out of breath and they'd not even covered a quarter of the distance.

They could hear the turbines spooling as they sprinted to the waiting shuttle, the crew chief frantically waving them in. They stomped up the back ramp and threw themselves into their seats, feeling the engines build power before the rear hatch had even swung shut and locked. By the time Jackson had secured his restraints, the turbines were howling as the shuttle climbed up and away from the slick at a steep angle.

****

Jackson barely remembered the shuttle ride back to the ship. He was vaguely aware it took them longer than it usually would because the small craft had to build up a lot of speed before it could change orbits and approach the *Blue Jacket* as she streaked over the planet. He snapped back to alertness once he felt the gravity inside the shuttle increase as it slowly reversed into the gaping maw of the destroyer's launch bay. The jolt of the ship's docking mechanism as it grabbed the shuttle and snugged it up against the airlock marked the end of a horrific mission in which Specialist Lott was the first person Jackson had ever lost under his command.

"Maintain quarantine protocols on those samples," he said quietly over the noise of the shuttle. "There will be a mission debrief in one hour, conference room on deck one-bravo. Everything that took place on the surface is classified until further notice."

He didn't wait for their acknowledgements. Instead he climbed out of his seat and motioned for the crew chief to open the rear hatch so he could get away.

"*Blue Jacket*, arriving." Somehow the passionless voice of the computer had an accusatory tone to it as it announced his return.

He fled the small craft and the staging area as fast as he reasonably could without actually running. In his mind he felt the accusing stares of the crew. *You took them down there. You let him die.*

By some miracle he made it to his quarters without being stopped or his comlink requesting his presence. He locked the hatch and violently ripped his rank insignia off his collar before tearing his uniform off with no less vigor. Once inside the private head he turned the water in the shower up to the hottest setting and stepped into the stream, not even flinching as it scalded his skin.

He leaned forward and let his forehead slam into the hard composite of the stall, letting the blistering stream run down his back. After an indeterminate amount of time he shut the water off and stepped out into the steam-filled head, the mist swirling as the small fan tried to pull in the moisture so the environmental systems could extract the water. His skin was bright red where the too-hot water had hit him, but he barely noticed. The screams of Specialist Lott came unbidden to his mind and he turned quickly, vomiting into the toilet.

It was some time later when he felt ready to dry himself off and get into a clean uniform. He walked out into the bedroom of his quarters and saw his comlink flashing with messages from Commander Wright and Commander Owens, the ship's Chief Medical Officer and Specialist Lott's superior.

He entered a quick response to both requesting they be there for the mission debrief and left it at that. As he pawed through his wall locker for another set of fatigues, he saw the box on the bottom shelf. Four small, round caps looked back up at him from the case that had twelve slots. He stared at the one in the top right corner for a full minute with longing, debating with himself how much time he had before he had to be in the conference room. He was the captain, after all. Wouldn't the briefing wait for him?

With waning resolve, he pulled his uniform out of the locker and firmly shut it. Even though he didn't know Lott, and couldn't have picked him out of a lineup, he wouldn't piss on the man's memory by showing up to the mission debrief and talk about his death with glassy eyes. He dressed quickly with a mechanical efficiency born of twenty-three years of repetition. Once his boots were on and had tightened themselves down on his feet, he inspected himself in the mirror while reattaching his rank insignia on one side of the collar and the *Blue Jacket's* crest on the other. Steeling himself, he keyed the hatch open and walked out into the deserted corridor.

****

"I know emotions are high and nerves are frayed right now, but let's try and get through this without missing anything," Jackson began once all the required attendees had filed into the conference room. As the hatch slid closed he took a deep breath and began recounting the mission on the surface to his staff. He was able to make it through the events of the day without interruption or anyone pointing an accusing finger at him.

"So you're under the assumption that this is a biological weapon of some sort?" Commander Owens said after Jackson had finished the recounting and had shown them the recordings from the tech teams' helmet cameras.

"Assumption may be too strong a word," Jackson said. "It's a working theory at the moment."

Commander Owens seemed to be less interested in the death of one of his specialists than he was in knowing what Jackson intended to do with the samples sitting in Medical.

"As you know, Captain, we have no staff able to test the samples brought back," Owens said. "I would suggest we jettison them or put them in cryogenic storage for the trip back to Haven."

"That's not technically true, Commander," Celesta said, speaking up before Jackson could answer. "There's a microbiologist and an expert on infectious diseases on your staff. You also have an ISO-2 clean room at your disposal which would be sufficient for an agent that isn't even airborne."

Commander Owens looked like he wanted to leap across the table and strangle Celesta.

"Your experts will have plenty to do just going through the remote probe data the team collected," Jackson said, heading off an argument. "While I don't foresee the need to directly test the samples right now, I want them put into cryo storage and preserved. We will not be jettisoning them off the ship."

"Of course, Captain," Owens said, appearing mollified.

"If there is nothing else, you're all dismissed," Jackson said. "Commander Wright will coordinate the memorial service for Specialist Lott and I will prepare a briefing for the crew. It's time everyone knows what we do about what is happening."

****

"Lieutenant Peters," Jackson said as he walked onto the bridge. "I want one of our com drones prepped for flight. It will be a direct course for the Alpha Centauri system. I will update you on the package contents shortly. There are to be *no* unauthorized communications loaded onto the drone, and I *will* be checking."

"Yes, sir," Peters said. "Sending the command now to pull a drone out of storage. It will take a few hours before it's ready to launch."

"That's fine," Jackson said. "Lieutenant, you have the bridge. I'll be in my office. Commander Wright will be coming on duty shortly."

He retreated to his office and pulled up a connection to the secure server all the mission data had been stored on. After sifting through it he decided to simply include everything they had, even the horrific video recordings of Specialist First Class Lott's death, in a compressed folder he added to the com packet he would eventually forward to OPS so that it could be loaded into the com drone.

He again reflected on the "gift" Admiral Winters had given him. In her need to gloat about the demise of his career, she had freed him to respond in ways he never would have before. For instance, he most likely would have tried to suppress the associated imagery of Lott's death for fear his actions leading to it would harm his career or cost him his command. With such considerations no longer hanging over his head like an executioner's axe, he felt he was able to consider the problem with an untainted point of view. He would include everything from the ground mission, in all its gory details, along with a synopsis of his planned actions afterward. He was more concerned about how his crew would react to what he was planning to do next than he was about an admiral sitting over a hundred lightyears away.

Chapter 10

"I'll make this as quick as I can since we all have a lot of work to do and not a lot of time to do it in," Jackson said, sitting behind his desk and talking to the camera set up in front of him. "I'm sure there are rumors flying around about what we've found in this system, on Xi'an, and even the loss of a crewmate.

"Five days ago we transitioned into the Xi'an system and found it deserted. No ships, no satellites, no com drone platform. As we made orbit we found the destruction was absolute all the way to the surface. Not a single resident of Xi'an was left alive, no structure was left standing, and very little evidence was left to tell us who was responsible." He paused as the pre-arranged images he'd loaded of the destruction scrolled across the monitor.

"It is also with a heavy heart that I tell you about the loss of one of our own. Specialist First Class Davis Lott was killed in action during our investigation of the anomaly found on the surface. Details of his memorial service this evening are posted on the shipwide message board. Specialist Lott was a well-respected member of the *Blue Jacket's* medical staff and will be missed.

"Since we're still not sure what, or who, caused this disaster we are pressing ahead with our investigation. CENTCOM will be notified of our findings and we will soon be breaking orbit for our next destination. I'm going to be straight with you. The evidence and intelligence we have available to us points to a faction within the Warsaw Alliance. To confirm or disprove this we will be departing for Oplotom, a world right across the accepted border, as soon as Chief Engineer Singh clears the ship. We owe it to every one of the citizens on Xi'an to find out who did this before they have a chance to strike again.

"These are events unprecedented since humanity first ventured away from Earth and later, Haven. I expect, and know, that you will rise to the occasion. That is all."

The red light over the camera winked out and Jackson leaned back in his seat, letting out an explosive breath.

"I thought that was just the right tone, sir," Celesta said. She and Ensign Davis were the only other ones in the office, the former to observe and the latter to manage the extra imagery Jackson had included in his presentation.

"It will hopefully answer enough of their questions without raising new ones," he shrugged. "The rumors had enough traction that anything less than near-full disclosure would have only fanned the flames."

"That's likely true," Celesta conceded. "I think we'll have to warn the department heads to be extra vigilant anyway. Something as incredible as a planet-sterilizing attack may create some unexpected reactions within the crew. Especially since spacers in Black Fleet are pulled from all parts of the Confederacy. It would have been entirely possible to have Xi'an citizens serving onboard."

"There aren't any, are there?" Jackson asked, wanting to kick himself for not having thought of that himself.

"No, sir," Ensign Davis spoke up. "I did a search on the crew personnel files when we first entered the system and detected something might have happened to the planet. I informed Commander Wright we had no crew from Xi'an aboard."

"Thank you, Ensign," Jackson said with a nod. "That was some quick thinking."

"Thank you, Captain," Davis said with a slight smile. "If there's nothing else?"

"No, Ensign, you're dismissed," Jackson said.

"Commander," Davis nodded to Celesta as she walked out the hatch. After it closed, Celesta looked to Jackson speculatively.

"She's really quite good," she said. "Why didn't you promote from within and give her a shot at Executive Officer? She has the experience and routinely has overwatch anyway."

"I did push for her," Jackson said with a humorless smile. "I was overridden."

Celesta suddenly looked wildly uncomfortable and shifted in her chair. "I wasn't aware—"

"Of course you weren't," Jackson said, waving her off. "It would have been impossible anyway. She'd have to be step promoted to at least lieutenant commander and it would bounce her right over Peters. As for your recommendation, it was a little bit of inside politics that you got caught up in, but it wasn't your fault. I didn't mention it to you because I didn't want you to begin your first stretch as XO feeling like you were resented and with a target on your back. You've done very well and you're already a far more effective XO than Stevenson was ... you've earned your position."

"Thank you, sir," she said, obviously wanting nothing more than to change the subject.

"Have you looked over the reports from Singh yet?"

"Yes, sir," she answered. "It still looks like another four days of repairs at least."

"That's what I figured when I read them," Jackson nodded. "No matter. We'll break orbit within the hour and just use a slower flight profile out to our jump point."

"The jump point is relatively far out in the system," Celesta said. "We should have plenty of time for Engineering to wrap up everything on the schedule."

"I'm sure you're right," Jackson said, not sure whom he was trying to convince more.

It was another twelve hours after the memorial service for Specialist Lott when the *Blue Jacket's* main engines fired and began to lug her up the gravity well, breaking orbit from Xi'an. Jackson sat pensively on the bridge as he ran the calculations in his head again, hoping to have his armament at least fifty percent functional by the time he would need to put on a final burst of speed to hit their transition point at the correct minimum velocity.

The crew seemed tense and unsure and, unfortunately, Jackson had no way to reassure them since he shared their misgivings. All the years on the bridge of starships and he'd never had to try and calm down a spooked crew or project a front of calm he didn't feel. Annoyingly, Commander Wright seemed to be able to do just that. She sat in her seat, almost serene as the rumble of the mains drowned out the ambient sounds of the bridge equipment.

****

The four-day flight to the edge of the system passed unremarkably. The crew seemed to settle down from the sudden loss of one of their own, and Singh's department, tasked with a real challenge for the first time in a decade, far exceeded the chief engineer's most optimistic schedule projections and, frankly, shocked the captain with their efficiency. They'd implemented creative solutions and had all of the *Blue Jacket's* forward-facing weaponry fully active. Point defense was still an issue and there was practically zero coverage on the aft end of the destroyer, but Jackson couldn't complain with the results considering where they'd started.

"I feel like the sense of purpose has done the crew a lot of good," Celesta remarked one evening as she sat in the wardroom grabbing a light lunch.

"It's only been a few days," Jackson said. "I'll admit the technical staff has wildly exceeded my expectations, but we'll see what happens when we hit the Oplotom system. I don't think a Terran starship has fired a shot in anger in over two hundred years."

"You're still convinced it's the Alliance?" Lieutenant Peters said as he scrolled through the drink menu on the automated dispenser.

"It's currently the most logical answer," Jackson said, washing out his coffee mug and frowning at the film that had formed on the interior between infrequent scrubbings. "But nothing would make me happier than to be wrong about that. Breaking a centuries-long peace is not how I envisioned ending my career."

Celesta looked up sharply at that comment and he kicked himself for his careless tongue. He'd had no intention of letting her in on Admiral Winters' little love letter until the cruise was on its final leg back to Haven.

"Captain Wolfe, please report to the bridge," the monotone summons from the ship's computer droned over the intercom.

"On my way," he said, killing any further automated messages. "Lieutenant Peters, I want you in CIC during both transitions, but especially when we pop out in that Alliance system."

"You got it, Captain," Peters said casually, drawing an irritated look from Celesta.

"What is it, Ensign?" Jackson asked as he walked back onto the bridge.

"We're less than two hours from the jump point," Davis reported. "We've accelerated to transition velocity and we're ready to shut the mains down and deploy the warp drive."

"Very well," Jackson said. "I also assume you've called me up here because you're ready to launch your com drone."

"Yes, sir," she confirmed. "Drone is loaded with the package and is locked out from further incoming data. Your clearance code is required for the final interlock."

"Stand by," Jackson said as he pulled up the correct menu on his own display, verifying that everything Davis had told him was true.

It was all there. The data packet to CENTCOM as well as a hidden burst transmission that would ping a certain CENTCOM Intelligence Section comlink address, a message that would propagate out along the com network until it was received and confirmed. He placed his thumb against the biometric reader while simultaneously entering his passcode with his left hand. The credentials were accepted and the screen disappeared.

"Thank you, sir," Davis said as her panel chirped. "Drone launch will commence in fifteen minutes, destination Haven."

"What's the ETA on that?"

"Two days, sir," she said.

He tried to crunch the numbers in his head, but he still marveled at the superluminal speeds the smaller drones were capable of, many times higher than even the fastest starships. He sat and began running back over the engineering reports even though he had already looked them over thoroughly hours before. With only two hours until their jump point he didn't feel like moving off the bridge.

"XO to the bridge," he said into the intercom. They'd be deploying the warp drive and transitioning the ship soon. May as well give Celesta the experience, though it was like a hot knife in his guts to follow Winters' orders, even if it was what he would have done anyway. "I hope that woman dies a horrible, slow death," he muttered.

"Sir?" Davis said uncomfortably.

"Oh, it's nothing, Ensign," he said quickly. "Just thinking aloud."

"I see," she said, seemingly even more disturbed by the explanation as by the comment itself.

Celesta marched onto the bridge and quickly took charge of the situation after Jackson gestured to his seat. Even though it helped that his first watch bridge crew was on duty, he was still duly impressed as she ran down her self-made checklist and was able to smoothly reconfigure the *Blue Jacket* for warp flight. Celesta was so prepared for her task that he didn't have to utter a syllable, not even a grunt, as she ran the crew through their paces and, without incident, transitioned the destroyer out of the Xi'an system in a blinding flash of light.

Chapter 11

"Report!" Jackson barked, waiting as the main display came back up.

"All departments have reported in," Ensign Davis said. "Successful transition. Nav is verifying position now."

"Position is verified," the spacer sitting at Nav reported. "We're sitting in the outskirts of the Oplotom system just outside the orbit of the seventh planet."

"Secure the warp drive and get the mains started," Jackson said. "Coms, what do you hear?"

"Nothing, sir," Lieutenant Keller said tensely. "I don't have any intersystem chatter or the clock signal from the con drone platform."

"This can't be happening again," the helmsman said loudly enough to be heard by everyone.

"Focus on your jobs, everyone," Jackson said. "Coms, same drill … have your shop verify that the gear is working correctly, but do not transmit any signal from this ship. Internal loopbacks and visual checks only."

"Aye, sir," Lieutenant Keller said, getting his department started verifying the equipment even though everyone was certain there was nothing wrong with the ship.

"Warp emitters are stowed. Mains are coming up now," Ensign Davis said. "Main thrust available in ten minutes."

"Begin visual scans of the system with the high-power optics," Jackson said. "I know the light is old, but maybe there's something there to give us a bit of a heads up."

It was a tense couple of hours as the ship sat on the outskirts, watching and listening. The mains were vibrating the ship softly, pushing the ship at minimal thrust, just enough to clear them out of the area of the jump point. Even though the flash from their transition would be clearly visible to anyone looking, Jackson didn't want the *Blue Jacket* roaring into the system, engines lit up and transmitting on every band, without at least getting some passive recon of the surrounding space.

"This seems to shoot some holes in your theory about the Alliance being responsible for Xi'an," Celesta whispered, her lips barely moving.

"Yeah," Jackson agreed. "You know when I said I hoped to be proved wrong about that? Now I'm not so sure. Could this possibly be Tsuyo Corporation?"

She only shrugged, not speculating on the wild theories put out by a CIS operative.

"Captain, initial scans of Oplotom with long-range optics didn't look good," Davis called out. "We're approaching their dark side and there are no visible lights."

"This is a planet of over one billion people," Jackson said. "There's no way every city lost power at the same time on one-half of the planet."

"What do you want to do?" Celesta asked.

"Coms, ping the drone platform and then ping the orbital traffic controller," Jackson said. "One challenge each. Let me know when the response is overdue."

"One ping each, aye," Lieutenant Keller said. They all waited another tense few hours until it became obvious they weren't going to receive a response to their challenge.

"No response, Captain."

"Helm, set course for Oplotom," Jackson said. "All ahead three-quarters."

"Ahead three-quarters, aye," the helmsman answered, pushing his throttles up and eliciting a harsh rumble from the engines. The *Blue Jacket* surged ahead and everyone on the bridge looked at each other with varying degrees of dread, knowing there was likely another dead planet ahead of them.

"We've crossed the fifth planet's orbit," Davis said some hours later. "Oplotom is coming up."

"Anything on the optical scans?" Jackson asked.

"Nothing yet, sir," she said. "We're chasing the planet around its orbit, so we'll be able to see the terminator soon and then the daylight side."

"Keep looking," Jackson said. "We stay silent until I'm convinced we're alone out here."

"Might it not be prudent to bring the weapons online?" Celesta asked quietly.

Jackson just shook his head. “The projectors on the forward beams will leak when sitting at full power,” he said. “It’s not much, but there is a detectable source there if someone is looking.”

“I’m surprised that’s an issue,” she said.

“It’s an issue on this ship,” Jackson said sourly. “The projectors are decades old. It’s a matter of decay, not design.”

“Budget?”

“Budget.”

“We have … something … coming up over the horizon,” Ensign Davis said. “It’s big.”

“General quarters!” Jackson said sharply. “Set condition 1SS.”

“General quarters, general quarters, set condition 1SS,” Ensign Davis’ voice could be heard throughout the ship. Crewmen who were already loitering near their work areas on alert sprinted for their battle stations and began to configure the destroyer for ship-to-ship battle.

“Tactical, go active,” Jackson was saying. “Get me resolution on that target. Bring all available weapons online and be prepared to fire.”

“Target and scanning radars going active,” the tactical officer said. “Weapons are going live … status is on the board.”

Jackson looked up on the main display and saw their list of available weapons come up and begin to populate with percentage and readiness statuses. He was more interested in the radar scans that were coming up, displaying in a window that popped up on the display in front of the looming shape of Oplotom.

It was enormous. It was also irregularly shaped, so much so that Jackson thought it might have been an asteroid or other natural formation that had been caught in the planet's gravity.

"Sir, target is maneuvering," Tactical reported. "It's coming about to face us."

Never mind.

"Bracket that target, main beams only," Jackson ordered. "Coms, begin transmitting all Confederacy challenges simultaneously along with the first contact package."

"You can't think—" Celesta's voice trailed off as she stared at the monstrosity on the display turning slowly to face them.

"I don't know what to think," Jackson snapped. "All I know is humans don't build ships like that. Range?"

"Six hundred thousand kilometers and closing," the tactical officer reported. "Target is not moving to break orbit. It's now station-keeping and facing our approach."

"Helm, braking thrust," Jackson said, staring at the display. "Cut our velocity by half."

"Aye, sir," the helmsman said, reconfiguring the engines to reverse thrust. They were all pitched forward momentarily as the ship began dramatically decelerating; the object in orbit simply kept rotating to keep them both aligned.

"Range?"

"Still over five hundred thousand kilometers," Tactical reported. "Given our deceleration curve we won't be within heavy beam range for another seven hours."

"That gives us some time to think, at least," Celesta said.

"It also gives them time to scan us with impunity," Jackson said. "They've not answered any challenges and they're in orbit over a Confederate planet that also isn't answering any challenges. Not even an automated reply. Tactical, update the target's status for the computer. It is now considered a hostile."

"Aye, sir," the tactical officer reported. "Updating target status now. Weapons are now locking on and calculating range."

"Load four Avenger missiles into the forward tubes," Jackson ordered. "Target the hostile and put the range countdown on the main display."

"Are you really going to fire without any provocation, sir?" Celesta asked.

Jackson looked over and saw the fear in her eyes and could hear the uncertainty in her voice.

"I have two dead planets, Commander," he said to her quietly. "Over a billion provocations between the two. This is what being a captain is all about: the hard choices. I can either sit back and see if they'll fire on us, which would likely destroy us given what we've seen so far, or I can hit first. My first responsibility is to the crew. If I'm wrong I will deal with the consequences."

She swallowed hard, but nodded and settled back into her seat.

"Captain, the target is beginning to drift toward us. Direct course," Tactical reported.

"Define 'drift,' Mister," Jackson snapped. "You mean it's changing orbits?"

"No, Captain," the tactical officer said, looking over his shoulder at Jackson as he did. "It's simply changed direction and slowly drifting onto an intercept course. No means of propulsion detected."

"A reactionless drive?" Jackson said, standing up and walking towards the main display.

"That's my assumption, sir," Tactical confirmed.

"Who would have technology like that?" Ensign Davis said with concern.

"Not us," Jackson said, the impossible truth of the situation becoming more clear. "Ensign Davis, prepare a com drone for a quick launch, same com addresses as the last one. We need to inform CENTCOM that we've encountered a new enemy, and they're not human."

Chapter 12

"Aye, sir," the normally unflappable Jillian Davis said in a trembling voice. "Drone is ready, message uploaded along with our preliminary sensor scans."

"Launch it. Now!" Jackson said. While the ship was at general quarters and he was on the bridge he didn't have to enter his passcodes to authorize something as mundane as a com drone launch. He needed to ensure that CENTCOM was aware of the situation. His last message would be worthless without the context of the new information he now had.

"Drone is away," she said. "It's free floating until its engine fires, but it's out of the ship."

"Good enough," Jackson said. "Tactical, what's our range?"

"We're at three hundred and eighty thousand kilometers and closing. Heavy beams are in range at two thousand kilometers, but they'll spread a lot that far away."

"Understood," Jackson said, exasperated he had no standoff weapons at his disposal. "What is the optimal range for the Avengers?"

"We're within their accepted envelope now," the tactical officer said. "They'll fire an initial burn and then accelerate into the target once they break fifty thousand kilometers."

"Lock on all four missiles and fire," Jackson said, his jaw set. "Reload the tubes once they're away."

Everyone on the bridge seemed to freeze.

"Sir?" the tactical officer said hesitantly.

"I SAID FIRE!!" Jackson roared, coming out of his seat. "You send those missiles or I will have you arrested for treason and find someone who will!"

"Missiles away!" the officer said, his hands shaking as he manipulated the fire controls.

"Reload and track," Jackson said, sitting back down. He waved off the Marine who had run onto the bridge when he heard yelling about someone being arrested.

"Birds are flying hot and clean," Ensign Davis said once she realized the tactical officer seemed completely locked up. "No reaction from the target. Final course correction in one hour. Impact estimated in one and a half."

"Thank you, Ensign," Jackson said, watching the seemingly pathetically slow tracks creep across the main display as the computer opened another window to show the *Blue Jacket* in relation to the enemy ... construct. He had a hard time calling something that big a ship. It was irregularly, asymmetrically shaped but roughly resembled an almond. It was just over three kilometers in length and two at the beam. He wasn't even sure how you'd safely bring something that big into such a close orbit with a planet without it simply falling from the sky. But then again, he'd just witnessed it sit in space and perform maneuvers as if it could care less that the planet's gravity well was there at all.

"Target is moving!" the tactical officer said, finding his voice again. "It's now accelerating along its original course. It's coming right at us at over two hundred G's of acceleration."

"The thing is no slouch," Jackson grumbled, surprised at how calm he felt staring down a planet killer as it raced to meet him. "Are the missiles updating their targeting profile?"

"Yes, sir," Tactical reported. "They corrected and fired their engines again two minutes ago to compensate for the target's movement. Impact will now be in ten minutes."

"What will four Avengers do to something that big?" Jackson asked quietly to himself.

"Piss it off," a voice said from his right. He looked and saw Chief Kazenski standing there, his eyes fixated on the main display. Jackson had almost forgotten about the wayward senior enlisted man.

The alien didn't try and dodge or intercept the missiles bearing down on it. The hardened nose cones of the weapons slammed into the organic-looking hull of the target, the motors firing one more time to try and maximize the penetration before the binary high-explosives ignited. Once the flash cleared the *Blue Jacket's* optical sensors were able to see that the alien hull was peeled back on the nose, but the ship was so large it barely looked like they'd scraped it. Looks were deceiving, however, and the Avengers did what they were designed to do and got some penetration, causing more damage beyond just the point of impact.

"We've done significant damage to the target's nose, sir," the tactical officer said. "Laser range in two minutes."

"Target where our missiles did the most damage," Jackson said. "I want all beams concentrated on the hull openings."

"Aye, sir. Updating targeting data now."

"Helm, push our nose to starboard by three degrees and kick her in the ass," Jackson said. "All ahead full."

"Ahead full, aye," the helmsman reported. The ship began to shake as the engines came to full power and the *Blue Jacket* surged towards their target.

"Our shot window just narrowed with the velocity change," Tactical warned.

"Then don't miss," Jackson said. "Nav, once we pass the target I need a course that slings us around the planet and out the other side."

"We're running?" Celesta asked.

"We're collecting invaluable data," Jackson corrected. "Going out in a blaze of glory by slugging it out with a ship twenty times our tonnage is not helpful to anyone. We make this pass, see if we can bloody their nose, and then run for it."

"If we survive the first pass," she said.

"If we survive," he agreed. "But they've spotted us and they've shown their propulsion is much more advanced than ours. This initial engagement is going to happen no matter what."

"Agreed," she said.

"Davis!" Jackson called. "Make sure we have as good a sensor picture as we can of the target on this first pass. I don't expect to make another one. Make sure we're recording all sensors all spectrums."

"Aye, sir," she called out, the fear in her voice that was there previously fading away as she became too busy to reflect on how scared she was.

They all watched the display tensely as the alien … ship … was resolved in greater detail. Thermal optics showed all the strange aspects of the asymmetrical hull, but failed to show anything resembling a drive output or weapons emplacement. Jackson had no doubt that they'd kicked over the hornet's nest with this one. For centuries humans had become complacent in the fact that nobody was in the neighborhood that could cause them any trouble. That misconception had just ended, and hard.

"Firing heavy beams!" Tactical called out, startling anyone who hadn't been watching the range countdown. The power draw for the forward heavy beams was so great that other systems began to drop out as the MUX determined who needed the power the most. Jackson watched as the beam projectors heated up under the continuous fire, but he was also watching the nose of the alien ship warp and slough away as terawatts of power per beam were poured into the breaches created by the missiles.

""We've got a thermal buildup along the target's port side," Davis called out.

"Let's get a—" Jackson's command was cut off as a brilliant flash lanced out from the alien ship and hit the *Blue Jacket* full on the prow. The main display winked out and the illusion of a window was shattered as if they were staring at a blank wall. All the other sensor feeds also were cut in an instant. Alarms were blaring on the bridge and the displays that were still working were scrolling a seemingly endless list of warnings.

"Some sort of high energy thermal blast right on the prow!" Davis yelled over the chaos. "Most of the sensors are out!"

"Go to backups," Jackson said, blinking as his eyes adjusted. "Get damage control parties to the prow and get me a casualty report. We're still alive so we can assume the ship has overflown us. We need to see where we're going and we need to see what's around us."

Armored hatches opened up along the forward edge of the superstructure and auxiliary radar and optical sensors deployed. Soon the main display popped back up and showed that the ship had executed its predetermined course and shot them around the planet and had them speeding along on an escape vector, still under full power.

"How are we still alive?" Celesta asked.

"Because they were as curious about us as we were about them," Jackson said. "I'll bet we're the first humans to fire at them. They wanted to see what we were capable of."

"Not much, it would seem," Ensign Davis said. "Enemy vessel is continuing along their original course, but they've accelerated to over six hundred G's. They don't seem to show any interest in coming back around for another shot."

"That's good news, I suppose," Jackson said. "Maintain sensor contact with the target and stay at general quarters. Tell Engineering to begin charging the warp drive capacitor banks."

"Do you think it's over?" Celesta asked as he walked back to his seat.

"For the time being," he said. "But I think something much, much worse has just started."

****

The trip out of the Oplotom system was fairly anticlimactic. They lost contact with the alien ship soon after they accelerated away from the planet, but it had been flying away from them at an incredible rate of speed when last they saw it. Using the backup optical sensors they were able to identify the nearest jump point and plot a direct course, wanting to warp out of the system before the aliens could change their minds.

****

"What hit us?" Singh asked as he looked over the reports coming in from his crews working in the prow. He and Jackson were standing outside of the hatch that led into the CIC.

"Some sort of high energy plasma discharge if I were to take a guess," Jackson said. "That was just a single shot."

"Impressive," Singh said impassively. "It turned almost every antenna on the prow to slag and destroyed all the bulkhead pressure fittings so completely I'm not sure we can repair very much of this damage."

"New pressure fittings?" Jackson asked. "Those can't be too difficult to fabricate.

"Not especially," Singh agreed. "But the heat from whatever hit us also deformed the outer hull to the point that we need to figure out how we're going to remount everything."

"It seemed like we were giving as good as we got on that first pass," Jackson sighed. "But this data is telling me they gave us as much attention as you would to swat a fly. One little parting shot and they've damn near crippled and blinded us."

"So are we heading back to Haven?" Singh asked.

"No," Jackson said. "We're on our way to Podere. It's a relatively advanced world and we should be able to at least get some basic repairs done before tackling the longer flight back to Haven."

"Maybe," Singh said, unconvinced. "You're still chasing this thing, aren't you?"

"No," Jackson said honestly. "Our single destroyer will not be able to go toe to toe with whatever the hell that was. We're going to get ourselves into a little bit better shape and then we're going to bug out."

"I'm mildly relieved to hear you say that," Singh admitted. "This is something better left to First or Fourth Fleet."

"Yeah right," Jackson scoffed. "If CENTCOM pushes too hard to deploy those fleets away from Britannia or New America I think we'll begin to see the breakup of the Confederacy."

"Truly?"

"If Haven calls on either of those governments to deploy their ships to the AU or the Alliance because of a new, super powerful alien threat, how do you think that's going to play out?" Jackson asked.

"I guess I've never looked at Fleet as part of all the political wrangling between enclaves," Singh admitted. "CENTCOM will have nothing left but a handful of old ships in Black Fleet that will answer the call, but every human world could be at risk."

“Let’s not get ahead of ourselves,” Jackson said. “It’s a single ship … or whatever it is … operating out along the frontier. This could either be an unfortunate misunderstanding, a declaration of war, or simply an incredible failure to communicate.”

“Which one do you think it really is?” Singh asked, ignoring the crew walking around them.

“I honestly don’t know,” Jackson sighed. “But we’ve been expanding with abandon for a couple hundred years. Our exploratory method leaves much to be desired and I think we’ve stretched ourselves too thin and too far for the level of technology we’ve achieved. We sent one deep space vessel out centuries ago and when it never came back we simply turned our eyes towards the easy targets: all those habitable worlds the warp drive put right within our reach. I don’t know … I feel like this was more or less inevitable.”

"Profound," Singh said sarcastically. "I wasn't aware you were such a philosopher."

"Right now I'm the CO of a badly damaged ship that's running scared," Jackson snorted, ignoring the barb. "I'll leave the philosophy of it to the politicians. Can we successfully transition with the backup sensors?"

"Certainly," Singh said with confidence. "This ship was designed with the assumption the prow was going to take some hits. You could have retracted everything but the targeting sensors before the engagement, but given the power the alien ship put out it wouldn't have made a difference. The outer armor was so badly warped the carriages to bring the assemblies back into the inner hull were nearly vaporized."

"Terrific," Jackson said. "I'm going to get us to the jump point as fast as she can get us there. Just keep the repairs up and keep your people busy. The less time they have to reflect on what's happened the better."

"I don't see that being a problem," Singh said, watching crewmembers scurry past them with a nod of acknowledgment to Jackson as they went about their business. "I'll admit ... when I heard you decided to make a head on pass with the old girl at an unknown alien hostile I was a bit apoplectic. But, despite the damage to the prow we're still quite capable. Powerplant and propulsion are one hundred percent, sensor backups are functional, and we still have some teeth. We lost the forward projectors but my crews have been steadily getting our lateral beams operational."

"How long?"

"You'll have a full port broadside available within another two days," Singh answered, consulting his tile. "I've kept the crews that were already on that job there since cramming the forward compartments with bodies doesn't necessarily help the work on the new damage go any faster."

"And the mag-cannons?" Jackson asked, not really putting too much stock in what he considered to be an antique of a weapon.

"All the accelerator rails in each gun were fully functional, shockingly," Singh said. "We're recalibrating the turret actuators and they should be fully operational. You really think we'd need such a short range weapon?"

"Given the distances involved in space warfare, *all* of our weapons are more or less short range," Jackson said. "Just let me know when you have them functional so I can have Armament bring the rounds up from the magazine and into the loaders."

"Will do," Singh nodded. "We'll be using the warp flight to catch up on a lot of the repairs and then hope that Podere has an orbital platform capable of some repairs to the nose."

"Keep at it," Jackson said, draining his coffee mug. "I'll be up on the bridge until we've transitioned out."

"That's a long watch," Singh noted.

"You can say that again."

****

"Chief Kazenski," Jackson said loudly. "A word, please." The senior enlisted man, despite having a clean and pressed uniform on, still appeared scruffy and unkempt.

"Yes, Captain?"

"There's not much you can do on the bridge right now," Jackson told him, deciding to forego another lecture on dress and appearance. It wouldn't do to appear so petty while they were facing such dire circumstances. "I want you to make your presence felt down on the lower decks in the shops and work centers. The crew will need reassurances and that should come from you."

"What should I tell them?" Kazenski asked. The man's utter stupidity set Jackson's teeth on edge. He let out a calming breath before answering.

"You should tell them the truth," he said. "We were in a brief engagement with an unknown hostile and now we're going our separate ways. We'll be transitioning to warp soon and then we'll begin making our way back to Haven."

"That's all?"

"What more is there, Chief?" Jackson asked. "The details of the engagement are highly classified. There will be no saving you if I find out you're divulging the information of the encounter to junior enlisted spacers." The implied threat seemed to penetrate the fog Kazenski perpetually lived in.

"I ... think I understand, sir," he finally said.

"That's good," Jackson said, looking past him. "You're dismissed."

"Is he always so—" Celesta trailed off, unsure how to complete her sentence.

"Useless?" Jackson supplied, not caring who on the bridge heard him. "Yes. But I'm stuck with him thanks to his family connections."

Celesta stared at him in open-mouthed shock. He never was so candid in front of her, much less sitting in the middle of the bridge. She looked over as Ensign Davis suppressed a small giggle at the comment. Apparently the operations officer was the only one who'd heard.

"I see."

"OPS," Jackson said, ignoring her tone. "Anything new in the area?"

"No, sir," Davis said. "We've been running active sensor sweeps and we cannot locate the enemy vessel."

"Could they have left the system?" Celesta asked.

"Since we don't know how their propulsion works we can't begin to speculate if they're still around or left the local star system," Jackson said, standing up to stretch his legs. "I suspect that they're sitting still out there in the asteroid belt watching us, not making any motion that the computers will flag."

"Should we still be broadcasting our position with active sensors?" Davis asked, speaking up in a rare instance of questioning anything Jackson did.

"We're running our mains at full power," Jackson said to her. "Anything even casually looking for us will see the light and thermal energy they're putting out. I want the best chance available to see them coming so we'll keep up active scans for now."

"Yes, sir," she said.

"How long until we hit the jump point?" Jackson asked.

"Another three hours, sir," the Nav station operator said.

"Warp drive capacitors are fully charged," Davis said. "Engineering reports the drive fully functional and ready for deployment."

"Good, good," Jackson said absently. "We're going to perform an emergency transition; that includes the fast-deployment of the drive. All of you should brush up on the procedure since we haven't practiced it in a couple of years."

The bridge crew took him at his word and all of them were ready when the call came. The warp emitters were deployed and charged in less than five minutes as the *Blue Jacket* was quickly reconfigured for warp flight. With one more quick "look" behind them with the aft tactical array, the ship vanished from the devastated Oplotom system in a brilliant flash of energy.

At nearly the same instant an enormous, tumbling asteroid, shaped roughly like a lopsided almond, stabilized its flight and began to move towards the Oplotom/Podere jump point at an acceleration unattainable by human spacecraft. Unlike the long, slender iron ship that had preceded it, the enormous vessel didn't disappear in a brilliant flash of wasted energy. The space around it seemed to fold and tear until it simply slipped through the opening without so much as a stray photon to mark its passing.

Chapter 12

"I'm telling you ... he doesn't have a clue."

"Shut up, Kazenski. Isn't there a batch of latrine gin somewhere with your name on it?"

"Mock me all you want," Ed Kazenski said, his hair disheveled and his eyes wild. "I was up there and he just drove this tub right at that big bastard. He even fired first! For all we know he just started an interstellar war!"

"Didn't you just tell us that Xi'an and Oplotom were both wiped out?" one of the junior spacers in the crowd asked.

"But the point is we don't *know*," Kazenski pleaded. "He says we're headed to some other Alliance planet for help before heading back to Haven. What if we're actually chasing after this ship that hammered us so bad in one shot?" His question had the desired effect on the small group that had gathered around him, mostly junior spacers that had no specialty rating. He seemed to pick up on the fact that they were swaying his way. "James," he said, pointing to a spacer third class who looked like he could still be in his teens. "Didn't you just propose? Don't you want to see your fiancé again?"

"Just get to the point, Kazenski. What are you selling?"

"All we have to—"

"That will be enough." Everyone simultaneously snapped their heads over to where the voice with the air of command had come from. Many blanched as the *Blue Jacket's* XO walked from around a stack of equipment racks with two Marines in tow. "This ship is at general quarters and we're in a declared state of emergency," she said. "What are all of you doing just standing around?" Like roaches scurrying when the lights come on, almost all of the junior enlisted ducked and raced away from the area as fast as their legs would carry them.

"Commander Wright," Kazenski said, trying to appear calm. "Just doing what the captain asked ... getting a feel for the crew's mood."

"Master Chief Edward Kazenski," she said, ignoring him. "You are under arrest and charged with violation of Article Six-B of the Terran Confederate Starfleet Code of Conduct. Sergeant, search and detain the chief."

"Yes, ma'am," the burly sergeant to her left said, roughly grabbing a gaping Kazenski. After an equally rough search that turned up a small vial of unmarked pills and an illegal atomizer used to inject them right into the bloodstream, Kazenski had his hands bound behind his back and was marched over to stand in front of the commander.

"It looks like I'll have a few more charges to add to the list before it's all said and done," Celesta said, looking at the pills the Marine sergeant had placed in her hand.

"I can explain those."

"Don't bother," she waved him off dismissively. "These are the least of your problems. You were warned about divulging details of the incident. Not only did you disobey that direct order, you've been quite busy trying to stir up a mutiny."

Kazenski's face contorted in fear at the word. Mutiny on a Fleet ship was something even his family would be helpless to deflect away from him.

"No! I never did that!"

"It's possible the captain was right and you're simply too stupid to understand the most basic details of your job, but holding impromptu meetings to suggest technicians drag their feet in making vital repairs to this starship along with disobeying their superiors is, in fact, mutiny," she said, walking up and putting her nose almost against his. "The fact that you're a pill popper just makes those charges a little easier to stick. This is going to go very, very badly for you ... I promise." She stepped away before nodding to the Marine escorts.

"Straight to the brig with him, gentlemen," she said. "Be sure to remove his rank and ship marker before tossing him in the cell."

"Yes, ma'am," the sergeant said before grabbing Kazenski up under the arm and marching him out of the area, the former chief blubbering and begging the entire way.

"Specialist Han, thank you for alerting me to the problem," Celesta said to one of the spacers who hadn't fled when she'd arrived. "I will make sure your service to your ship and to your captain are annotated in your record."

"Thank you, ma'am," Specialist Han said, bowing his head slightly. "I was only doing my duty. He's been down in all the key departments today trying to tell us that if the ship wasn't repaired there could be no way we would have to face off with the alien ship again."

"How was this received? Did people seem to react favorably to his ideas?" she asked.

"It is hard to say, ma'am," Han answered honestly. "The crew is scared and we don't feel like we really know what is going on."

"Thank you for your honesty, Specialist," she said. "You're dismissed." She stood there for a moment more looking lost in thought as the spacer hustled back to his work center.

****

"Black Fleet is still a military organization, Commander," Jackson said, his irritation evident. "I'm not about to disregard about a dozen OPSEC regulations because the crew is feeling jumpy. The details of this encounter need to be contained for the time being. I applaud your instincts on throwing that sack of shit Kazenski in the brig—and I wish I'd been there for it, oh so much—but I'm not getting on the shipwide and pleading or cajoling them to do their jobs."

"I understand that, sir," Celesta said. "But even you've admitted ... this ship, this fleet, has been little more than a courier service for decades. I fear the resolve and the instincts needed for a situation like this simply aren't there. I'm not saying you need to divulge details, but simply informing them of the current plan might go a long way."

"That was what that idiot Kazenski was supposed to be doing," Jackson grumbled. "Fine. You put together an intel brief for the department heads, I'll approve it, and you can post it up for general dissemination. Would that satisfy you?"

"I believe it would, sir," she said, leaning back in her seat.

"If that's all," he said, standing up and locking out his terminal, "I'm going to take a look at the prow section and see how the engineering crews are coming along with repairs."

****

The *Blue Jacket* burst into the Podere system with much less of a perceptible shudder. Daya Singh's team had recalibrated the warp drive emitters back to at least where they were before the ship had gone into dock at Jericho Station.

"Coms?" Jackson asked, his mouth dry.

"I'm receiving the clock ping from the com drone platform!" Lieutenant Keller said, the relief plain in his voice. "Platform status is normal. I'm also getting all the standard com traffic you would expect from a populated world."

"That is good news indeed," Jackson said. "Announce our arrival to the Eighth Fleet listening station and to the Poderen government."

"Aye, sir. Standard com package transmitting."

"Nav, set a course of the planet. Standard orbital insertion. Helm, when you have thrust you're clear to execute at one-half thrust," Jackson said. "Stand down from general quarters. Set condition 1-Bravo." 1-Bravo was normal watches, but a heightened state of alert shipwide. He received a symphony of confirmation of his orders while he watched the warp drive already being retracted into the hull.

"What do we know about this planet?" he asked Celesta. "I've just read the broad overview."

"Settled by the Warsaw Alliance in 2205," she began. "Mostly immigrants from what would have been Italy on Earth. They had made the trip to New Georgia and decided they wanted a world of their own. They paid handsomely for the right to colonize, but they quickly turned a profit from the fact Podere is able to grow enough food to feed half this sector. In fact, this planet is almost entirely dedicated to agriculture."

"Shit," Jackson muttered. "I suppose it would have been too much to ask for them to have heavy ship construction facilities."

"They do have substantial orbital repair facilities," she said. When she saw the skeptical look he gave her she explained, "They support an enormous fleet of cargo ships that come and go almost constantly. If one of these merchant vessels isn't flying it isn't making any money. The facility is quite modern."

"I wonder how willing they'll be to help us," Jackson said. "We're not here under any official capacity and I'm not about to tell them we just escaped from a planet-killing alien ship."

"That brings up an interesting point," Celesta said, trying to keep her voice down when she saw Ensign Davis' not so subtle attempts to eavesdrop. "We do have some obligation to warn them that *something* may be turning up on their doorstep."

"True," Jackson said, considering the problem.

"Captain," Lieutenant Keller interrupted his thoughts. "The com platform has forwarded three messages, all encrypted and addressed to you as high priority. They're all classified as well."

"Thank you," Jackson said. "Forward them to my personal address. I'll take them in my office."

As soon as he sat down in his seat and unlocked his terminal he knew he was in for an unpleasant time. One message from an anonymous address, which was unusual, and two from an address he knew very well. He started with those.

"Captain Wolfe," the puckered, humorless face of Admiral Winters filled his screen. "It has taken me some time after reviewing the ... report ... you sent to craft this response. The disjointed jumble of incoherent data and mad ramblings were quite a chore to get through. I did take away that you managed to get a crewman killed while taking an unauthorized trip to the surface of Xi'an.

"Both of these actions are punishable under the Code. As for the rest ... I'm not sure what to make of the fact you're claiming the entire surface of Xi'an has been obliterated. The fact that there were no com platforms in the system leads me to believe the *Blue Jacket* somehow transitioned into the wrong system or there is much more to the story that you are leaving out. Either way, I will get to the bottom of this.

"I've dispatched the cutter *Constantine* from the Haven Defense Force so that I can get a clear picture for myself what is going on. Consider yourself put on notice. When I have the truth of this debacle I am sure that it will have a negative impact on how you leave the Fleet. Winters out."

"What the unholy hell?" Jackson muttered, utterly astonished. He'd sent a concise and detailed report along with all the raw data. What the hell was she blathering on about? Confused, he opened the next message.

"*Captain* Wolfe," Winters began again. "You have simply gone too far this time. As you may have guessed, I have had all the operational reports coming from the *Blue Jacket* flagged and sent to me first before they go to the archives. I am the one doing your mission analysis on this last cruise.

"Aliens? Aliens, Captain Wolfe? And to add insult you've included another jumble of data files, ostensibly to support your absurd, asinine report. I was able to glean that you were in the Oplotom system, *far* off-mission and possibly damaging already delicate relations between the Alliance and Haven.

"I have not forwarded any of these reports from your ship to the archives as I'm undecided as to what to do with you. It appears you have suffered some sort of break with reality and it unfortunately means I cannot allow you to remain in command of the *Blue Jacket*. As of receipt of this message consider yourself relieved from duty. Commander Wright is now captain of the ship and will be responsible for executing her new orders: Return the *Blue Jacket* to Jericho Station.

"While you aren't under arrest as this point, understand that you will be facing criminal charges when you return."

Jackson watched as Winters struggled to keep the smile off her face.

"Admiral Winters, out."

"Well ... that was interesting," he said. A single knock at his hatch interrupted him from getting ready to put his fist through his terminal monitor. "Enter!"

"Captain," Celesta said uncomfortably.

"Sit down, Commander," he said wearily. "I'm sure you're here to tell me about a message you received that was on a time delay from the com platform. From Admiral Winters."

"Yes, sir," she said as she slid into the seat.

"What's your take on it?"

"I'm not sure what to say," she said. "In her message to me she admitted that she'd only read the cover sheet from you with the synopsis and hadn't bothered to open up any of the data files. She thinks you're making all of this up, sir, and as long as she's blocked the reports from going to the data archives the regular Fleet analysts will never see it."

"That's about the long and short of it," Jackson said. "Shall we talk about the eight hundred pound gorilla in the room?"

"Ah ... yes," she said, squirming. "I know you think that I'm on this ship because she and I have some relationship that would give her cause to do me a favor at your expense."

"The thought had crossed my mind," he said drily.

"She did approach me," she admitted. "She utterly despises you. I mean she truly hates you with religious fervor. I was never comfortable with the things she told me about you, real or not, but the opportunity to be an exec was enough for me to overlook what was obviously an egregious abuse of power by a senior officer to punish a subordinate she had a vendetta against."

"That's plain enough," Jackson said in disgust as his suspicions were confirmed.

"I have no intention of obeying her orders, sir, and trying to take command of this ship," she said. "The *Blue Jacket* is yours. Knowing what you do now, I'll understand if you think it's best I remove myself from duty."

"You came clean when the cards were on the table," Jackson said after a moment. "You're a good XO and I'm going to need you before this is all over."

"Thank you, sir," she said.

"But," he said, holding up a finger, "I will understand if you don't want to risk your career by defying Winters. I can have you removed from duty and confined to quarters until we reach Haven. It will give you plausible deniability and your record won't be tarnished."

"While I appreciate the kind offer to have me arrested, I would rather remain at my station."

"Don't say I didn't warn you," he said with a laugh. "Oh ... there was one more message and I think I know who it's from. You'll probably want to stay for this." He twisted the monitor around so she could see it and keyed up the next message. It was from whom he had suspected. He heard a slight gasp from Celesta as she saw whom it was. Despite the apparent recent lack of grooming and hygiene, there was no mistaking the face.

"Hey, Captain," Agent Pike said. "Got your message. So it was really fucking aliens? Wow. I didn't see that coming. Anyway ... as you've probably already seen there isn't much of a Fleet presence out there. I'm moving this up my channels here to try and kick Eight Fleet in the ass and mobilize them, but I'm stuck on some shithole world in New Europe. The Commonwealth hasn't been very diligent in maintaining the drone network so I'm not sure if my messages are being propagated out or dying two systems over.

"I also heard from a little birdy that you've got serious trouble coming. Admiral Winters was heard to be storming the halls of Jericho muttering about being able to finally put that Earther where he belongs. I'm guessing the Earther is you and I can only imagine where she thinks you belong. If my source is to be believed, and she usually is—at least about work—Winters is going to try and get Celesta Wright to take command of the *Blue Jacket*.

"I'm not sure if this is because of what you've reported back or in spite of it, but either way I'm hoping you'll take steps to ensure you stay in command of that ship. Despite your lack of tactics you showed some serious balls charging that thing over Oplotom. You very well may be the only warship out there standing between that monstrosity and another massacre. No pressure.

"Anyway ... I'll work this on my end through my connections. You need to stay out there. Do whatever it takes to make sure that thing doesn't cut a huge, bloody swath through the Confederacy and I'll buy you a beer afterwards. Assuming you survive. Out."

"Who the fuck was that?" Celesta blurted when the video winked out.

"Why, that was Mr. Aston Lynch, junior aide to Senator Augustus Wellington," Jackson said with a straight face.

"Captain—" she began hotly.

"That was Agent Pike," Jackson said, laughing and holding his hand up to head her off. "He's a super spook for the CIS. Mr. Lynch is one of his many personalities as I understand it."

"So that whole time he was a CIS agent just bumming a ride from us?" she demanded, seeming to be very angry about the whole thing. Jackson narrowed his eyes speculatively.

"He sent you another message as Lynch, didn't he?" he asked shrewdly "One that just came in because we've been out of contact with the network." Celesta became flustered and her cheeks burned bright red. "No need to answer, Commander," he said. "But yes, he's a legitimate agent and he's been a help on this mission. Sort of."

"So what is our next move?" Celesta said. "If Agent Pike"—she practically spat the name out—"is to be believed we may be the first and last line of defense out here."

"That's a terrifying prospect," Jackson said. "We're in no shape to fight right now and I don't think that monster will take it so easy on us this time around."

"You really think it was holding back?" she asked.

"Not a doubt in my mind," he said. "It let us get close to take a shot and learn what sort of threat we were. As it turns out, not much of one. I have a feeling if we meet again we'll be fighting for our lives."

"*Captain to the bridge*," the computer announced, interrupting Celesta before she could ask her next question.

"We'll discuss this further," Jackson said as he rose from his seat and straightened his utilities.

"We're entering Podere's orbit, Captain," Ensign Davis said as they walked back onto the bridge.

"Have we had any contact with the local government?" Jackson asked.

"Yes, sir," the second watch coms officer said. Jackson turned around at the feminine voice, taking note of the crew change at the coms station. "They welcomed us into their space and asked that we maintain a high orbit to stay clear of the cargo ships coming into port."

"It's a start, I suppose," Jackson said. "Tell them that I need to discuss an urgent and delicate matter with a representative that is capable of making decisions on their behalf."

"Aye, sir,"

"If we can't at least get the damage on the prow cleaned up we're going to be in a bad way," Celesta remarked.

"Not necessarily," Jackson said. "This ship is made to take a punch on the nose. Losing the forward targeting radar is a bit of an inconvenience, but our lateral beams are almost all functional on the port side. That's a lot of firepower in a single pass."

"True," she said. "It would still be nice to at least get some of those sensors working again."

"No argument there," Jackson said.

"Captain, a representative from the surface will be available to speak with you in nine hours," the com officer said, sounding almost apologetic. "They say they're entering night hours and everyone has gone home. I tried to stress the seriousness of the situation but they seem to be brushing it off."

"Thank you, Ensign," Jackson said, leaning back in his seat. "Nine hours? We have to cool our heels in high orbit for nine hours because someone doesn't want to be late for dinner?"

"Not to mention that's nine hours in which the *Blue Jacket* is not being repaired," Celesta said, equally annoyed.

"Coms, tell them we expect to hear from them as soon as possible," Jackson said. "Reiterate that there is a credible threat to their planet that we need to discuss. Ensign Davis, use our credentials and open a channel to the com drone platform. Keep access limited to my personal codes only for right now."

"It will take me a moment, sir," Davis said.

"I'll forward you the data packet and addresses to send them to momentarily," Jackson said. He was already furiously typing on the terminal attached to his seat's armrest. He didn't need to bother with video for what he was doing. By the time Ensign Davis had negotiated with the com platform Jackson was just finishing his correspondences, attaching the applicable data files, and sealing them into encrypted data packets.

"The files are on the way to you," Jackson told her, walking over to the OPS station. "Use our Fleet override and make sure a drone is launched immediately."

"Yes, sir," she said, her hands flying over her terminal screens. "Drone will be launching in five minutes."

"How many of our own com drones do we have left?" he asked.

"Internal complement of drones is down to eight, sir," Davis said.

"Okay everyone," Jackson said, walking to the middle of the bridge. "Call up your watch reliefs and get some food and rest. It appears the Poderen government is going to make us wait for a third of a day and I want you all rested when that happens. We'll either be docking for repairs or we'll be exiting the system."

There was a mild commotion as calls were sent out to the relief watch and the bridge crew began gathering up the random collection of coffee mugs and other personal items that they brought with them during long shifts. Jackson watched them as they briefed their replacements before leaving to go eat, reconnect with friends, and grab some rack time. He felt a pang of guilt for not telling them that they might not be leaving the area until the politicians could sort everything out and get a Fleet presence out to the frontier.

Beyond the guilt, however, was a gnawing feeling that overshadowed everything. The fear that the alien ship would find this system was causing him physical discomfort to the point that he hadn't been eating or sleeping regularly since they'd arrived in the Xi'an system. He was also suffering through mild withdrawal symptoms as that same fear had kept him away from his illegal bourbon stash for longer than he could remember in recent years. The combination had resulted in a low-grade headache which had settled in his temples and made the beeps and chirps that were a constant on a starship bridge almost unbearable.

He knew he could drink just enough to normalize himself, but he was too afraid to do anything that might compromise his ability to command the ship. The fact he was the only starship captain in the last two hundred years with any actual combat experience, even after only a single pass, single volley with an enemy, was terrifying. As the reality of that fact sank in he realized there would be no cavalry swooping in. There was no battlegroup out there with a crusty old fleet admiral that had the experience to take on an unknown enemy and not be surprised by anything it could throw at him. He was it.

"Are you okay, sir," Celesta said quietly, snapping him out of his thoughts.

"Of course, Commander," he said, clearing his throat. "Why?"

"You just turned very pale and began sweating," she said. "Maybe you should get some rack time yourself. I'll take the first half of this watch and then call Lieutenant Peters up."

"That's not a bad idea," he said, trying to hide his relief. "You have the bridge, Commander." He could feel her eyes on his back as he walked off the bridge, trying not to appear like he was hurrying.

Instead of going back to his office like he'd planned he found himself taking the left two decks down and walking to his quarters. He pulled the utility top off and tossed it on a chair, sinking down wearily on the bed. Before he had too much time to think about it, he kicked his boots off and lay back.

"Set wake up," he said to his comlink. "Five hours from now." There was a chirp from his comlink and a softer acknowledgement from the ship's computer letting him know it was aware of his intentions. It would hold all non-priority message traffic and let him get a few hours of uninterrupted sleep.

He drifted off to an uneasy sleep full of images of another dead planet.

Chapter 13

-Beep beep-

Jackson wasn't aware how long the computer had been trying to get his attention. He sat up groggily and felt more exhausted now than when he'd gone to sleep. Looking at his clock he saw it had only been three hours ago.

-Beep beep-

"Go!" he called out, rubbing his eyes.

"Captain, this is Lieutenant Peters," the disembodied voice of one of his operations officers floated from the speakers in the ceiling. "I'm sorry to disturb you, sir, but we've had something odd happen."

"Define odd, Lieutenant," Jackson said.

"The tracking signal from an automated mining rig in the outer asteroid belt just dropped off," Peters said. "I've contacted the surface and they told me it's prone to this sort of intermittent failure. They won't send anyone to check on it unless it stays out for more than six hours."

Jackson's blood ran cold. "We both know that's bullshit, Peters," he said, grasping for his boots. "Go to general quarters. 1-SS. I'm on my way. Get your ass to the CIC once Davis gets there."

"*General quarters, general quarters!*" the call blared over the shipwide. "*All crew to battle stations! Set condition 1-SS and prepare the Blue Jacket for imminent combat operations!*"

Jackson rolled his eyes at Peter's embellished call to action as he yanked on his utility top and felt his boots automatically snug around his feet. He could feel the full day's worth of growth on his face and knew his breath must smell like a trash can. Irrationally he felt some resentment towards the aliens for attacking before he could shower and get something to eat as he rushed out of his quarters and raced for the bridge.

"Report!" he barked as he stormed onto the bridge.

"No contact with the alien ship yet," Ensign Davis said, still trying to fasten the buttons on her own utility top. "The signal from the mining platform hasn't come back up either."

"Is the com drone platform still singing?" Jackson asked.

"Yes, sir," Lieutenant Keller reported. "Clock and status signals are still strong and steady."

"I'll bet they're going for those first," Jackson said, thinking hard as he looked at a two-dimensional representation of the system imposed over the view of the main display. "They would have had to learn at least that much about us to hit the long-range coms before moving on the planet." He thought about it for a moment longer before he was sure he was right.

"Helm! Heat up the mains and prepare to break orbit," he said. "Coms, tell whoever the hell is answering calls on Podere that we have a potential hostile ship in the system and we're moving to intercept. Nav, give me the most efficient course that swings us out to the com platform."

"We're going to attack?" Ensign Davis asked. "In our condition?"

"Our condition, Ensign, is that we're the only human ship in this system with any teeth," Jackson said with a confidence he didn't feel. "I'm not inclined to abandon these people to certain death because we got scraped up in our last fight with this thing."

"Course is plotted and the mains are online, sir," the helmsman reported.

"Very well," Jackson said, sitting in his seat to keep from fidgeting. "All ahead, full."

"Ahead full, aye," the helmsman said, smoothly pushing the throttles up to maximum. The bridge vibrated harshly as the mains shoved the *Blue Jacket* forward and began getting them up to breakaway speed.

"OPS, we need all weapons charged and ready," Jackson said. "Inform Engineering I want all four reactors running at eighty percent and all capacitor banks charged. Tactical, verify weapon statuses as they become available. Have the forward tubes loaded with Shrikes."

"Shrikes, sir?" the tactical officer asked in confusion. "Not Avengers?"

"I know the Avengers are the heavy hitters, but the Shrikes are faster and have better range," Jackson explained, trying to remember they all lacked experience as he fought to not reprimand the junior officer for questioning him. "We'll have time to reload with the big boys after we test the waters with the smaller missiles."

"Yes, sir. Requesting Shrikes for all available forward tubes."

Jackson looked up at the display again and saw they were going to have to swing all the way around the planet before they could break and head for the com platform. It would be at least nine and half hours before they were even within range of the damn thing to scan it with the backup targeting radar.

"Should we have the platform launch a few drones now with a warning before we lose it?" Celesta asked. She looked as haggard as everyone else on the bridge and Jackson remembered that she had just gone off shift when general quarters was called.

"To whom?" he asked, trying to keep his voice neutral. "Any com traffic with our codes is being held up at a ... chokepoint. Besides which, there's every possibility this is a false alarm."

"Do you really think that?"

"No I don't," he said with a sigh. "I led them right to this system. I may have killed every man, woman, and child on Podere with my carelessness."

****

"Com drone platform has just stopped reporting," Lieutenant Keller stated. They'd been steaming hard for that point in space for over three hours, the harsh vibrations of the mains at full power numbing them in their seats.

"Update our plot," Jackson said. "Assume the enemy is within a sphere radiating one hundred thousand kilometers from the platform's last reported position. Helm, adjust your course accordingly; we want to keep our nose on that bastard."

"Aye, sir,"

"Nav, what's our acceleration?"

"We're at five thousand one hundred meters per second delta-V, Captain," the chief sitting at the nav station reported.

"Helm, cut the mains," Jackson said as he crunched the numbers in his head. "Zero thrust, maintain course."

"Zero thrust, aye," the helmsman reported. "Mains answering idle condition."

"We're not getting much more speed for the amount of propellant we're burning," Jackson explained to Celesta. "Not only that, but we're lighting ourselves up like a mini-nova running the engines so hard."

"We have to assume we've already been spotted," Celesta said.

"Oh it knows we're here, all right," Jackson said. "If it follows the pattern we've gotten from the tiny amount of data we have it should be coming right for us after the com platform is destroyed."

"Comforting," she answered, the tension in her face at odds with the flippant tone of her comment.

"Tactical, you're cleared to run up the active arrays when we approach within sixty thousand kilometers of our projected engagement sphere," Jackson said. "While I'm sure we've been spotted after such a violent ascent from around Podere, there's no point in broadcasting our exact position the entire flight. OPS, tell Chief Engineer Singh I want a status report on all primary flight and tactical systems sent to my terminal within the next fifteen minutes."

The next two hours passed uneventfully as the ship drifted towards where they assumed the com platform had been located. He resisted the urge to hover over his crew, pace, or give unnecessary orders or encouragement as they went about their jobs. The status update he'd received from Singh showed that, despite the previous damage, the *Blue Jacket* was probably more ready to fight than she had been over Oplotom.

"Contact!" the tactical officer called out. "Debris field along the projected course of the com platform. Density readings are consistent with the platform's construction but there isn't nearly enough to account for the entire structure."

"Same as all the others," Jackson said. "At least we're now one hundred percent certain who we're dealing with. Go to high-power mode on all the active sensors. Find this son of a bitch."

"Going active."

"Helm, pitch the nose down seven degrees and engage the mains, half-thrust," Jackson ordered as he studied the disbursement of the debris field. "Let's fly underneath all of that before it gets too close and spreads too much."

"Ahead one-half, aye," the helmsman said. "Helm answering to new course."

Jackson watched as the dotted lines of their new projected course were populated by the computer on the main display, verifying that the ship would clear the navigation hazards with a comfortable safety margin.

"New contact," the tactical officer said with some hesitation.

"Well?" Jackson said, not quite snapping. "What is it?"

"The computer is having trouble resolving the returns. It's like it isn't constructed with any metal alloys."

"Just put it up on the display," Jackson said. He looked as the ghost of a sensor return was imposed just behind the debris of the station, keeping precise distance and pacing along just behind it. It was also much, much closer than they'd expected it to be. Jackson thought he'd have had a bit more warning.

"Target the sensor anomaly and fire the Shrikes!" he barked. His outburst seemed to fluster his tactical officer, who held his hands frozen over his terminal and had a look on his face of sheer panic.

"Fire, damnit!!" Jackson practically screamed. When the officer didn't seem to be responding, Jackson leapt towards the tactical station and grabbed him by the shoulders. "You're relieved of duty. Out of the seat. Now!!"

The flustered officer was nearly flung out of the seat as Jackson slipped into it and began bracketing the anomaly with the Shrikes' targeting system, overriding the computer's protests that it wasn't a valid target. Less than ten seconds later he flipped open the protective red cover of the hooded fire control switch and flicked it up, authorizing weapons release.

Four high-velocity, low-yield Shrike missiles streaked out of the lateral launch tubes, two on each side. Even as the missiles streaked towards the target Jackson sent the request for Avengers to be reloaded into the launch tubes.

"Target is maneuvering," Ensign Davis said. "It's dropping down and below the debris field and accelerating towards us."

"Helm, all ahead emergency!" Jackson called as he peered over the Tactical console at the display. "Get us under that ship."

"All ahead emergency, aye," the helmsman said as he overrode the safety lockouts on the throttles and pushed the engines beyond their accepted performance envelope. The vibration and sound on the bridge was horrendous.

"Target is slowing and there's a massive thermal buildup on its nose," Celesta called out. When Jackson moved to Tactical she had jumped into the command chair and was trying to control the flow of information to him so he could concentrate on fighting the ship.

"It's going to take out the Shrikes," Jackson said as he operated the *Blue Jacket's* sensor suite, recording as much data as he could as they roared by. Sure enough, there was a flare of energy that washed out their forward sensors and the status links to their four missiles winked out well before they would have impacted the target.

"They're not going to fall for that again," he said, keying in the targeting data for the Avengers.

"We're going to pass beneath them still well out of heavy beam range," Ensign Davis said, doing as much as she could from OPS to assist Jackson.

"Acknowledged," he said. "Helm, keep an eye on the engines. If the plasma chamber temps start to fluctuate don't bother alerting me. Pull the power back."

"Yes, sir."

"Another plasma burst is building up on the target's starboard flank," Davis warned. Jackson looked at their range and saw they were still nearly seventy thousand kilometers apart. With the *Blue Jacket* under emergency acceleration they would pass within minutes at their closest point, forty-eight thousand kilometers, before the range would begin to increase again. Even with a reactionless drive he didn't think the massive alien ship would be able to turn and pursue before they could get a decent lead on it.

"Maintain heading," he said. He received an alert that the forward-facing missile tubes were loaded, but they'd closed the range so much that he had no chance to fire and allow them to track into the enemy. The Avengers were interceptor-type missiles that worked best when able to cross an incoming ship's course in a head-on pass. Jackson looked over at the armament panel and saw he had no heavy beams available on his forward starboard quadrant. Whatever the enemy was about to do he had nothing to answer with.

"Target is accelerating tangentially from its original course," Celesta called in alarm. "It's closing the range quickly!"

"Helm, fire starboard thrusters, fore and aft!" Jackson ordered. He wanted to crab the *Blue Jacket* away from the incoming behemoth, but the small attitude thrusters were only meant to change the orientation of the ship, not push it onto a new course.

"No effect, Captain," the helmsman reported. "Her inertia is too great."

"Cease thrusting," Jackson said in irritation. "Commander Wright, send localized warnings to the compartments on the starboard side. Tell them to get out of there and prepare damage control teams. This won't be an exploratory jab like the last hit was."

"Enemy ship is firing," Davis said, her voice tight with fear. Jackson watched on the display as the high-energy thermal distortion on their sensors heralded the destructive plasma charge that was bearing down on them. He looked on in helpless frustration. The *Blue Jacket* could do nothing to alter her course in time to avoid the incoming fire. "Impact in seven seconds!"

"Sound the alert," Jackson said even as klaxons began to wail throughout the ship.

There was a few seconds of silence before it felt like a vengeful god struck the destroyer amidships, the hull ringing and warping from the blow. Alarms blared on the bridge and warnings scrolled across every display.

"Direct hit on the starboard flank!" Davis yelled over the alarms. "Hull breeches reported in the affected area. Sections twenty-seven through thirty-five, decks four through seven are open to space! Inner hatches are sealed and damage control teams have been notified."

"Casualties?" Jackson asked, trying to concentrate on tracking the enemy ship.

"Nine crew unaccounted for," she said.

Jackson swallowed down the bile that rose in his throat.

"Confirm what the tactical array is showing," he said. "Is the enemy slowing down and coming about?"

"Confirmed," Celesta said from the command chair. "It's not only coming about, it's accelerating at a rate we can't match. Five hundred G's and increasing."

"That's impossible!" the operator at the Nav station hissed.

"Apparently not," Jackson said grimly. "Ensign Davis, get ahold of someone in Armament and find out if the rear launch tubes are still unavailable. I've got no status on my display. Helm, how are the engines holding up?"

"I had to throttle back to eighty percent, Captain," the helmsman said apologetically. "Plasma chamber temps were reaching critical and output on number two was starting to fluctuate."

"Very well," Jackson said. "Keep me informed." He knew Engineering would already know about the engine status so he didn't bother to call down and harass Singh in the middle of a gunfight when the *Blue Jacket* had just had her hull peeled back like a tuna can. The stress of trying to command the ship while having to concentrate on operating the tactical station was beginning to take its toll. The only thing he knew for certain was that this engagement would be over soon ... one way or another.

"Enemy ship is approaching on an intercept angle that will put them off our starboard flank in two minutes," Celesta said, watching all the sensor feeds from her station.

"Helm, go to zero thrust," Jackson said. "Spin the *Blue Jacket* about one hundred and eighty degrees along her Z-axis and then engage the engines, full astern."

"Yes, sir," the helmsman said, foregoing the traditional command responses as he frantically executed the maneuver. The *Blue Jacket* swung around ponderously until she was flying backwards, her nose now pointing at the pursuing alien ship. There was a change in the pitch of the engines as they came back up, their thrust now accelerating the destroyer backwards at full power.

"Go ahead and cheat her a little to starboard," Jackson said as he selected his armament. "I want to take them down the port flank if possible."

"Yes, sir."

"Enemy vessel will overtake us in seventy seconds," Davis said tightly. Jackson selected all the heavy beamers on the port flank, eighteen pulse laser projectors that made up a nearly two hundred petawatt broadside, enough to boil away meters of starship hull material in seconds. The projectors would feed off the massive capacitor bank that would be drained after two volleys, after which the *Blue Jacket* would try to break contact and use its other armament to keep an enemy at bay while the reactors recharged them.

Unfortunately, the capacitors were as old as everything else on the ship, and just as neglected as the rest of the weapons, so he was counting on a single, partial volley before the system melted down. Nevertheless, it was the most potent weapon he had and he planned on bringing it to bear. He selected cascading fire mode, highlighted the incoming target, and specified the area along the port flank where the plasma bursts seemed to be generated from.

"I'm going to try and hit it as they fly by," Jackson said. "Be ready to reverse thrust and begin braking."

"Sir, the alien ship is slowing down," Celesta said. He looked at his own display and saw the ship decelerating violently and at a rate that would put it at a relative stop only fifteen hundred meters off their port side.

"I've got a bad feeling about this," he said. "They may be trying to capture this ship."

"Why?"

"We can discuss the enemy's tactics in debrief, Commander," Jackson said shortly. "Stand by for a shoot and run maneuver and you'd better go ahead and alert Major Ortiz he may be repelling boarders." He waited quietly as the enemy slipped into range, watching it edge close, careful to stay just behind the missile launch tubes.

"Helm, zero thrust," Jackson said. "Steady as she goes and be ready for a hard braking maneuver."

"Yes, sir," the helmsman croaked, looking in horror at the display as they could actually see the alien ship looming out of the black towards them.

"Sir?" Celesta whispered, as if irrationally afraid the enemy could hear her.

"Firing!" Jackson said, flipping the switch again to let loose a massive broadside.

There was a flash on the leading edge of the enemy ship and then a fresh barrage of alarms. Quickly looking at his terminal, he realized only two projectors had fired one pulse each before the power system failed. His heart sank as he looked at the feed from the optical sensors trained on the target and saw the shot had barely blown a divot out of the oddly textured material.

"Engineering is reporting the power trunk to the port side capacitor bank has failed," Celesta said quietly. "Fifteen capacitors exploded and there was a powerful enough arc from another that it killed a technician and destroyed the control system to the amidships thrusters."

Jackson stared at the ship off the *Blue Jacket's* port flank before slamming his fist into the tactical console in such a rare emotional outburst that everyone on the bridge actually jumped despite the danger lurking just outside.

"Suggestions?" he asked his crew, turning the seat to face them. Nobody spoke for a long moment.

"Don't let them take us alive, Captain," the chief sitting at the navigation console said.

"We can't even scuttle the ship," Celesta argued. "We have no nukes, nothing that can take her out."

"That may not be true," Jackson said, bringing up a submenu on his display and entering all the credentials needed to access the system that nobody but him knew about.

"Sir, the enemy is moving again," Ensign Davis said. "They're drifting in closer to us. Ten meters per second closure rate."

"The arrogant bastard knows we can't hurt him," Jackson ground out. As he began carefully entering a command sequence, ignoring the questioning looks from his crew, he saw a green indicator wink on from the display to his left. He looked at it and blinked in disbelief. "Why the hell not?" he muttered, pausing the script he'd been entering on the right terminal.

"Sir?" Ensign Davis asked, her voice strong and steady but her eyes wide and hands trembling.

"Helm, stand by," Jackson said. "I'm going to be feeding you course corrections fast and furious in a few minutes."

"Standing by, Captain."

He selected the blinking green indicator on his armament panel with a certain amount of doubt. He doubted that the system would actually work and, if it did, that it would actually do any damage. Looking up through the "window" of the main display he could see the two barrels of the upper mag-cannon turret give a twitch as power surged into the system. It was a promising sign that he hoped was mirrored by the belly turret.

He selected deep penetrator, high-explosive rounds for all four cannons and selected the spot on the enemy ship he wanted targeted. The enormous ship was still drifting in at its leisurely rate and tendrils could be seen beginning to break away from the hull. Jackson figured they were grapplers that would be grabbing the *Blue Jacket* in a few minutes if his idea didn't work.

"Say a prayer to whoever the hell it is you believe in, everyone," Jackson said, his finger hovering over the execute button. He pushed it down firmly and watched as the upper turret swung quickly to the left and the barrels gimbaled down slightly. There were brilliant flashes of light and the ship shook with tremendous *booms* as the fifteen-hundred-millimeter cannons spat out hardened shells at hypersonic velocity directly into an enemy ship that was far too close to dodge or intercept them.

The damage was incredible. Each shell blasted into the ship leaving a neat, circular entry hole as the four cannons peppered the port side of the target with over sixteen shots before the first shell's timed fuse ran down and the high-explosive charge detonated. This heralded the beginning of a cascading explosion that could be seen rippling underneath the skin of the ship's hull, the light from the explosions actually shining through it. Twenty shells fired in total before the cannons fell silent and the powerplant ramped up to begin recharging the capacitors.

Despite the devastating attack, the affected area was still relatively small compared to how large the vessel was. It was apparently enough to give it second thoughts, however, and it lurched away from the *Blue Jacket*, streaming some sort of viscous substance that froze when it was ejected into space.

"Target is moving away!" Ensign Davis nearly shouted in relief. "No detectable plasma charges on its surface. I don't think they're going to return fire."

"Stay sharp!" Jackson cut off the few tiny celebrations that had begun to break out on the bridge. "Where's it going?"

"Tracking," Celesta said, studying the sensor data. The enemy had already put a lot of distance between itself and the destroyer and was still accelerating. "It looks like they could be heading back to Podere."

"You're certain about that?" Jackson asked, climbing out from behind the tactical station.

"Not completely certain, no. But that's the only thing along that trajectory," she said. "If they simply wanted to put distance between us and them it would have been easier to accelerate along the course we were already on. They have to know we can't match their acceleration."

"Helm, turn us back around," Jackson ordered, ordering Celesta out of his seat with a wave of his hand. "Nav, plot us a course back to Podere that takes advantage of the velocity we're already carrying. We can't afford to stop and accelerate back towards the planet."

"Course plotted, Captain," the chief said. "We'll need to accelerate along this arc and get an assist from the fifth planet. That will swing us back around on an intercept course with Podere."

"Very well. Helm, get us moving on that course, ahead full."

"Ahead full, aye," the helmsman said as the *Blue Jacket* finished spinning about so her nose was pointed back in the direction she was flying.

"Verify target's position," Jackson ordered.

"Target is verified at seventy thousand kilometers and increasing," Ensign Davis said. "Their acceleration profile is only fifteen percent of what we've seen before but they're turning directly towards the planet."

"That will still put them there ahead of us, but not by much," Celesta said. "Do you think we damaged their drive?"

"I wish I knew," Jackson said, feeling lightheaded as he came down off such an enormous adrenaline rush. "Those shells seemed to get pretty good penetration at that range. The fact it didn't return fire makes me think we scrambled something in there. Maybe their power system."

"That was some last minute tactic," Celesta said quietly. "But that wasn't what you were originally working on at the tactical station, was it?"

"We'll discuss it later," Jackson said, cutting her off. "Since we're getting some distance let's start rotating people out for breaks. It will be quite a while before we're heading back to Podere."

****

"Holy shit, that was lucky," Specialist Ormond remarked as they rotated out of their work area for a short break.

"There are more than a few dead spacers who would disagree with you," Chief Cullen said from beside him. The pair had been able to get out of the starboard engineering compartments before the first blast had opened the ship up. "That incompetent Earther has let this ship get into a close engagement with a superior enemy twice now. If you ask me he's chasing this thing."

"He seemed to do pretty well," Ormond said without much conviction. He had been awake for nearly thirty-six hours and most of that spent under the tension of potential combat. He never realized how terrifying it would be ... stuck in the lower decks, hearing the ship getting hit and taking damage without being able to know what was actually happening. Cullen grabbed him around the shoulder and roughly guided him into a small alcove in the work center that was lined with lockers and had a single bench.

"You can't really believe that?" he asked, staring intensely at Ormond.

"All I know is I'm tired, Chief, and I could use something to eat," Ormond said, wanting to get away.

"You know Wolfe had Chief Kazenski locked up, right?" Cullen asked.

"Yeah ... for trying to start—"

"He wasn't starting anything," Cullen snapped. "He was doing his job. If you have some rogue CO putting the entire ship at danger, not to mention our lives, it's his responsibility to take action. Is it not?"

"I ... suppose," Ormond said, looking around and hoping nobody would hear the conversation.

"Damn right," Cullen whispered so savagely that spittle flew from his mouth and landed on Ormond's cheek. "Listen ... there are some of us who aren't real keen on dying so our token Earther CO can prove he deserves his seat. We have a plan where nobody gets hurt, nobody gets in trouble. Can we count on you?"

"What would I have to do?" Ormond asked.

"I asked a yes or no question," Cullen said.

"Uh ... yeah, Chief," Ormond said, feeling utterly helpless. "You know you can always count on me."

"That's what I told everyone else," Cullen said with a sudden smile. "Since you work in the MUX control room we have a special job for you. But don't worry ... with the damage we've taken hopefully even someone as dense as Jackson Wolfe will know it's time to fly us back to Haven and call in the big ships to deal with this thing."

Cullen walked out of the alcove without another word, leaving Ormond standing there with the burden of a terrible choice on his shoulders.

Chapter 14

"Have a seat, Lieutenant Barrett," Jackson said as his still-shaken tactical officer stepped into his office. He waited until the young officer was seated and settled before continuing.

"I'm not one for tiptoeing around a subject, so what the hell happened out there, Lieutenant?"

"Captain Wolfe," Barrett said, looking Jackson straight in the eye, "I can only apologize for my performance, but I offer no excuses. I failed and I will accept the consequences of that."

Jackson had started out furious at Barrett, but he grudgingly had to admit he was impressed that the young man didn't come in with a list of excuses as to why he'd frozen up. It was a trait he appreciated.

"Michael, I'm looking at your drill scores and your training records," Jackson said, idly flipping through the file on his tile. "You've consistently been my top performer and have had an exemplary record while serving aboard the *Blue Jacket*. The lack of disciplinary action alone makes you a standout." Sadly, that hadn't been a joke.

"I'm going to be straight with you ... I don't have anyone else to replace you with. We're chasing this thing across the system in the hopes we can close on it before it can wipe out Podere like it has Xi'an and Oplotom. I can't be tied up at the tactical station and Commander Wright doesn't know the system well enough yet to run it in combat."

"I can do my job, sir," Barrett said with conviction. "I won't let you down again."

"We're all scared, Lieutenant," Jackson said. "Here is where I would usually give you a stirring speech about rising to the occasion and not letting your fear own you, but I think you'd only feel worse after that. All I'm going to say is this: Get your ass back to your station, Lieutenant, and study the previous engagement. Learn everything you can about it and you damn well better not lock up on me again. Am I clear?"

"Crystal clear, Captain," Barrett said sharply.

Jackson stared at him for a moment longer.

"Dismissed," he said finally. "Send Commander Wright and Ensign Davis in on your way out."

He watched Lieutenant Barrett hustle out and felt like he was making the right choice. At least he hoped he was.

"Ensign Jillian Davis, reporting as ordered," his operations officer said, coming to attention in front of his desk.

"Ensign Davis," he said, watching as Celesta walked into the room and leaned against the rear bulkhead as the hatch slid closed. "Hell of a day, wasn't it?" he asked, not offering to let her stand at ease or sit down.

"It was indeed, sir," she said, still staring at the spot directly over his head.

"Some of us performed better than others," Jackson said, leaning back. "You just saw Lieutenant Barrett leave. Did he look happy?"

"No, Captain, he did not."

"That's because when tested in the crucible of combat, he cracked," Jackson said, his voice even. "Not everyone is fit to serve on a warship, wouldn't you say?"

"I ... would have to agree, sir," Davis said with uncertainty in her voice.

"Take that ensign bar off your uniform, Davis," Jackson said with a dramatic sigh. To her credit, she reached up and tugged off her rank insignia without so much as a twitch of her eye, though Jackson could see the red flush creeping up her neck.

"Commander Wright, did you get what I asked for?" Jackson asked.

"I did," she said simply, putting a silver bar in his outstretched hand. He walked around the desk, standing to Davis' side as she stood at attention, still staring forward.

"For exceptional performance of duties and gallantry in the face of the enemy, you are hereby promoted to Lieutenant, Junior Grade," Jackson said, pinning the bar on her right collar. The ship's crest was still on the left. "XO, note the time and date in the ship's log."

"Yes, sir."

"At ease," Jackson said, smiling slightly as Davis reached up to touch her new bar. "Congratulations, Lieutenant Davis."

She looked like she was about to try and put her arms around Jackson and hug him before her military bearing took over again and she straightened up. The move didn't go unnoticed by Commander Wright as her right eyebrow went up a tick.

"Thank you, Captain," Davis said, shaking his hand instead. "I won't let you down."

"I'm sure you won't," he said, smiling indulgently. "Now get your ass back to your station and review the sensor logs. Find me something useful. Dismissed."

Lieutenant Davis spun smartly on her heel and exited the office with a certain bounce in her step.

"Interesting time to be doing field promotions," Celesta remarked. "Complete with a little hazing to boot."

"To be honest, Commander, we'll probably all be dead within a day so I figure it couldn't hurt for at least one person on this ship to be happy," he said, sinking back into his chair.

"Not much optimism? Even after the mag-cannons did so much damage?" she asked.

"Realism trumps optimism every time," he sighed. "The math isn't on our side. Even if we pumped the rest of the shells in the magazines into that monster we simply aren't carrying enough destructive force aboard to kill it. It's just too big. There's also the fact that it's been learning after every engagement, adapting even. I don't think we'll have the same luck if we meet again."

"Which begs the question: Why are we still chasing it?"

"As long as we can provide some cover for Podere I'm willing to stay," Jackson said. "If it makes a move to leave the system we'll reevaluate the situation."

She made no move to leave despite having no further protests to air out.

"Was there something else, Commander?"

"What were you doing before the mag-cannons came online, sir?"

Jackson tried to stare her down, but when she wouldn't budge he shrugged his surrender. "I may have not been completely honest when I said there weren't any nukes aboard," he said. "There are, in fact, four. Four very big ones."

"You mean the main reactors," she said, narrowing her eyes.

"Very good, Commander," he said with a nod. "There is a procedure that isn't in any Fleet manual or technical data for the *Raptor*-class ships. It's something that's passed down orally to each captain when he, or she, assumes command. It was a backdoor left by the designers to be used in only the most dire of emergencies.

"There is a way to disable all the safeties on the reactors and send them critical. It happens quite fast if you also shut down the pumps for the cooling jackets."

"I see," she said, emotionless. "And you'd have been willing to blow the *Blue Jacket* up to stop that ship?"

"Yes," he said simply.

"Good," she said, pushing herself off the bulkhead. "I will admit to worrying that you may have been doing this for the wrong reasons before."

"But not now?" Jackson asked.

"Not now," she confirmed. "I'll see you on the bridge, Captain."

After she'd left and the hatch sealed he stared up at the ceiling for a moment, slightly confused by the exchange. The mag-cannons had been an utter stroke of luck, but he couldn't deny how good it had felt seeing those shells ripping the port side of that ship apart. They were still seven hours away from Podere, but the enemy ship was only four hours away. He wasn't sure how it had actually been killing planets, but he hoped it wasn't something that could be accomplished in a few hours.

With the short respite in the battle he'd ordered the crews to get rested and fed and took care of some light administrative work, like promotions, to keep himself busy and try to raise the spirits of the crew a bit. Celesta had taken the liberty of piping the sensor feed of the mag-cannons shredding into the enemy ship to all the departments. The more he'd thought about it the more he liked the idea. At least give the technicians in the lower decks some hope that they'd come through this, even if their captain had none for himself.

****

"Captain, I might have something for you," Lieutenant Davis said as soon as he stepped back onto the bridge.

"Good news?" Jackson asked.

"It's ... news," she said evasively. He walked over behind her station to see what she was talking about, ignoring the clear regulation violations in the form of personal photos lining one side of the console.

"Show me what you've got."

"I began looking over all the high-res optical data we collected on the enemy ship between engagements," she said. "Here is a still shot after the Avengers opened its nose up during that first pass."

"Right," Jackson said impatiently. "So?"

"Here's another shot of that same area," she said, pulling up another image. "This was as it made its approach during the last engagement."

"What the hell?" Jackson muttered, squinting at the image.

"That's not been repaired, Captain," she said. "It was ... healed."

"The implications of this are somewhat profound. And disturbing," Jackson remarked.

"I would say so," Davis said. "This ship, or at least its hull, is an organic compound that shows signs of being alive."

"This mission is getting more bizarre by the minute," Jackson complained under his breath. "Log this data and put it in on the secure server. This changes nothing, so keep it quiet for now ... I don't need a damn philosophical debate in the middle of a battle, and even if that ship is 'alive' it has still killed millions of humans."

"Yes, sir."

"Make sure you tag the data where you can find it quickly," he said, still keeping his voice down. "I'm going to have you launch another com drone right before our next round with this thing. The data is going to a specific address that I'll give you in a moment, not to CENTCOM."

"Sir?"

"It's ... complicated," he said. "Just believe me when I say that if we're going to get any help with this we need to stay off the main channels for now."

"Yes, sir."

"One more thing," Jackson said, leaning back away from her console. "Finish your analysis of the ship, but then I need you to put that knowledge to practical use. Put together a targeting package and send it over to Tactical. Even with the unique features we're seeing in this hull material I would assume that port side is still blasted open. We want to put more shells into that if it'll let us."

They were still two hours away from Podere when the news went from bad to worse.

"We're getting a burst of com traffic from the planet," Lieutenant Keller reported. "Some trying to contact the com drone platform, two specifically to us, and a jumble of calls for help over the general band."

"Is the alien ship firing on the surface?" Jackson asked.

"No, sir," the officer said, the dread evident in his voice. "If I'm understanding this correctly it's landing troops at every major settlement in the eastern hemisphere."

"Helm! Full emergency acceleration," Jackson called out. "Tactical, start getting your targeting scripts loaded and ensure the mag-cannons are ready to fire."

After a pair of confirmations the ship began to rumble violently as she strained past her designers' limits.

"OPS, give the helm real-time updates on the target as we get closer," Jackson said, swaying slightly on the harshly vibrating deck. "We may only get one pass at this, and it will be a small targeting window. We can't afford to waste the time it will take to decelerate to be able to enter orbit over Podere, so you'll have to shoot during a high-speed flyby." He walked back over to his seat and jabbed the intercom button.

"Engineering, Lieutenant Commander Singh ... I need more speed, Daya," he said.

"If I give you any more the engines are literally going to tear off of the pylons," Singh said, his voice almost drowned out by the sounds of the machinery in Engineering. "She's giving everything she's got, Jack. Singh out."

Jackson drummed his fingers against his chin, staring off out the main display. It had nothing to do with the abruptness of his chief engineer over the intercom and everything to do with the fact he knew Podere was being ravaged that very second and there was almost nothing he could do about it.

Chapter 15

"She's giving everything she's got, Jack. Singh out."

Daya Singh was standing in the middle of the operations center for the Engineering Department, looking harried. So far the ship's powerplant and engines had responded to the call and the high-output they'd been running at for the last few days didn't seem to be straining any of the individual components. If anything, the techs swore the ship was running better than she had in years now that they were running her harder than any of them could ever recall.

"Chief Cullen," Singh called out. "Run over to reactor one and make sure they're installing that bypass correctly on the water jacket. They've never done this and I don't want someone getting their skin peeled off by high-pressure steam because they don't have the valves configured correctly."

"Yes, sir!" Cullen called, hardly believing his good fortune. He called over a specialist first class and told him to man the instrument-monitoring station. "Just keep an eye on these parameters," he told the young spacer. "If they start to creep up make sure you let the chief engineer know." Cullen clapped the specialist on the shoulder and darted out of the room before he could be asked any questions.

He practically ran down the corridor, stepping aside as pockets of traffic rushed by to one task or another. Pulling his comlink out, he selected a batch message to a list of thirty-eight addresses that simply said, "Check junction 117-3B." The innocuous message that looked to be in engineering jargon was a prearranged signal. That goddamn Earther was pursuing the alien ship *again* after they'd barely survived the last scrape. Cullen wasn't fooled by that doctored bit of video they were running on a loop that showed the mag-cannons shredding the alien at close range. If anything, he felt insulted they would attempt such a lame deception. How could guns that were so outdated even at the time of their manufacture be able to do so much damage to something that chewed up entire planets?

"Ormond," he said, popping his head into one of the main work centers. "You still good down here?"

"Yes, Chief," Specialist Ormond said, paling slightly as he knew exactly what Cullen was referring to.

"Good," Cullen said, ignoring the other spacers in the room. "Don't fuck this up." He stepped back out into the corridor and took a ladder up a deck and headed forward towards one of the security checkpoints to talk to a Marine corporal who was also instrumental to their plan. He hoped those idiots working on the bypass on number one didn't kill themselves or vent into the room before he could make it back down there.

****

"Captain, I think we may have an opportunity here," Lieutenant Barrett called out from the tactical station. Jackson walked over to stand behind the chair, resting his hand on the back.

"What've you got?"

"If you look here, the target has taken up a stationary position over the area where it's been deploying ground forces," Barrett said. "Given the rotation of Podere, that will put it in our direct line of sight within the next forty-five minutes if we bear a few degrees to port."

"I'm listening," Jackson said, intrigued where this might be going.

"I propose we purge the mag-cannon loaders and reload with solid core rounds," Barrett went on, talking more quickly as his enthusiasm for the plan started to peek through. "If we fire them dead ahead while the *Blue Jacket* is still at full power—"

"The rounds will be near relativistic speeds when they hit the target," Jackson finished for him. "Can you hit it at this range even if you know where it's going to be?"

"It will be close," Barrett admitted. "The system isn't designed for this type of long-range shot, but if we fire a full spread and space the shots out along this line—" his finger traced an imaginary line along the screen to illustrate his point, "we won't risk hitting the planet and we'll still have enough time to reload the high-explosive rounds and recharge the cap banks."

"Call down to Armament and have them change the load out for the mag-cannons," Jackson said, making the decision quickly as the clock counted down. "You stay here and check, recheck, and then check one more time to make sure your firing solutions are airtight. One stray round at that speed could wipe out an entire city on Podere."

"Yes, sir," Barrett said, turning to his console and beginning to enter he parameters so the computer could crunch the numbers for his plan.

"This is an interesting plan," Celesta said quietly as he retook his seat.

"It's solid," Jackson said more defensively than he needed to. "Kinetic weapons have been a tried and true staple for human warfare. They're just a bitch to aim at these ranges." The mag-cannon targeting actuators were designed to be able to target a fairly large ship at a relatively close range. Hitting something even as big as the alien ship at the distances and speeds they were dealing with would, on the surface, seem impossible. But Jackson was hoping they were due for some good luck, preferably a miracle, sometime in this mission.

"I'm not disparaging the idea," she said. "If it doesn't work we haven't lost anything but a few tons in useless solid core rounds. If it does work this could be quite spectacular."

"Yeah," Jackson said, mulling it in his head. "Twenty rounds ... that's not a lot of chances to hit this bastard at this range even as big as it is. If it sees them coming and just nudges itself to a higher orbit they all miss."

"Like I said, no harm done," she insisted.

"Maybe," Jackson grunted. "It does feel good to take the initiative though."

It was another thirty minutes before the armament crew had swapped the load out and Barrett had absolute confidence in his numbers. Jackson discreetly had Lieutenant Davis check them to make sure there wasn't any obvious error. He appreciated the effort Barrett was making to redeem himself, but his previous performance earned him a “trust, but verify” treatment until he proved otherwise.

"Helm, bear two degrees to port and pitch down three degrees, no change in engine power," Jackson said.

"Aye aye, sir," the helmsman said, "bearing to port and pitching down."

"Tactical, the stage is yours," Jackson said, flipping a switch on his own console. "You are authorized weapons release for upper and lower mag-cannon turrets at your discretion."

"Aye, sir," Barrett said. "Aligning cannons now and turning over fire control to the computer."

Jackson stood up and watched the barrels of the two upper cannons twitching as the fine correction motors adjusted the weapons a thousandth of a degree at a time. There would be a sweet spot where the *Blue Jacket* would line up with the moving alien ship and the computer would begin the firing sequence without waiting for him or the tactical officer to initiate.

Most of the bridge crew watched, transfixed on the barrels of the guns that were lit up by the ship's external running lights. The near hypnosis was broken when the first gun lit off with a mighty *boom* that shook the ship. The rest of the twenty shots followed quickly, the recoil of the guns shaking the ship. The bridge crew shielded their eyes as the trace amounts of trapped gas in the system ignited while escaping the barrels and flashed brightly on the main display.

"All shots away," Lieutenant Barrett reported, all business as he checked his displays. "Reloading with high-explosive rounds. All four mag-cannons still show fully functional."

"Very good, Lieutenant," Jackson said. "Prepare for your next volley as we close on the target. OPS! Monitor the enemy ship and check for impacts. How long?"

"Rounds will reach the enemy in thirty-three minutes," Davis said. Jackson just raised an eyebrow. If the *Blue Jacket* could achieve those speeds, at least without killing the crew during acceleration, he could have beaten the enemy ship to Podere and made his stand there.

Jackson forced himself to leave the bridge and head to the wardroom to grab a quick bite to eat and refill his mug with water. He'd had so much coffee the last couple of days his hands were shaking and he felt like it was eating a hole through his stomach lining. Although both of those could be attributed to stress. After the initial bout of panic had subsided when they first encountered the alien ship over Oplotom, he was somewhat surprised that he'd been able to hold things together as well as he had. While he would never say it out loud, he had always assumed that, save for a few exceptions, his crew was a collection of misfits and fuck ups. In those same moments of candor with himself he would also have to conclude that there was some truth to the rumor that he'd lucked into a command slot that he possibly didn't deserve.

But they were now steaming towards their third engagement with the enemy after bloodying its nose and, despite the fact they would almost certainly be destroyed if the thing gave chase, he felt pretty damn good about it. It'd been a long time since he, and likely any of the crew, had felt anything to be really proud about. The *Blue Jacket* may have left the Sierra Shipyards over forty years ago with much fanfare, but she'd been little more than a glorified messenger and a slowly rotting relic of a time nearly all humans thought long gone.

Jackson topped off his water again after that sobering thought. Humans had, by and large, eschewed warfare in all its forms over the last two hundred and fifty years or so. As a species they congratulated themselves on attaining the next step on their way to enlightenment and sat around pulling the scabs off old wounds as they talked about the barbarism of their ancestors. That, more than anything else, was probably why Earth was excluded from the conversation, her citizens looked upon as pariahs when they dared venture into the more civilized realms of man. Earth still bore the scars of past wars and the old, familiar landmasses reminded everyone that it hadn't really been all that long ago that the species had been killing each other by the thousands over reasons so obscure they no longer made sense.

That was all bullshit, of course. At least in Jackson's mind. The enclaves had largely been separated along the ideological and ethnic dividing lines that had existed when the serious colonization had begun, and they had remained separated from each other for the most part for all this time. Hell, Earth was now the most diverse place in the galaxy.

But either way, the rules had irrevocably changed when that alien ship had made orbit over Xi'an and launched an attack. He had no delusions that this could be some isolated incident. This was a probe by a single scout ship to test the waters. The fact it had played cat and mouse with the *Blue Jacket* and even tried to capture it only confirmed that fact in his mind. He hoped his species was ready for what was coming. No matter what the outcome with this single-ship incursion the die had been cast ... humanity would have to fight for its survival, or at least its right to exist among the stars.

****

"Report," Jackson said as he climbed back into his chair.

"Eleven minutes to impact," Lieutenant Davis said, her eyes not leaving her screens.

"New firing scripts are updated and loaded, Captain," Lieutenant Barrett said. "Armament crews are reloading the turrets now."

"Excellent," Jackson said, sitting down and forcing himself to remain seated. He passed the remaining minutes by idly scrolling through status reports from his department heads, wondering about what would happen to him should they actually survive the coming battle. He'd openly defied Admiral Winters and so had Celesta Wright. No matter how justified it had been, he had no doubt that they would both have the hammer dropped on them by a CENTCOM board of inquiry. The prospect almost made him hope the alien would make short work of him.

"Impact plus one," Lieutenant Davis said, indicating that it was one second after the expected time of impact. "Waiting for the light to reach us."

When it did, they didn't need her instruments to let them know. A bright flash lit up visibly on the main display from the direction of Podere.

"Holy shit!" Lieutenant Barrett exclaimed before looking at Jackson sheepishly, but the captain was out of his seat, staring at awe at the fading point of light.

"Sift through all that for me, Lieutenant," he said to Davis.

"Two impacts," she said, squinting at her display. "One round took a fair-sized chuck off the tip of the nose, the other ... the other—" she trailed off as she ran the optical data back a few more times and looked again.

"Lieutenant?" Jackson said impatiently.

"The second round punched all the way through," she said finally, putting the video up on the main display. "Large entry damage at the point of impact and then, as you'll see as she spins from the hit, there's an enormous area blasted out on the opposite side. The enemy ship is still spinning. Looks like it's beginning to stabilize."

"Holy shit," Jackson said matter-of-factly, mimicking his tactical officer. "OPS, keep updating Tactical with the new course projections for the target. Tactical! Adjust your firing sequence to take advantage of the gaping hole you just created. Arm up the Avengers too." There was some quiet cheering and high-fives going around on the bridge and Jackson let them have their moment.

"Captain," Lieutenant Keller said, "we're getting some calls from the surface. They want to know what we did. Besides the flash in the sky they say the ... let's just call them troops ... on the ground are being collected and taken back up."

"What are they calling them?" Jackson asked.

"They keep calling them worms," she shrugged. "But it's clear the worms were deployed from smaller landing craft that came from the enemy ship. Either way, now they're leaving."

"It's a recall," Jackson said. "They're leaving this system. I hope we damaged their propulsion or we're not—"

"Enemy ship is breaking orbit," Lieutenant reported. "Acceleration profile is barely a tenth of what it was when it retreated from our last engagement. I think it's damaged, but still flying."

"Lieutenant Davis, send an intercept vector to the helm and continue tracking," Jackson said urgently. "Helm, steer to follow target, ahead full." They'd pulled the power back on the engines after their slingshot around the fifth planet. The mains had pushed them up as fast as they could and they were already caught in Podere's gravity.

"Helm is not answering new course, sir!" the helmsman said.

"What?!" Jackson asked in disbelief. His mind raced as he tried to think of what would cause the computer to ignore a course correction. They weren't about to do anything that it would forbid and there were no associated warnings. Even as he was considering what to do the sound of the engines suddenly died, leaving an eerie quiet on the bridge.

"Captain, I can't raise Chief Engineer Singh," Celesta said. "In fact, all the shipwide coms are down."

"Son of a bitch," Jackson said, realization dawning on him. "Nav, will we clear Podere with our current course and speed?" he asked.

"Yes, sir," the chief at Navigation said. "No problem."

"Sentry!"

"Yes, sir?" the Marine corporal said, walking onto the bridge.

"Nobody is to be given access to the bridge," Jackson said as he stormed to the hatch. "Shoot anyone that comes down that corridor that isn't authorized."

"Sir?" The response came from more than a few people, including the XO.

"Isn't it obvious?" Jackson spat. "We've been sabotaged. There's a mutiny in progress."

Chapter 16

"OPS, bring up the internal security feed," Jackson said. "Main display. Show me the Engineering Operations Center." Lieutenant Davis numbly entered the commands and the video feed popped up on the main display. The scene was utter chaos. There were obviously two factions as some spacers fought to keep the mutineers out of the room, but they were at a significant disadvantage since the attackers were armed.

"Either they've taken over the armory or some of Major Ortiz's men are in on this," Jackson said, pointing to the infantry carbine one of the specialists was carrying.

"There's Lieutenant Commander Singh," Celesta said from beside him, pointing to where Daya lay on the floor, his limbs spread out like he'd been unconscious or dead before he hit the floor. A moment later the video feed blinked off.

"I'm losing control of some of the internal systems," Davis said when Jackson glanced over at her.

"Which ones?"

"Internal video feeds, shipwide coms, and remote hatch control," she said.

"They're on their way," Jackson said, turning to leave.

"Where are you going, sir?" Celesta asked.

"I'm going to even the odds a bit," Jackson said. "You stay here and attempt to retake control of this ship." He hustled over to the Marine sentry who now looked very uncomfortable.

"Seal this hatch when I leave. Nobody gets in here except me. Understood?"

"Understood, sir!" the Marine said, much happier now that he had been given orders from a superior officer. When he'd lost contact with his own command structure he'd not been sure what was going on or what he should be doing.

Jackson ran to his office and sealed the hatch behind him. He went to his terminal and began executing a set of subroutines that would allow him access to the computer despite the mutineers' best efforts otherwise. It was another aspect to the *Blue Jacket's* system architecture that wasn't widely known. He went in and made sure that, first and foremost, the ship was safe. All the reactor readings were within limits and there didn't appear to be any issues with life support or gravity, so he let that go for now.

Pulling up the security feed he saw that a team of six men, led by a chief petty officer he didn't recognize by sight, were all heading towards the bridge, all armed with Marine carbines. As he expanded another menu he could see how they'd pulled it off so fast. Most of the major access corridors had been sealed off by activating the airtight hatches, effectively sealing the crew in their work centers so they couldn't interfere.

He took this as a good sign ... it meant this was likely a small group of people and not half the damn ship. On a whim he pulled up the feed for the brig and, sure enough, Ed Kazenski wasn't in his cell. The Marine on guard was lying on the ground and blood was pooling underneath him. Jackson hoped he could reestablish control in time to get him medical attention.

"Time for a little surprise," he said grimly, entering three commands into a separate window. He then went to his wall safe and quickly opened it, pulling out an ancient weapon that, while comparatively primitive, would be more than adequate. It was a twin to the one in his desk drawer, but this one worked. There was also a modern, Fleet-issued sidearm in his safe, but he knew it would be useless.

He looked at the smooth sides of the slide, running his hand over it. It was an exact replica of a Colt 1911 .45 ACP service sidearm that Singh had painstakingly recreated for his friend from drawings he'd found in an archive. He'd made the weapon after he learned of Jackson's interest in the Second Great World War and, in particular, the weapon designs of John Browning. It was meant to be a display piece, but on some shore leave they'd gone ahead and fabricated ammunition and had great fun shooting at empty beer bottles out in the desert.

Jackson quickly loaded the two magazines he had, each holding seven rounds, and slipped one into the pistol's handle. He worked the slide to chamber a round and flicked the safety up, keeping the hammer back so the single-action weapon would be ready to fire quickly.

Slipping out of his office he reflected on how surreal the whole thing was. An actual mutiny on a Terran Confederacy starship. He edged around the corridor and saw the armed party was already at the hatch leading onto the bridge, arguing about how best to get past the barrier.

"Didn't quite plan on that part, did you?" Jackson asked casually, his voice steady despite the seething rage he was feeling. He kept the .45 down against his side.

"Stay right there, Earther," the chief said. Jackson could now read "Cullen" on his utility nametag. "Tell your Marine to open this hatch."

"Why would I do that?"

Cullen walked up to within three paces of Jackson and aimed the carbine at his head. "Because I'll blow your goddamn Earther brains out if you don't," he said.

"A fairly stupid tactic in hostage negotiation," Jackson shrugged. "But do what you have to do, I suppose."

Cullen closed his eyes and actually flinched before squeezing the trigger. Nothing happened. Culled looked at the carbine and squeezed the trigger a few more times, looking at it in confusion.

"It worked when you shot Kazenski's guard, no doubt," Jackson said, watching as the other five began to approach. "But I disabled all handheld weapons on the ship. They're tied to the main computer, you stupid bastard. But this one works just fine." Before Cullen could react, Jackson flicked the safety off the .45 and shot the chief right in the forehead.

The thunderous report of the gunpowder-propelled shot had the desired effect on the other five. That and being sprayed with what used to be inside Cullen's head. Jackson kept the weapon trained on them as the chief's body slumped to the deck, blood pooling from the horrific wound the .45 round had inflicted.

"Any more of you traitors want to try your luck?" Jackson asked the now terrified group in front of him. They all dropped their rifles and put their hands up. "Lay face down on the deck and put your hands over your head. Marine! Get out here and restrain these vermin!"

The hatch to the bridge slid open and the Marine jogged out, recoiling at Cullen's body. To his credit, he grabbed flexible restraints from a cargo pocket in his fatigue pants and began securing their arms behind their backs.

"Now that this mutinous traitor can't answer any questions, which of you wants to be the one who begins to put things right?" Jackson asked as Celesta walked from the bridge, her hand flying over her mouth at the sight.

"I'll talk, sir," came a muffled voice from the floor.

"Turn him over," Jackson told the Marine. The sentry grabbed the spacer by the ankles and twisted quite roughly until Jackson was looking down into the face of a terrified spacer. "Your name?"

"Specialist Ormond, sir."

"I don't think you need to worry about your rank anymore," Jackson said, waving the pistol around and causing Ormond much anxiety for it. "Start talking."

"Master Chief Kazenski put it all in motion," Ormond said. "Chief Cullen approached me and said I was vital since I work in the primary MUX control center. He said you'd gone rogue and we were chasing an alien ship for a personal vendetta of yours. He told me that we needed to stop the ship to keep us all alive."

"You do realize that the alien ship is *still* out there, right?" Celesta said, her eyes cold and completely without compassion. "You cowards have disabled us right as we are making a high-speed approach towards a hostile, powerful ship."

Ormond paled as the reality of what they'd set in motion sunk in.

"You and your friends may have killed us all, not to mention every living human on Podere," Celesta finished.

"How many were there?" Jackson asked him.

"Thirty-eight Fleet personnel," Ormond said. "I don't know how many Marines."

"Major Ortiz?"

"No. Just the guards from the armory. We sealed the hatches shut to the Marine garrison before beginning."

"What did you do to the ship?"

"Disabled steering and manually shut the valves to the primary propellant manifold to start with," Ormond said. "We began shutting down individual subsystems after that."

"Who can restore all ship functions?" Jackson asked. When Ormond hesitated, he pushed the barrel of the .45 into his nose. "Who?"

"Lieutenant Peters," Ormond said, tears beginning to stream down the sides of his face. "He was our man in the CIC who could re-route command functions from the bridge. Other than the propellant valves and the breakers for the attitude jets he can put everything back. He was going to take command after we secured the bridge."

Jackson stood up, looking down at Ormond in disgust. "You know I'd be on the right side of the Code of Conduct if I blew your brains out, right?" When Ormond nodded Jackson continued. "For your sake, you better hope I can regain control of my ship before that alien bastard figures out we're adrift. I'm going to the CIC. You and you ... with me." He pointed at Celesta and the Marine sentry before turning and walking off to the lifts.

"If Peters has control of all internal systems he knows we're coming," Celesta said, pointing at the security camera in the corner of a hatchway.

"I've disabled all the cameras," Jackson said. "There were some backdoors into the system Peters wasn't aware of."

"Another captain secret," Celesta said nodding. "Those have been useful."

"I hope to keep us all alive long enough for you to get some of your very own one day," Jackson said as the lift doors closed.

****

"Lieutenant Peters, I'm still not getting anything from the bridge. Should we send a runner?"

"As you were, Specialist," Peters said. His face was flushed red and he was sweating profusely. It had been twenty minutes past when Cullen was supposed to check in telling him Wolfe was in custody or dead. He'd watched the captain run from the bridge to his office alone and couldn't believe his luck, but when he'd tried to call Cullen he found he couldn't raise the chief's comlink despite entering the address as an exception to the com blackout in the computer. Once all the internal camera feeds dropped simultaneously he began to feel the first twinges of a panic attack coming on.

He looked to the two armed Marines guarding the entrance to the CIC for some reassurance. It hadn't been easy to convince the two to go along with the plan, but Kazenski was able to bring them onboard and even got them to open up the small arms locker at one of the checkpoints.

"Sir, I can't raise Engineering," another specialist said. "In fact, I can't access anything."

"It's a temporary glitch," Peters said loudly. "Everyone stay at their stations and be quiet until it's sorted out."

He heard one of the guards shout something unintelligible before an explosive roar just outside the hatch made them all jump and one of the Marines slumped over onto the floor, blood spreading across his fatigues.

"Drop that weapon, Marine, or I'll put you down too," he heard a familiar voice outside and nearly fainted. Before he could react he saw Jackson Wolfe and Celesta Wright stride into the CIC, the captain holding some sort of blocky sidearm with smoke curling out of the barrel.

"Francis Peters, you are under arrest for mutiny, treason, and whatever else I can find that will stick," Jackson said, walking up to the trembling officer. "The sentence for such crimes during combat is a summary execution." He raised the pistol. "I'll delay sentencing and just toss your ass in the brig for now if you turn around and restore control of the ship to the bridge."

"I'm not sure I know what you're—"

"You have five seconds," Jackson said, cutting him off. The rest of the crew in the CIC was sitting and staring at the interaction in open-mouthed shock. Wordlessly, Peters moved over and began entering commands into his terminal. Jackson watched and could see at once how the operations officer had bypassed the normal failsafes. They were meant to protect against a technical failure, not a deliberate act of sabotage. Once the scripts to counter those commands had executed he shoved Peters out of the way, and not gently, so he could use the terminal and enter his own command codes to fully restore ship functions.

"Bridge," he said after a moment, "this is the captain. What's your status?"

"*Captain!*" Davis's voice came over the intercom. "*Everything is coming back online up here, but that ship has slowed again and is turning toward us.*"

"Range?" Jackson asked as he keyed in the commands to unlock the Marines still stuck in their garrison two decks below.

"*Two hundred and fifty thousand kilometers and closing,*" Davis said. "*It's still hurt, but it's coming.*"

"I'll be up shortly," Jackson said. "Tell Tactical to get the mag-cannons ready to fire. CIC out."

"You need to get back up there," Celesta said. "I'll go get Major Ortiz and get steering and propulsion back."

"Very well," Jackson said. "Restrain this scum along with that other Marine outside. Once you're with Ortiz, tell me and I'll reactivate his weapons. Let him know what's happened. And get Daya to Sick Bay!"

"Yes, sir," she said, motioning for the bridge sentry to bind Peters and the remaining guard who was still lying face down.

Jackson raced back to the left that would take him back into the superstructure so he could be on the bridge as the alien approached again. He held the .45 at low ready, trying to remember the smatter of tactical training he had received with personal weaponry. Even with recapturing the CIC he wasn't sure if there were collaborators still roaming the corridors that wouldn't hesitate to take him out. The only way he'd get the names of everyone involved was to take Kazenski alive, wherever he was hiding at.

Chapter 17

"Range?" Jackson barked as he ran back onto the bridge. He flicked the safety back up on his pistol and stuffed it into his pocket as he went to his terminal and began entering commands.

"One hundred and ninety thousand kilometers," Lieutenant Barrett said. "Cannons are armed and trained on the target. Capacitors are charged so we're ready to fire at your command, sir."

"Excellent," Jackson said, the relief washing over him as he learned that his ship was able to at least defend herself. "I'm working to get maneuvering and propulsion back. There's still a pocket of mutineers in the engineering spaces."

"I can't believe we're dealing with this on top of an alien ship in human space," Lieutenant Davis remarked acidly.

"That makes two of us, Lieutenant," Jackson said absently as he scrolled through the menus to reactivate the ship's internal security systems.

"*Captain, XO*," Celesta's voice came over the intercom. "*We've released Major Ortiz and his men. They're armed and ready to go.*"

"Reactivating their weapons now," Jackson answered. "Get the mains back online as fast as you can. Maneuvering jets don't take as long once power has been restored to that system."

"*Yes, sir,*" she said. "*I'll let you know as soon as we have anything to report. XO out.*"

Jackson had waffled about enabling all the small arms on the ship. He was sure the Marines could rush in and take a bunch of Fleet techs unarmed, but the mutineers were smart and determined ... there was no way to tell what sort of improvised weapons or traps they'd been able to rig up. He also didn't want a melee down in Engineering. Better to trust Major Ortiz to do his job and give him all the tools he needed to secure the ship.

"Lieutenant Davis, I assume you've been taking this opportunity to get detailed recordings of the enemy as it does its slow approach?" Jackson asked.

"Yes, Captain," she said.

"Good," he said. "Package that data up and add it to what I've already given you. Load it all to a com drone and launch it as soon as you're ready." He leaned back in his seat and tried to relax and refocus as the enemy approached. They didn't know full range of that damn plasma weapon, but he had to assume the giant tunnel they'd blown through the ship had to negatively affect it. There was nothing he could do until the *Blue Jacket* could move under her own power, so he forced himself to sit and wait while his crew tried to rectify the situation.

****

"Commander, we have a group in the compartment ahead," Major Ortiz said as he looked at the security feed on a small tile he was holding. "Three of them are armed. How do you wish to proceed?"

"Are any of them Master Chief Kazenski?" Celesta asked.

"No, ma'am."

"Secure the compartment however you see best, Major," she said, swallowing hard. "Lethal force is authorized."

"Yes, ma'am," Ortiz said, also not looking pleased about the situation. "Alpha Squad, you're up. Three targets, no hostages that I can see. Breech the compartment and dispatch all three hostiles. Do NOT damage any of the equipment in there."

The eight Marines that made up Alpha Squad quickly deployed around the entry hatch to the compartment, making almost no noise. The hatch was standing wide open, but the ambient noise of the ship would have masked their approach. On a signal from their squad leader the two on either side of the hatch stepped back and angled their weapons into the room, each taking out a target on the opposite side of the room. Two more Marines rushed in past them, the first killing the last hostile standing while the second swept the room for anyone who may have been missed.

"Clear!" the shout came after less than ten seconds.

Celesta and Ortiz rushed into the room as the other members of Alpha Squad grabbed and detained the other three spacers who had been in the compartment. They'd just secured the Engineering Operations Center and from there would be able to reinitialize the remaining systems the attempted mutiny had knocked out.

"Major, check on Lieutenant Commander Singh," Celesta ordered as she began checking to see exactly what they'd done. Trying to decipher the information without Daya Singh was a bit frustrating as she still wasn't completely familiar with the systems. "And find out where they put the second engineer, Lieutenant Caldwell. He should be here to help get everything back up and running."

As she continued to muddle her way through the process of restarting their maneuvering systems, she heard a Marine roughly questioning one of the restrained techs.

"All the crew that weren't part of this are being held in a storage compartment one deck up, ma'am," the Marine reported after he'd slapped around a blubbering specialist second class.

"Go get them," Ortiz ordered. "Ma'am, we need to press on to the shut-off valve to get the engines running. Lieutenant Commander Singh is still alive. I'll have him taken to Doctor Owens."

"Right you are, Major," Celesta said, stepping away from the console. "Let's move."

"Bravo Squad, let's go!" Ortiz bellowed as he walked out of the Operations Center.

****

"Captain, propellant pressure is coming back up in the mains," Lieutenant Davis said. "We should be good for engine start in less than five minutes."

"Not a moment too soon," Jackson said tensely. They'd been watching the enemy creep closer and closer. It hadn't been accelerating, which was good. After the initial burst of energy to change its direction it had just been drifting towards them. "How's its wound looking?"

"It's still opened up to space, but it's closing rapidly," Davis said. Jackson swore under his breath. They'd had a real chance to finish it off when Barrett's Hail Mary shot had punched a hole clean through it, but whatever it was that performed the extraordinary damage control on the strange ship had already begun to work its magic.

"Lieutenant Barrett," he said. "Go ahead and fire the Avengers. Let them cold coast most of the way and then accelerate into the opening on the starboard side."

"Yes, sir," Barrett said. "Updating missile programming now ... firing."

Jackson could just see the four points of light as they raced away from the destroyer before they went dark to cover most of the distance on inertia. He was glad he'd taken another chance on his tactical officer. After his bout with near-crippling panic the young lieutenant had performed flawlessly, not only proficient at his job but devising successful strategies with what little he had to work with on the stricken destroyer.

"Engines are coming online, sir," Davis said. "Plasma chambers are all heating up within limits and magnetic constrictors are fully engaged."

"OPS, give the helm an updated course that will allow us to bring our guns to bear on the most heavily damaged side of the target," Jackson said. "Helm, as soon as you have engines I want one-quarter thrust until we clear around the target's nose and then go to full power."

"Aye aye, sir," the helmsman said, shifting around in his seat and adjusting his controls now that he was back in business. The telltale rumble of the mains igniting vibrated the deck and to Jackson there could have been no sweeter music at that moment. She was beat up, but the *Blue Jacket* was ready to go one more round.

The helmsman nudged the throttles up and angled their course over to come across the target's nose and bring them up on the more damaged starboard side. Jackson looked up at the information Davis had projected onto the main display and saw that they were only forty thousand kilometers from each other. Once the helmsman kicked her in the ass the *Blue Jacket* should be able to cover that distance in a relatively short sprint.

"Target is maneuvering," Davis said. "It's reversing course and coming about."

"Shit!" Jackson said, standing up. "It's running now that we're underway again. Tactical, send a signal to the Avengers: hit that ship wherever they can land a hit and get ready to let 'em have it with the mag-cannons."

"It's too far out of range," Davis said. "We can't land a cannon shot at this distance."

"Not for long," Jackson said through gritted teeth. "Helm! Run that bastard down!"

"Yes, sir!" the helmsman said with enthusiasm as he pushed the throttles all the way to the stops. The *Blue Jacket* responded with a roar as her mains ran up to full power and she leapt ahead, chasing the fleeing ship.

"We're closing the gap," Davis said. "Helm, come starboard four degrees and you'll have the inside line to come up alongside."

"Adjusting to starboard," the helmsman confirmed.

"Rate of closure is decreasing," Davis said. "The target is now almost matching our acceleration." Jackson frowned at that.

"Where is it going?"

"Unknown," she said. "It's not angling back towards Podere ... looks like it may be running for open space."

"Or it's getting ready to go FTL and leave the system so it can lick its wounds and come back," Jackson said. "Status on our missiles?"

"They expended their fuel before they could catch the target, sir," Barrett reported. "I ordered them to detonate so they weren't a navigation hazard."

"Good thinking," Jackson said absently as he watched the target's acceleration creep up to match theirs, causing a stalemate. He looked over as Celesta walked onto the bridge.

"All guilty parties have been rounded up and detained," she said. "The ones left alive anyway. Lieutenant Commander Singh is in Sick Bay and Commander Owens said his injuries were non-life threatening."

"All good news," Jackson said with obvious relief. "Outstanding job taking the ship back, Commander."

"Thank you, sir," she said, clearly taken aback at such a generous compliment from a CO that barely acknowledged when someone went above and beyond save for Davis' field promotion. "Major Ortiz deserves much of the credit. He and his Marines minimized loss of life and avoided damaging the ship while suppressing the mutiny."

"I'll make a note of that," Jackson promised. "If we ever make it back to Haven I'll do what I can to see he's recognized."

Celesta nodded, knowing the part he left out was that the both of them might not be in a position to recognize anyone as they were likely to be arrested as soon as the *Blue Jacket* was dragged into port.

"Sir," Davis interrupted both their internal musings. "There is something up ahead on this course. It's the jump point from Podere to Nuovo Patria."

"That's one of the oldest colony worlds in the Alliance," Celesta said. "There are tens of millions of people there."

"Could this thing really be going to try its luck in another system after all the damage we've done?" Jackson asked. "I would have thought it'd try to run for home, not push deeper into human territory."

"Depends on what its mission is," Celesta said. "Maybe it was sent to test our resolve and see just how much destruction and death it could wreak before we mounted an effective defense."

"A suicide bomber strategy?"

"Basically."

"Let's see if the old girl has one more left in her," Jackson said. "Helm, full emergency acceleration."

"Aye aye, sir." As the *Blue Jacket* strained with everything she had to catch the fleeing alien, Jackson could see they were beginning to close the gap again.

"If you two are right, we have another problem," Jackson said to Celesta and Lieutenant Davis. "Our jump points are just arbitrary points in space, they don't mean anything other than we know the warp lane is clear to the destination point. The lanes are created by sending automated ships to make short hops all the way to the target and document or clear any hazards. If this thing knows about the warp lanes it knows a lot more about us than it should."

"It did just take out two planets by landing ground forces," Davis said. "It's possible it was able to access the computer networks."

"Maybe," Jackson grunted. "It'll all be academic soon. We're closing the gap quickly."

"We'll be within firing range in less than—"

"Massive thermal build up on the starboard, rear quadrant!" Davis' shout ran right over time of Barrett. "They're going to fire!"

"Hard to port!" Jackson yelled. "Break off, break off!"

It was too late and a blinding flash of light streaked towards them, encompassing the entire main display as the *Blue Jacket* had just begun to swing her nose over. There was a horrendous impact and everyone was thrown from their seats. Jackson had been standing so he was sent airborne until he impacted the row of consoles next to OPS. Alarms began blaring loudly accompanied by red strobes.

"Report!" Celesta struggled to get out as she saw Captain Wolfe was not getting back up.

"Damage reports coming in," Davis said in a shaky voice. "Massive damage along the starboard side. Two hull breeches along the rear quarter and outer hull damage on the entire flank. Engine four is ... gone!"

"What?!"

"Engine four has been blasted clean off the ship," Davis confirmed. "Half the pylon was taken with it. Emergency shut-off valves engaged and saved most of our propellant."

"We're in a tumble, ma'am," the helmsman reported. "I'm trying to straighten us out."

"Where's the target?

"Not showing up on our sensors," Barrett said. "Radar shows it disappearing right as we were hit. I can't confirm with optics because they were washed out by whatever hit us."

"It jumped to FTL," Jackson said, struggling to get to his feet. Blood was running freely down the left side of his head and he looked to be in considerable pain. "Helm, straighten this damn ship out. Nav, set course to take us back around the system towards Podere. OPS, prepare a com drone for Nuovo Patria. We need to warn them about what's coming."

"Com drones are unavailable," Davis said apologetically. "The hit on the starboard side partially liquefied the upper armor of the hull. The hatches for the com drones are welded shut."

"Can we cut through them?" Celesta asked.

"I'm receiving no status from any of our remaining drones, ma'am," Davis said.

"Have Commander Juarez deploy a crew in EVA gear to the internal maintenance hatches for the drones," Jackson said. "If they're still viable we'll worry about cutting the hull away then. Am I to understand we're down to three engines?"

"Yes, sir," Celesta said. Jackson went to run his hand over his head and winced, pulling away a hand covered in blood. "You need medical attention, sir."

"No argument there," he said. "I don't think a compression bandage will help with this. Commander, you have the bridge. I'll be in Sick Bay and then we'll figure out what we're going to do to unfuck this mess."

He turned before he could see Celesta's jaw drop at his profanity.

As the rolling battle moved along, the forced professionalism of the captain in front of the crew was beginning to crack and peel. The mutiny had shaken him up more than he was letting on, and he wanted nothing more than for this nightmare to be over. Unfortunately, a happy ending didn't seem to be in the cards. If he could only catch a break on this cursed cruise ... he'd give anything for just one thing to go right.

****

"Captain! Are you okay?" Commander Owens, the *Blue Jacket's* chief medical officer, just happened to be walking by the entrance to Sick Bay as Jackson walked in.

"I've been better," he admitted. "Can you get one of your techs to patch me up?"

"Of course," Owens said. "This way, sir." The doctor led him back into a room and indicated a chair for him to sit on. He began inspecting the wound and pushing around the affected area, causing Jackson to grit his teeth.

"It's deep, but nothing a new skin bandage can't take care of," Owens said. "I'll have Specialist Ki come in and take care of it and then we can talk."

"Thanks, Doc," Jackson said. Specialist Ki, a woman so youthful looking he would have sworn she was too young to wear the uniform, gave him a shy smile as she entered the room and began cleaning the wound and getting it ready for the bandage coated in an organic substance that would promote healing.

For so much blood the cut was actually fairly small, barely an inch long and not especially deep. The med tech had him patched up and out of the room within twenty minutes. He hadn't heard any klaxons or announcements indicating the enemy ship had come back to finish them off. He debated just leaving, but he'd sort of agreed to talk to Commander Owens. When he found the doctor, and who he was attending to, he was glad he had stuck around.

"How are you feeling?"

"Good, Captain," Daya Singh said. "They're just keeping me here as a precaution. I heard you lost one of my engines?"

"I'll get you a new one," Jackson promised.

"So what's the plan?" Singh asked, trying to prop himself up.

"Right now we're simply trying to staunch the bleeding," Jackson admitted. "We're beaten up, missing an engine, and streaming atmosphere from about a hundred places. Currently we should be back on course for Podere to check on the population there."

"Starships are always leaking atmosphere," Daya said, waving him off. "That's why we carry so much oxygen and nitrogen on every cruise to replace it. I heard a rumor that ship may have jumped to FTL heading for another Alliance planet."

"How the hell are you hearing all these rumors?" Jackson asked, only half-joking.

"I still have my comlink," Daya said. "You gave me access to the ship's log last year and I've been reading the entries. That's not the point. What are we going to do about that ship going after another human planet?"

"I don't know what we can do at this point," Jackson said, spreading his hands helplessly.

"The warp drive is still functional, isn't it?" Owens said, speaking up for the first time.

"I'm under the assumption it is," Jackson said.

"Then I think you know what has to be done," Singh said. "We need to loop back around and hit the Nuovo Patria jump point and try to get there before this thing does."

"So you two called me in here for a pep talk and to encourage me to continue on with this suicide mission?" Jackson said, rising from the seat. "I'll keep what you've said in mind. When we pass by Podere and are lined up for a run, assuming the *Blue Jacket* can even achieve transition velocity at this point, I'll make my decision." He nodded to them both and walked out of Sick Bay.

As he walked down the corridors, his utilities caked with dried blood, he passed a score of crewman hustling about their duties. Each gave him a respectful nod as they rushed off to perform some task to keep the destroyer flying. He didn't see panic or sullenness. He didn't even really see much fear. If he had to put a name on it he would have to say the faces of his crew were set with a grim determination as he passed them.

He felt his resolve begin to harden as he watched them, nodding back to each in turn but offering no empty words of encouragement. They didn't need it. They may have started this cruise as a collection of castaways that were just waiting out their time or looking for the easy road, but now they were the most battle-hardened crew in the Fleet. A cynic would point out that fact was true when the first shots were fired in anger, but Jackson could see the truth of it while walking through the lower decks. Despite the mutiny and the horrific damage the *Blue Jacket* had suffered, the crew would follow him no matter what he decided. As the lift doors closed to whisk him back up to the bridge he knew exactly what it was he had to do.

Chapter 18

"OPS, give me a status on the warp drive," Jackson said as he strode onto the bridge.

"Ordering a diagnostic on the drive components now," Davis said, yawning hugely. "But I can say for certain the starboard hatches are welded shut over the emitters. Also, Commander Juarez confirms all our remaining com drones are damaged beyond repair."

"Get Engineering to put a detail on it," Jackson said, ignoring the news about the drones. "It doesn't have to be pretty, just cut the damn hatches off and jettison them if they have to. Just free up the emitters."

"Yes, sir."

"The warp drive, sir?" Celesta said. "Are we taking a trip to Nuovo Patria?"

"We are," Jackson said.

"It would probably help if you addressed the crew now," she said.

"I was thinking the same thing, Commander."

****

"Hello." Captain Wolfe's face appeared on every non-essential monitor shipwide, prompting everyone to pause what they were doing and pay attention.

"As you all are well aware, we have been in a prolonged and costly battle with an unknown alien ship that has invaded the Terran Confederacy, leaving a path of unimaginable destruction through the Asianic Union and into the Warsaw Alliance.

"We've lost crewmates along the way. Friends. The *Blue Jacket* has been battered and is limping across the Podere system now, barely able to defend herself. The logical thing to do would be to make orbit over Podere and wait for help, or possibly push on to Haven ourselves, but there's a problem with that. The enemy ship has left the system on a course that will almost certainly take it to Nuovo Patria, an Alliance planet with over thirty million people living on it. It might run into the Eighth Fleet there, it might not, and we have no way of warning them what's coming.

"Things have not gone our way in this battle. We've had to fight outdated systems, fight poorly maintained weaponry, and even fight ourselves. But I've watched this crew rise to the occasion in spite of all that. I've watched spacers swallow their fear and do their duty in the face of an implacable and terrifying enemy. I have no right to ask any more from you than what you've already given. But I'm not asking. The people of Nuovo Patria are asking. The people of Podere are screaming for justice as they pick through the ruins, and the memories of Xi'an and Oplotom are demanding vengeance.

"It doesn't matter that we've had more than two centuries without armed conflict. It doesn't matter that most of you joined with no expectation or desire to see combat. Despite all of that ... this is still a warship, a ship of the line, and the fight has been brought to us. We will not shrink from our duty and we will *not* fail in our mission." His voice had been rising as he spoke, and every officer, every enlisted spacer could feel the will of their captain emanating from the monitors and speakers.

"We will be coming around for a pass of Podere to gain velocity for a warp transition," Jackson said, calming down as he began the details portion of his briefing. "We'll hit the Nuovo Patria jump point and hopefully get there in time to stop the enemy. We've already done significant damage and I'm fully confident we can disable or destroy it during the next engagement. Listen to your officers. Get the ship, and yourselves, ready to finish this mission. Your names will be talked about for generations ... the crew of the *TCS Blue Jacket*, the destroyer that stood alone against an alien juggernaut. Let's get to it. CO, out."

****

"How was that?" Jackson asked after the camera light winked off.

"Very good, sir," Celesta said. "It set the right tone, I think."

"We'll see," he groused. "If they storm the bridge again we'll know it wasn't all that inspirational."

"Coms has been pulling in messages from Podere," she said, steering the conversation into a different direction. "Three cities are a total loss, but they've gotten some good data on what it was that turned all those other cities into the slicks we found on Xi'an."

"That's something I suppose. That was beyond luck that the aliens pulled their ground troops before breaking orbit. We have nothing onboard to try and rout out an enemy on the surface, and Podere has no standing army."

"Luck had to break our way sometime," she shrugged. "Do you want to respond to Podere?"

"No," Jackson said after a moment. "We've got enough problems as it is without trying to deflect some regional governor's plea for aid. If they have a smart one he'll invoke a little know treaty clause that would more or less force us to stay and help out."

"I think we're well beyond playing by the rules at this point," she reminded him.

"True," he conceded. "Even if the *Blue Jacket* survives the two of us are screwed."

"That's the way I see it as well."

"Go get some sleep, Commander," Jackson said. "You can relieve me in four and then we'll both be fresh for the transition. After that we have a fifty-two-hour warp flight, assuming the drive and powerplant can sustain our highest velocity."

****

"The crews are almost done cutting the hatches off the starboard drive emitters," Singh said, slowly stirring his tea. "The emitters themselves along with the deployment arms look completely undamaged. I had been worried that heat great enough to liquefy our hull armor would have fused the joints on the arms, but we appear to be in business."

"How much longer?" Jackson asked, his eyes feeling gritty from being up so long. He was on the bridge by himself until Celesta and Barrett came back on duty. He had ordered Davis to her quarters despite her strident protests that she was fine. With Peters in the brig she had been on shift for nearly thirty-six hours.

"A few hours," Singh shrugged. "We're not even near the jump point yet. What's the hurry?"

"I can't begin to accelerate to transition velocity until they're off the hull," Jackson said.

"Why are you accelerating so soon?"

"We're missing an engine, in case you forgot," Jackson said, slightly exasperated.

"Three main engines is more than enough," Singh said, still unconcerned. "Even if another drops off we have the auxiliary boosters."

"I'm not sure I trust a fifty-year-old rocket booster to fire when I need it," Jackson said, his vision beginning to blur from the fatigue. "How shorthanded are you after we rounded up that mutiny?"

"Unfortunately there were a lot of my people involved," Singh said, wincing as he did. "That doesn't say much for my ability as a Starfleet officer I'm afraid. You really shot Chief Cullen in the head with that 1911?"

"Yes," Jackson said. "That's not something I'm especially proud of, but I'd have been less proud to have millions die because I let six traitors bludgeon me to death in the corridor."

"True," Singh said. "Well ... as much as I'd love to keep you company I'm afraid this is where I must leave you. I'd like to at least get a few hours of sleep before we see if the warp drive will transition us or shred the ship to individual molecules."

"I'm not really sure which is the worse option there."

"Goodnight, Jack."

"Sleep well, Daya."

****

"Here goes nothing," Jackson said, settling into his seat and feeling immensely better after a shower and a hot meal despite only getting a couple hours of sleep. As Singh had said, the *Blue Jacket* easily surged to transition velocity on her three remaining engines. The warp emitters had successfully deployed and were beginning to glow a bright blue, going on pure white.

"Five seconds to transition!" the chief at Nav said far more loudly than necessary. Jackson watched as the distortion ring began to form around the front of the ship and a few seconds later he felt the violent buffeting as the *Blue Jacket* transitioned out of the Podere system.

"We're on our way, everyone," Jackson said, standing up. "Continue what repairs you can while we're at warp. XO, let the department heads know that I favor resting the crew over any heavy maintenance or repairs they may want to make. I'd like to be on normal watches by the time we hit Nuovo Patria."

"I'll let them know, Captain," Celesta said.

"Captain, I don't have a relief watch anymore," Lieutenant Davis said.

"You and Lieutenant Barrett will alternate watches with each other until we're ready to transition back into real-space," Jackson said. "When we arrive I obviously need you both on duty. You have first watch, Davis. Barrett, take a walk with me. XO, you have the bridge."

Lieutenant Barrett rose out of his seat with a concerned look on his face and hustled off the bridge to catch up with the captain.

"Yes, sir?" he said, falling in beside Jackson.

"I just wanted you to know that your performance after our last talk has been exceptional," Jackson said. "I held off entering the previous incident into your record since you accepted full responsibility, and I figured that alone earned you a shot to prove me wrong. You've done that and then some." He stopped in the hallway and held out his hand to the young lieutenant. Barrett shook it with a bit of a shocked look on his face.

"I've never been so happy to be wrong about a junior officer," Jackson said. "If we make it through this I'll be putting you in for a promotion."

"Thank you, sir," Barrett said. "When this is over, I hope I have the opportunity to continue to serve under you."

"I would like nothing more myself, Lieutenant," Jackson said, keeping his face neutral. "Carry on."

Chapter 19

"... *the devastation is simply indescribable. We have no landing craft aboard so we have no way to verify that there are no survivors, but the damage looks absolute. As of right now I'm declaring Xi'an a complete loss. There are no signs of any other ship in the area and the debris in orbit is inconsistent with a Raptor-class destroyer. We will continue our survey before moving on to Oplotom. We are using our only com drone to send this message so we will be out of contact until we reach a world with a drone platform still intact. Captain Jegg of the TCS Constantine, out.*"

The ball of ice that had been forming in Admiral Alyson Winters' stomach did a slow roll as the images from the cutter, *Constantine*, scrolled across her monitor after the captain had signed off his communiqué. With shaking hands she pulled up the operational reports filed by the *Blue Jacket* over a week ago and compared the images.

Unsurprisingly, they were an exact match. The only difference was that Captain Wolfe had been much, much more thorough in his investigation than Captain Jegg had been. The bile rose in her throat and she felt her temples throb with the fast onset of a tension headache. She would like to say it was because of the magnitude of the tragedy she was looking at, but that would mostly be a lie.

She was fucked. Truly and properly fucked.

So confident that Wolfe had either gone completely off the reservation and lost his mind, or was playing some sort of bizarre game, she hadn't even thought to look more carefully through the *Blue Jacket's* reports before filing them away. She'd saved them in a hidden file on her personal computer, relishing the fact that the damning documents would be all she'd need to make sure the disgusting Earther would never step foot on a starship again and would likely be sent back to Earth with a no-travel restriction hanging around his neck.

Now ... Now it looked like she would be the one answering some uncomfortable questions as evidence of an attack on no less than two Terran planets had been covered up by her hold order on any communications from the destroyer. Now that the *Constantine* had verified that something had likely attacked and wiped out Xi'an there would be no way to keep a lid on it since the Senate Intelligence Committee was waiting on word from the frontier regarding rumors of unrest along the AU/Alliance corridor.

But ... what were the odds Wolfe would emerge victorious against such an overmatched opponent? She scrolled through the reports and saw how much damage the old *Raptor*-class ship had taken in a single pass against the alien ship. The damn fool appeared to be pursuing it across the Alliance. In fact, she hadn't heard from the ship for nearly five days. It was possible, even likely, that the *Blue Jacket* was nothing but wreckage by now.

She closed all of Wolfe's reports, purged the data from her machine, and then quickly went into the data archives and removed all the exceptions she had put in when the *Blue Jacket* had departed. Winters had been a data clerk herself, never having actually left Haven her entire career. She'd never commanded a starship nor had she served as an actual mission analyst, but she did know exactly how to retrace her footsteps and eliminate any evidence she'd ever been in there. In fact, she was accessing the system using generic administrative credentials that would be difficult to trace. When everything came to light after the *Constantine* returned it would simply look like Wolfe had neglected to file regular operational reports. Given the man's past, it wouldn't be much of a stretch for an inquiry board to conclude it had been negligence on his part.

****

Jackson walked the corridors of the *Blue Jacket*, stopping to talk to crew or look in on a department that seemed to be having a particularly rough time under the circumstances. Even though the mutiny had been quashed he still felt a bit exposed, even with the Marine sentry tailing along behind him. He was still carrying the .45 under his utility top since the weapon's thin profile was easily concealable. The modern sidearm in his office was a bit more unwieldy, would have to be worn in an external holster, and could be disabled in the same way he'd deactivated the weapons the mutineers had been using.

From what he could see, the ship was in bad shape. The fact she was still flying and had a little bit of fight left in her was a testament to the designers at the Sierra Shipyards and the builders who'd put her together. They were less than a day from arriving in the Nuovo Patria system and he knew that if they met the alien again there it would be the last time, one way or another. The destroyer simply couldn't survive another beating, and if their high-explosive shells failed to disable or destroy the enemy they were out of ammunition anyway.

"So the port-side lasers are completely inoperable?" he asked as he walked alongside Daya Singh. They were in a large chamber that housed reactor three while the chief engineer inspected some maintenance that had been done to the fuel system.

"Total loss," Singh confirmed. "At least not without being in a shipyard with months of down time."

"That's unfortunate."

"We were actually lucky that when the power trunk exploded it didn't cause serious damage to the MUX and the subsystems located in that area," Singh shrugged. "As it is we don't even have enough raw material to try and effect repairs on the system, and even if we did there's no guarantee it wouldn't just happen again."

"Do we know what caused it?" Jackson asked.

"Design flaw," Singh said confidently. "For the laser projectors on our flanks the power is distributed in such a way that if the main feed breaks it kills power to the entire side. My guess is that, other than in testing, the system has never been up past ten percent capacity for the entire life of the ship."

"So we're down to a single salvo with the mag-cannons," Jackson said, shaking his head. "Not a scenario I had envisioned when I thought about deep space battles."

"How's that?" Singh asked disinterestedly as he continued to look over the work his crews had done earlier. Jackson answered him anyway.

"I always figured we would stand off hundreds of thousands of kilometers and lob long-range missiles at each other until someone got lucky," he said. "Despite the size and the velocity of the shells they can spit out, the mag-cannons are still basically thirteenth century tech ... you have to get in very close and you can't guide the weapon once it's fired."

"I agree there," Singh said, straightening up. "When I was first assigned to the *Raptor*-class I always thought the cannons were absolutely absurd. Although they would make a hell of a ship-to-surface weapon."

"A little like using a sledgehammer to kill an insect, but true," Jackson said.

"I've had crews inspecting the cannons and the turrets while we've been in warp," Singh said. "They'll hold up for this last fight. I can't promise the same about the rest of the ship."

"That bad?" Jackson said with a wince.

"Missing engine, leaking air from a few dozen hull breaches, power system fluctuating wildly, and significant structural damage just for good measure," Singh said. "No matter what happens at Nuovo Patria, this will be the old girl's last cruise."

"It already was," Jackson said, no longer seeing any need to keep the secret. "Ninth Squadron is being stood down. The *Pontiac* and the *Crazy Horse* are already heading to Sierra to be dismantled and scrapped."

"I guess we'll go out in style at least," Singh said.

****

"Stand by!"

The *Blue Jacket* bucked and shuddered under Jackson's feet as she transitioned back into real-space. Just as Jackson was about to order Nav to verify their position a flash outside blinded him. Before he could blink his eyes clear there was a tremendous *boom* felt throughout the ship and alarms began blaring.

"Are we under attack?!" he demanded.

"Negative, sir!" Lieutenant Davis shouted over the alarms. "One of the forward warp emitters broke loose from its mount and impacted the ship! We have breaches in the upper hull, outer and inner. Pressure hatches have failed and we're losing atmosphere on decks fourteen and fifteen."

"Seal off all pressure hatches on those decks!" Jackson snapped. "Try to contain this before we lose the whole damn ship!"

"Pressure hatches closed," Davis said. "We could only save seven compartments out of nineteen."

"How many crew?" Jackson asked, dread in his voice.

"Twenty-seven," Davis said quietly, her voice barely audible even with the alarms silenced. "Six were blown out of the ship when the hull was compromised."

"Daya! What the hell happened?" Jackson practically screamed into the intercom.

"*The forward dorsal emitter broke loose from the arm sometime during the flight*," Singh's voice came through the speakers. "*It was held in place by the distortion ring created by the drive and was released when we transitioned back to real-space. It was still charged and exploded when it impacted the hull.*

"*There's more bad news, however ... the emitter still had the power cable attached. When it hit the hull it blew out four main power junctions. The dorsal mag-cannons are inoperable until we repair or bypass the affected junction.*"

"Get to work on it NOW!" Jackson barked. "Get your crews in pressure suits if you have to, but I need those cannons online as fast as you can possibly manage it. Coordinate your efforts through OPS. Bridge, out." He leaned back and rubbed at his eyes before looking at his bridge crew.

"Does anyone have any good news?"

"I've verified our position, sir," the spacer at Nav said. "We're on target, seventeen kilometers away from our intended entry point."

"That's good," Jackson said. "Coms?"

"We're getting normal com chatter, Captain," Lieutenant Keller said. "Drone platform, ships in orbit ... everything looks quiet. There's even an Eighth Fleet cruiser in orbit over Nuovo Patria."

"Send them a flash message and warn them we may have an enemy combatant arriving soon or hiding already in the system," Jackson said. "Don't be too detailed until they ask."

"It'll be nice not to be the only ship in the fight this time," Celesta remarked.

"Don't count on it," Jackson said. "Odds are they'll run if the enemy ship appears in their sky."

"Whereas we no longer have that option," Celesta said, gesturing out the "window" of the main display to the crumpled arm that used to hold one of the four forward warp drive emitters.

"No we don't," Jackson said. "This is where we'll make our last stand. Tactical! Begin scanning the system. If that thing has been here trying to repair itself I'd rather find it sooner than later."

It was the better part of an hour of frenetic activity on the bridge when they received their first com signal.

"Captain," Lieutenant Keller said. "That cruiser is demanding we fly a specific route down to Nuovo Patria and prepare to be boarded."

"There hasn't been enough time for them to receive our signal and send a response," Celesta said with a frown. "They sent that as soon as they had positive identification on our beacon when we transitioned into the system."

"Tell them we're severely damaged and will not be flying anywhere at the moment," Jackson said. "After that ignore any further transmissions from them."

"Yes, sir," Lieutenant Keller said, clearly uncomfortable with the order.

"Could it simply be because we're not scheduled to be in this system on this cruise?" Celesta asked.

"I would normally agree with that assessment," Jackson said. "But the request to board is highly unusual. I can only imagine Winters has sent out standing orders to the entire area. The only thing that does surprise me is an Eighth Fleet cruiser skipper actually giving a damn what a CENTCOM admiral wants."

"So what do we do"?"

"Nothing," Jackson said with a slight shrug. "We press ahead with repairs and stall over the coms as long as possible. I still believe that bastard is on his way here or, more likely, sitting somewhere in the system waiting for us to show up."

"Could that cruiser be of help if they entered the fray?" Celesta asked, raising her voice so that the bridge crew would lose interest in their private discussion.

"That cruiser is a bit newer, but if a *Raptor*-class destroyer has been taking such a beating from the alien ship that smaller ship would likely do little more than slow it down," Jackson said. "I'd almost rather they stay out of it than risk their crew to a no-win situation." They fell silent as the soft, almost relaxed murmur of the bridge belied the gravity of their situation and the manic state of the engineering crews that were already entering the damaged forward sections to try and get power restored to the dorsal cannons.

"Tactical! Where's my update?" Jackson called out.

"Working on it, sir," Lieutenant Barrett said. "The emitter took out the auxiliary high-power array when it exploded. Slag from the hull took out most of the antennas. I'm working with what we have left."

"Will we even be able to target the enemy?" Jackson asked.

"Yes, sir ... but it'll be a lot closer than we would like before the shorter range navigation radars pick it up," Barrett said. "I'm working with OPS and Engineering to tie my station into their system now."

"Keep me updated," Jackson said, fighting to keep the resignation out of his voice. Finding out that they had even less warning than they had before wasn't welcome news. "Coms, is that cruiser still calling us?"

"No, sir," Lieutenant Keller said. "After our declaration of engine trouble they haven't responded."

"Very good. Commander Wright, you have the bridge. I'm going to be checking the damage firsthand," Jackson said, climbing out of his seat.

****

"When these compartments were breached the explosive decompression was enough to get them through the gap and out of the influence of the grav generator," Singh was explaining. "We hadn't increased back to one G after transition so that didn't help. It wasn't anyone's fault, Jack. It was an accident."

"An accident?" Jackson asked, incredulous.

"Yes," Singh said forcefully, "an accident. I've already looked at the damage to the truss for that emitter ... it didn't fail from any battle damage. This was a horrible, horrible coincidence. It likely would have happened even if we had flown to Xi'an and found nothing but a disinterested planetary governor and a boring few orbits before moving on. If anything this was my fault."

Jackson only then realized how personally the chief engineer was likely taking the mishap. "I didn't mean to imply—"

"I know that," Singh waved him off. "But I signed off on the drive against my better judgment. I could have insisted and sidelined the *Blue Jacket* once I realized we were bypassing months of testing and inspections after the clowns at Jericho Station had been climbing all over her. I didn't and now we know that was a lethal mistake."

"Sorry, Daya," Jackson said. "I suppose it's selfish of me to think all the guilt and regrets since this all started belong to me personally."

"There's plenty to go around," Singh agreed. "I'll let you know when we have a definite plan of attack. My gut tells me to lay new runs from the panel two sections back all the way to the turret. But if my guys tell me the lines are all still good and the junctions can be replaced that would be the quicker route."

"Thank for the tour," Jackson said, recognizing a dismissal when he heard one. "I'll be on the bridge when you determine what we should do."

He walked back the way he'd come, skirting around the worst of the damage and staying out of the way by moving back towards the lifts via the port access tube. Since most of the personnel and material were moving forward in the starboard tube the enormous tunnel was practically deserted.

That big bastard was out there somewhere ... waiting. Jackson knew that the alien ship had arrived at Nuovo Patria before the *Blue Jacket* had limped into the system. He could feel it in his gut. What he couldn't figure out was why it was waiting. That Eighth Fleet cruiser wasn't enough to pose any real threat to it even as badly as it had been damaged. So far as he knew the damn thing had already healed itself up and was sitting at full strength.

The only conclusion he could come to was that it was waiting for him. Or, more specifically, the *Blue Jacket* herself. He guessed that it had torn through two systems, at least two that he knew of, without ever encountering any real resistance. Then their single destroyer had fought it to a standstill on multiple occasions and had even punched a hole clean through it. It was probable that part of its mission profile during its sojourn into human space would be to analyze any potential threats. If it was sitting out there waiting for them it would only be because it hoped to capture the destroyer and either dissect it or (more likely) take it back to wherever it came from. Neither proposition sounded especially appealing.

****

"That cruiser is beginning to move," Celesta told him as he walked back onto the bridge.

"Direction?"

"It's breaking orbit," Lieutenant Barrett said. "It looks like they'll pick up some speed around Nuovo Patria before coming out to intercept us."

"How old is this information?" Jacksons asked.

"Just over four hours," Barrett said. "She's still broadcasting nav data on her transponder, so we're updating the plot as we receive it."

"Any messages from them?" Jackson asked over his shoulder to where the com officer sat.

"No, Captain," the officer said. "Still nothing but the automated transmissions from them and the com drone platform."

"They're more than a day from getting here at their current acceleration," Jackson said as he looked at the tracks crawling across the main display. "Keep track of it and alert me to any changes, but for now it doesn't factor in to our immediate plans."

"Aye aye, sir."

It was nearly four hours later when Jackson got the call from his chief engineer regarding the upper cannon turret. He had ordered the *Blue Jacket* into a wide, lazy arc that spiraled down into the system under minimal thrust. As a courtesy, he kept his transponder fully active so the cruiser would know that he wasn't trying to hide. In a worst case scenario the destroyer, even on three engines, could easily outrun the smaller ship and he had the advantage of the "high ground," able to use the star's gravity to assist his maneuvers while the smaller ship fought against it.

"What's the verdict?" he asked Singh over a video link. Both were seated in their respective offices.

"As I suspected, the damage to the power junctions was simply massive, far too great to attempt a repair and have any confidence of it holding," Singh said, sipping on a cup of tea and wiping the black smudges off his face with a rag.

"So you need to lay in an entire run from section fifty-five all the way to the turret?" Jackson asked. "Do you even have the right size cable in a length that great?"

"I do not," Singh said. "We're cannibalizing it from the starboard laser banks. There's a continuous run of cable that's actually larger than what we need. It's also not damaged like the run on the port side since we never got those projectors working."

"How long are we actually talking?"

"A little over fifty meters would be ideal," Singh said.

"I don't imagine that this cable will be easy to extract from the starboard side," Jackson said, rubbing his temples again.

"I'm throwing manpower at it to solve that particular problem," Singh assured him. "It's secured in there tightly, but we'll get it pulled out in the next couple of hours. We should be able to test the cannons within the next six."

"Let's hope the enemy gives us that much time."

"You still think it's already in the system with us?" Singh asked.

"I'm absolutely positive that it is," Jackson said. "It probably is trying to figure out what we're doing skulking along the edge of the system. Once it discovers we're severely damaged I have a feeling it won't waste any time launching an attack."

"Well, here's to hoping you're wrong," Singh said, mockingly saluting with his tea cup. "I'll let you know once my crews have pulled that cable and I've had the chance to inspect it. Engineering out."

Jackson spent the next few hours chugging coffee and studying the sensor logs from their past engagement with the enemy ship, hoping something would pop out that he'd overlooked before. He was desperate to find some weakness he could exploit. The problem was that he already knew the ship was susceptible to kinetic weapons and, conveniently, the mag-cannons were all he had left that was functional on his ship.

Given the sheer size of the enemy, however, he wasn't that confident that another full salvo would be able to permanently disable it even if every shell impacted the same area. Idly, he pulled up another screen and began running the calculations on a plan that was nothing short of insane. As his caffeine-addled mind looked at the results, he knew that it had at least a sixty percent chance of working despite how unworkable it was. He saved the program he'd constructed on the secure bridge server and switched off his terminal. Lieutenant Davis would be coming on watch so he only had around six hours to grab something to eat and get some rest before he was expected back on duty. With a weary sigh, he hauled himself up out of his chair and shuffled to the hatch. Living on adrenaline and coffee for the last week had taken its toll on his body and even his joints ached as he walked down the corridor to his quarters.

Chapter 20

"Tactical, we've just been given the go ahead from Engineering," Jackson said as he slid back into his seat six and a half hours after he'd last climbed out of it. "Begin running a full diagnostic cycle of the dorsal turret. Have Armament load in some solid-core shells and we'll test fire both cannons."

"Aye, sir," Lieutenant Barrett said. "Beginning dorsal turret self-test now and requesting solid-core shells for both cannons, one each."

"Sir, that cruiser is accelerating again," Lieutenant Davis said. "Still not pushing too hard but it looks like they're responding to our maneuvers."

"Let me know when they're in range for two-way communication," Jackson said. "What ship is that anyway? Who's the captain?"

"The *TCS Murmansk*," Davis said. "Captain Agapov commanding."

"Send any other useful information we have on the ship and her captain to my terminal," Jackson said. "Otherwise, proceed with our current course and weapons testing."

"Have you heard of Captain Agapov?" Celesta asked.

"No," Jackson said. "I haven't had much contact with Eighth Fleet. We've only been to Alliance space one other time. Most of our cruises are through New America and Britannia. You?"

"Never heard of him," she said with a shake of her head. "We never made it out this close to the frontier. But most Eighth Fleet COs I've been in contact with were a prickly bunch."

"That's been my experience as well," Jackson said as he watched the barrels from the dorsal cannons move left and right, pitching up and down as they did to verify their full range of motion. "I'll try to talk to him once they're within range, but I have a feeling we're going to be trying to avoid him."

"Another complication is something we don't need," Celesta said.

"I couldn't agree more, but unless I want to open fire on a Terran ship I don't have a lot of other options," Jackson said. "If my hunch is correct, the enemy will eventually come at us so the more distance between us and the *Murmansk* the better it is for them."

"Lucky them," Celesta remarked before turning back to the test data she had scrolling across her screen.

It was almost a full hour later when the rails on the cannons had fully charged and they picked out their test target: an irregular moon with nothing of interest on it orbiting the tenth planet, another uninteresting lump that was skimming along the very outer edge of the star's influence. The moon was over two hundred million kilometers away so they'd never see the impacts, but the point of the test was just to ensure the operation of the cannons.

"Firing solution confirmed and the rails are charged, Captain," Barrett said.

"Fire," Jackson said, averting his gaze from the blast he knew would be coming. Two *booms* rang through the hull as the two dorsal cannons fired in quick succession.

"Shots away," Barrett said. "Analyzing data now." The *Blue Jacket's* navigation radar was tracking the rounds to verify that they were fired at the expected speed and course.

"Engineering," Jackson said as he held the intercom switch down. "How did it look down there?"

"Gun number two is pulling a bit more current that it should be, but it's still within acceptable limits," Singh said. "We can make some adjustments and fire another test round—"

"Negative," Jackson interrupted. "Button everything back up. I want that new power cable secured. It doesn't have to be pretty, but it has to stay put. Weld the brackets to the damn deck if you have to. We're reloading the dorsal turret and going hunting."

"Sir," Davis said. "The *Murmansk* has just gone to full power and turned onto a direct intercept course."

"I guess they saw our test shots," Jackson said.

"At least they'll be in com range sooner," Celesta offered.

"I can't wait," Jackson said with resignation.

****

"Captain Agapov, it's a pleasure to talk to you," Jackson said. "Thank you for agreeing to this video communication." Jackson was sitting at his desk and looking at a man who appeared to be in his late fifties and was almost a caricature of what people thought of when they heard the name Warsaw Alliance, even down to the thick, well-manicured beard (something that was completely against Fleet regulations.) He had to wait for a few minutes for the signal to reach the *Murmansk* and then another few for the response to come back.

"Captain Wolfe," Agapov said, his Slavic accent quite thick. "We have much to talk about. Let us set aside the fact that you have appeared in the system unannounced and unscheduled, apparently to savagely attack one of our moons, and discuss the standing order from CENTCOM to apprehend you on sight. In fact, I shouldn't even be talking to you. My orders state the only command personnel on the *Blue Jacket* I should be talking to is a Commander Wright."

"I suspected as much," Jackson said when it was clear the other captain had finished speaking. "I'm guessing your orders come directly from an Admiral Winters. There are obviously some issues with CENTCOM I need to have straightened out, but none of that matters right now. I have strong reason to suspect that a powerful alien ship is in this system as we speak and has definite hostile intentions. We've been fighting it since we discovered its trail of destruction beginning in the Asianic Union. I would respectfully suggest that you return to orbit over Nuovo Patria and stand ready to fend off any attack on that planet."

"Yes ... the communication from CENTCOM indicated that you may have suffered a break from reality," Agapov said slowly. "Trust me when I say that the only surprising thing to arrive in this system in the last week has been you. Please make this easy on all of us, Captain, and heave to. We will allow you to depart your ship on your own when we dock and the *Blue Jacket* can be brought into orbit with Commander Wright on the bridge. Otherwise, we will be forced to apprehend you and risk the lives of both our crews."

"You're as stubborn and short-sighted as I'd feared you would be, Captain," Jackson said pleasantly. "As you are no doubt aware, your ship cannot run down a *Raptor*-class destroyer. Given the circumstances, I cannot allow you to board this ship and will make sure you never come close enough to try. For your own safety, and that of your crew, I repeat my suggestion that you return to Nuovo Patria until we subdue the enemy or are destroyed ourselves."

"You arrogant, crazy bastard!" Agapov said, his face turning an even brighter red than it had been with his ruddy complexion. "I will not be talked down to by some Black Fleet swine—" The video cut off abruptly, leaving only a few seconds of static before the terminal automatically closed the screen. Jackson frowned, unsure as to what that meant. As he was about to call to see if their equipment had failed he felt the harsh rumble of the *Blue Jacket's* main engines coming to full power.

"*CAPTAIN TO THE BRIDGE!!*"

Jackson sprinted from his office, dreading what he would find when he got back to the bridge.

"It came out of nowhere!" Celesta said as he ran onto the bridge like a wild man. "It took out the *Murmansk* in one shot!"

"Range!" Jackson said as he took his recently vacated seat.

"Five hundred and eighty-six thousand kilometers," Barrett said. "It's coming about onto an intercept course and is accelerating at one hundred and fifty G's."

"OPS! Were you able to see how much of the damage we inflicted is still there?" Jackson asked.

"The computer is cleaning up the images we were able to collect, but at this range it won't be much," Davis said.

"That's an odd way to word it," Celesta said, leaning in. "Do you really think they were able to effect repairs from such heavy damage this quickly?"

"This ship doesn't repair itself in the conventional sense," Jackson said quietly. "It *heals* itself ... and quickly. The outer hull appears to be organic."

"Why wasn't I aware of this, Captain?" Celesta nearly hissed.

"An oversight on my part. I kept it to myself to prevent a widespread panic before we knew what we were actually dealing with and then forgot to brief you once I'd had time," Jackson said, realizing he'd made a mistake in not bringing his XO into the loop right away.

"I see," she said icily.

"I apologize, Commander," he said quietly but forcefully. "It was a simple mistake that ultimately doesn't mean anything in our current situation. Get over it. We've got a bit of crisis going on right now and I need you focused."

"Of course, sir," she said, still obviously not happy but conceding that the conversation was quite low in priority at that moment.

"Tactical, can you get a firing solution with the sensors we have left?" Jackson asked.

"Negative, Captain," Barrett said. "I can track its progress, but I can't resolve it enough to allow the computer to begin running pinpoint firing solutions."

"So ... we have to let it get closer and hope that we can get a good lock and fire before it hits us with another of those plasma bursts," Jackson said, rising to pace along the bridge.

"Target has slowed its acceleration," Davis said. "It's now approximately two hundred thousand kilometers astern and has matched its velocity to ours."

"This is an interesting development," Celesta said. "It's changing tactics on us. Why?"

"I suspect it knows how badly we're damaged," Jackson said. "I also think it wants to take the *Blue Jacket* intact. If it has been watching us since we entered the system, it probably figured out we're no longer able to leave. It may be trying to just run us down until we run out of propellant."

"What *is* our propellant status, Lieutenant?" Celesta asked Lieutenant Davis.

"Less than twenty percent remaining," Davis said. "We've been expending it at over four hundred times our usual burn rate due to so much time at full power. We also lost a considerable amount when engine four was destroyed."

"Understood," Jackson said. "We won't need much. This will be over quickly. Coms! Send a flash message to Nuovo Patria to prepare for a possible attack and to launch com drones to CENTCOM informing them of the threat and the loss of the *Murmansk*."

"We're being jammed, sir," Lieutenant Keller said apologetically. "I've been trying to raise someone on the planet since the enemy reappeared. It's a barrage jam on all frequencies so strong we've had to attenuate our receivers to prevent damage."

"It's adapted again," Celesta said. "Just like the new tactic of pacing us."

"Yes, but it doesn't learn very quickly," Jackson said. "A high-power barrage jam is a crude method to suppress a radio signal. Its very existence lets you know you're being jammed. Maybe the operators on Nuovo Patria will be smart enough to know what that means and send a drone anyway. Coms ... a little more forthcoming with developing information pertaining to our current engagement, if you please."

"Yes, sir. Sorry, sir."

"Helm, adjust our current course to maintain this heliocentric arc," Jackson ordered. "I don't want to lead it down into the system if it's content to follow along out here. We'll adjust when it does, but we won't allow it to push us into a rash decision."

"Helm answering to new heading now, sir."

They led the enemy on a circuit around the system for over ten hours at a leisurely pace with no change. Jackson had even ordered a few velocity changes to try and force a reaction, but the enemy would simply accelerate or decelerate with them. All the while the barrage jamming was in place so they couldn't even receive an automated signal from the planet or the com drone platform.

He knew that the enemy was likely building a profile that would help predict human behavior based on the interactions they'd had so far. Unfortunately that meant the aliens knew far more about humans than the crew of the *Blue Jacket* knew about them. The crew had taken to calling the ship "it" and referring to it as a singular entity because it was so unnerving to face a silent enemy that seemed to be only motivated by killing as many humans as it could. The fact that there could be a full crew on the behemoth chasing them was somehow more terrifying than thinking of the ship as a singular, unstoppable titan.

The problem was that the enemy's new tactics seemed to show they were at least somewhat aware to how humans reacted to prolonged stress. The slow speed chase was fraying nerves, causing lapses in concentration, and making them more prone to rash action. Jackson had caught himself more than once on the verge of ordering the *Blue Jacket* to spin and perform an emergency deceleration to see if he could get the other ship within range of the mag-cannons. Rationally he knew there was no way the ship could perform the maneuver without the alien matching them and having enough time to hit them with another of those devastating plasma bursts. But that didn't stop Jackson from considering the order just to get the waiting over, even if it resulted in the destruction of the ship.

"Sir, we need to start swapping out the crew for rest periods," Celesta said, her eyes bloodshot and her face drawn.

"I know," Jackson said. "Try and work it out. They'll have to make do with short naps ... I can't afford to have people in their quarters asleep if this thing makes a run at us."

"I'll try and—"

"Enemy ship is decelerating!" Davis called out far more loudly than necessary.

"Just decelerating or changing course?" Jackson asked, moving over to look at the plots the computer was generating from their meager sensor data.

"Just decelerating," she said. "Correction! It's turning into the system and accelerating towards Nuovo Patria."

"Son of a bitch," Jackson said. "This was their game. Wear us out and then make a mad dash towards the planet in a maneuver that we can't duplicate. Nav! Plot me a course in, maximum performance on three engines. Helm! Come onto new course when you get it and accelerate ... ahead full."

The *Blue Jacket* shook and rumbled as the engines were once again asked to provide maximum thrust. Jackson noted that the tone and vibrations were becoming more pronounced and more harsh as the mission wore on. He wondered how much the ship had left to give. The fact she was now steaming full bore towards yet another engagement with the alien ship was a testament to her designers, who could have never imagined what their brainchild would be subjected to when they drew her up fifty years prior.

"How long?" he asked.

"Nine hours and forty minutes," the specialist at Nav reported. "I can't do much better, Captain. We're carrying a lot of velocity in a very wide orbit. I'm trying to conserve as much speed as I can while turning as tight as she'll let me."

"Understood, Specialist," Jackson said, frustrated at the disparity between the aliens' reactionless drive and what it could do while they were slaves to Newtonian physics. "OPS, work with Tactical and try to keep a solid track on the enemy. It may be trying to lose us in the system."

"So much for resting the crew," Celesta said as Jackson sat down.

"I'll have Commander Owens issue stims if this looks like it's going to keep dragging on," Jackson said. "It's not my first choice to have my crew jacked up on drugs, but there are three people just here on the bridge I simply can't be without. I'm sure it's the same story in the other departments."

"I'll go down to Medical now and give Doctor Owens a heads up," she said, rising from her seat. "It wouldn't hurt to take a walk through the other sections while I'm down there to get a feel for how the rest of the crew is doing."

"Outstanding idea, Commander," Jackson said. "Thank you."

****

Celesta rode a lift down from the superstructure to deck nine, jogging down the port service tube, heading aft towards Sick Bay. She was becoming increasingly worried about the stress being piled onto Captain Wolfe. He'd assumed the full weight of recent events onto his shoulders, taking the deaths at the hands of the marauding aliens as his personal responsibility. She was worried it was going to lead to lapses in judgment on his part.

So far, the man she'd been serving with was nothing like what was described to her by Admiral Winters when she'd first arrived on Jericho Station. She assumed that she'd be meeting a buffoon of an officer who would be able to teach her little. Winters had even hinted that Wolfe was such a liability that she might be forced to take command of the *Blue Jacket*. The admiral had even gone so far as to say that he was respected so little by his crew that they probably wouldn't even question her. The message she'd received when they arrived at Podere confirmed that she'd been played. Celesta wasn't sure she liked what it said about her that she'd been handpicked for the task of undermining Captain Wolfe's authority.

When everyone around him was falling apart, Captain Wolfe seemed to be able to hold his fear in check and think rationally. The fact they were still flying, let alone delivering such a beating when so severely outmatched, was a testament to his ability to adapt to the situation. She'd like to think she would have been so cool if she had been sitting in the seat, but she couldn't be absolutely certain. Either way it would be over sooner than later. With the warp drive completely inoperable they were left with only two options: win, or lose.

"Commander Wright," Doctor Owens greeted her as she walked into Sick Bay. "Are you feeling unwell?"

"As unwell as anyone right now," she said. She'd meant it as a joke, but the chief medical officer just nodded with an understanding frown.

"Anyway ... I'm here at the behest of the captain. He wants to know if there is a low-grade stimulant that you can issue to the crew that will stave off the symptoms of fatigue for the next day, at least."

Owens' frown deepened. "I'm not necessarily in favor of distributing drugs like this to the crew," he said. "If certain members wanted to come in and—"

"Doctor," Celesta said forcefully, "the ship will soon be engaging the enemy, likely for the final time. We can't afford to rotate key personnel out to rest them, and the other departments are just as shorthanded as the bridge crew is. I'm coming to you in good faith that you'll understand the unique situation we find ourselves in."

He seemed to think on that for a moment. "I detect an implicit threat in that," Owens finally said. "If I refuse he'll relieve me of duty and find someone willing to distribute the stim packs." He waved off Celesta as she tried to protest.

"He has his job to do and I have mine," he said. "I wouldn't be much of a physician if I did not at least voice my concerns and he wouldn't be much of a captain if he didn't utilize everything at his disposal. I do, however, understand the situation. I will have my staff begin packaging the stims into two different strengths. I'll be counting on the department heads and supervisors to provide the correct one to the crew. Will that satisfy Captain Wolfe's requirements?"

"It will," Celesta said. "Thank you, Doctor."

"I'm in this fight as much as anyone else on this ship," Owens said with a shrug. "If you'll wait for a few moments I'll give you the required dosages for the bridge crew."

****

Jackson tried to keep from drumming his fingers on his armrest and bouncing his leg as the stims Commander Wright had brought up from Sick Bay began to take effect. The drugs had dried his mouth out and hurt his stomach, but the fog that had settled on his mind had lifted and he felt like he was again able to think clearly and quickly. He noticed the rest of the crew experiencing varying degrees of the same effects.

"Com frequency jamming has stopped," Lieutenant Keller reported. "However, there is no response from the drone platform. I'm getting signals from the planet but I'm having trouble cleaning the data up."

"It just took out the platform so there's no need to continue suppressing all communications," Jackson said. "Try and get a boosted signal to Nuovo Patria on the emergency band. Just tell them an attack is imminent and if they have anything that can take out landing craft or fight the enemy on the ground now is the time to drag it out. Just repeat that message as we fly down the well towards them."

The *Blue Jacket* was now flying away from the planet as it gained velocity and prepared for a series of gravity-assisted turns that would bring them back on course for Nuovo Patria. While counterintuitive to be running in the opposite direction at full power, the amount of energy needed to stop the ship, come onto the new course, and then try and accelerate back towards the enemy would do nothing but waste time and propellant, both a real concern when facing an enemy that didn't need to play by those same rules.

To compound the problem, the jump point from which they entered the system was at thirty-seven degrees inclination from the ecliptic plane. This meant not only were they needing an assist to pull them back towards the inner system, they needed to majorly correct their course on another axis and try to maintain their velocity through the maneuver.

"We've been captured by the seventh planet," Lieutenant Davis said. "Helm, the countdown for our next course change is being sent to your station now."

"Confirmed," the helmsman said. "Reducing power and preparing to come about onto new course."

"Helm, you're clear to execute course change orders from OPS and Nav until we're making our final approach to Nuovo Patria," Jackson said. "Don't waste any time waiting for me to confirm what they're telling you."

"Yes, sir."

Jackson felt the pitch of the engines change and heard the ship groan as the thrusters fired, pushing her against inertia at the same time the engines were pushing against the pull of the gas giant they were blasting by. He idly wondered what the locals called it. Given how many systems humans had colonized, only the life-bearing worlds were officially named, the others left to the local government to name, or not name, as they saw fit.

Soon the *Blue Jacket* began complaining in earnest about the opposing forces she was being subjected to. The buffeting was so violent that Jackson considered ordering his crew into their restraints. As the planet streaked by and out of view the engines came back up and they were flung away from the gas giant at incredible velocity. The angle of deflection they'd achieved wasn't all that extreme and they would now be in a position to use the sixth planet, another, considerably larger gas giant, to come about on their final course towards Nuovo Patria.

The problem was that they'd be closing on the planet against its orbital path, not chasing it. This drastically shortened their firing window assuming they could even get a clear shot at the enemy ship. Jackson briefly toyed with the idea of trying Barrett's trick shot again with the solid-core shells, but the exploding warp emitter taking out their high-power array had essentially eliminated that as an option. They would be quite close before they would even be able to get a solid lock on the alien ship, for too short a time to fire and then reload with the high-explosive shells as well as recharge the capacitor banks.

"Tactical, what missiles do we have left?" Jackson asked after a moment of thought. "I know we're out of Avengers, but there has to be something left."

"We have seven Shrikes and ten Mark VIII strategic nukes," Barrett said, reading off the display to his right.

"The Shrikes won't be effective at this closure speed and we know the nukes are useless," Celesta said.

"Well, let's look at that for a moment," Jackson said, tapping his fingers against his chin as he always did when trying to work through a problem in his head. "The warheads are fake, but the missiles are still the same that the ship was originally loaded with. The

Fleet crews didn't bother to even take them out of the cradles when CENTCOM made the swap."

"I don't see how this helps us," she admitted.

"Those missiles are far more sophisticated than the dinky ship-to-ship stuff we've been lobbing at the alien ship so far *and* they're multistage," Jackson said. "Each missile has three sets of booster engines."

"While that's fascinating, sir, I still don't see what a missile without a warhead will accomplish no matter how advanced it is," she said.

"OPS!" Jackson barked, making Lieutenant Davis jump. "What's the projected time until our final course correction?"

"Fourteen hours," she said.

"Engineering, Bridge," Jackson said, stabbing the intercom button forcefully with his finger. "Daya, get your ass up here." The bridge crew stared at Jackson as if he'd lost his mind. They'd never seen him so brusque and unprofessional, much less over an open intercom channel.

"Lieutenant Davis, keep an eye out for any movement from the enemy. You have the bridge for now," he said, ignoring their looks. "Lieutenant Barrett and Commander Wright, you're with me."

Ten minutes later the three of them, and a visibly winded Daya Singh, were seated at the table in the conference room just aft of the bridge. Jackson ignored them as he began bringing up the specs for the MkVIII missiles they had sitting in the forward magazine.

"Lieutenant Commander Singh," he said, "tell me what explosives we have on board, or could improvise, that would fit in a cylinder five meters in diameter by thirteen meters high."

Singh just looked at him as if he'd lost his mind. "Have you been drinking, Captain?" he asked.

Jackson winced slightly at an accusation that struck a little too close to home even if it had been in jest, but ignored it. "Not even any of the rotgut your crew makes down in reactor room four," he said instead. "Now, what have you got for me?"

Over the next two and half hours the four officers argued, compromised, and finally agreed on a plan that the most optimistic of them thought could turn the tide of the battle while the most pessimistic felt it had an equally good chance of destroying the *Blue Jacket* before they even made it anywhere close to Nuovo Patria.

****

"You, you, you, and you. Follow me," Singh said. He'd walked into the break room just outside of the Engineering Operations Center and seemed to pick four specialists out at random. In actuality he knew they were among the more bright of the junior enlisted he had at his disposal. It was exceedingly convenient that the four had been trying to hide from their supervisor in the break room when he happened to walk by.

"What have you got for us, Cheng?" one of the specialists asked. The term "Cheng" was slang for Chief Engineer from so far back nobody could remember its exact origins. It had fallen out of disuse between officers but the enlisted crews still used it as a sign of respect. The name was one of those holdovers that had stuck around as individual ships were organized into fleets and a burgeoning Terran

Starfleet had to decide what rank structure it would use, which traditions to allow to stay and which to outright ban.

"Special project," Singh said. "Straight from the captain. Get your asses up to the forward magazine and meet with a Specialist Halsey and her crew from Armament. She'll let you know what needs to be done."

"This gonna help us kick some alien ass, sir?" another of the spacers asked.

"If it works," Singh nodded. "This could be a game changer, but I need you to be at your best."

"You can count on that, sir," the spacer said. Singh noticed the young man was almost vibrating in his boots as a result of the stim pack he'd ingested. He hoped their supervisors were watching their intake of the stuff closely. Owens had been pretty adamant that nobody overdose on the stim packs as they were strong enough to cause serious health problems if abused.

"Good. I'll be joining you myself after I pass some instructions on and check with the other groups," Singh said. "Go. Now. I'll let your boss know where I've sent you."

He watched them go before turning and walking into the Operations Center. There were three other groups he had to get moving simultaneously if the plan had any chance of coming together in time. While he had serious misgivings about Jack's plan, he had to admit that on the off chance it worked it would be a devastating blow to the enemy.

Chapter 21

"Commander Wright, we're nearly to our next course change," Jackson said, his voice conveying a calm he did not feel.

"*I'm well aware of that, Captain*," Celesta's harried voice came back. "*We're running the final test now before the program is uploaded. This wasn't as easy as changing a few parameters. We've essentially completely reprogrammed the weapons' entire software load.*"

"I fully appreciate the difficulty of your task, Commander," Jackson said patiently. "However, we are now committed to our current timetable."

"*We'll be ready*," she said shortly. "*XO, out.*"

"Lieutenant Davis, what's the status on the cargo hatch crew?" Jackson asked.

"Aft cargo bay has been cleared and the first four missiles are in position," Davis said. "The other six are on their way down the port access tube from the magazine. Engineering crews say it will be a tight fit but they should be able to queue the rest up for a quick reload."

"Very good," Jackson said, leaning back. The plan had so many moving parts and they had so little time that he had to try and relax and trust that his crew was doing everything they possibly could to ensure success.

The only sticking point so far had been the aft cargo bay since it was too small to fit all ten missiles into it. It was really only a staging area that was meant to receive material for Engineering from service ships or docks that required the *Blue Jacket* to back her stern into an airlock. The MkVIIIs were almost thirty-five meters long, meant to be fired from the periphery of a system before the ship hauled ass to its exit jump-point, and all ten wouldn't fit in the small area. Unfortunately, the regular launch tubes for the missiles, two on the ventral surface just aft of the nose, were forward-facing and wouldn't work for their needs. They'd had to improvise and modify the rear of the ship at the same time crews were modifying the missiles themselves, while another team simultaneously rewrote the weapons' operating code. It might not work at all, but at least it kept everyone's mind occupied as they closed the distance to Nuovo Patria.

"Coms, are we still receiving signals from the planet?" he asked.

"Yes, sir. It's mostly still indecipherable, but it's there," Lieutenant Keller said. "I still can't get a response to direct queries."

"Could the enemy ship have found a more precise way to disrupt our communications?" Davis asked.

"That's what I'm thinking," Jackson said. "It means they're not only adapting at an exponentially faster rate, I think we're being baited towards the planet."

"That would be the only logical answer to why we're still receiving some radio signals but can't get a signal in nor get a coherent message from them," Barrett volunteered. "Could they be able to adapt in other ways?"

"Such as?" Jackson prompted.

"We've hit them twice with kinetic weapons and caused a lot of damage, sir," Barrett said, turning in his seat to face the captain. "Do you think they can adapt to defend against the cannon shells?"

"I've considered it," Jackson admitted. "But since the mag-cannons are literally the only thing on the ship that can shoot, I've dismissed it. They'll either penetrate or they won't, but we're committed to this run either way."

"Yes, sir," Barrett said, turning back in his seat to continue his attempts at locating the enemy with their degraded sensor capability.

"*Bridge, Engineering*," Celesta's voice came over the intercom after another forty-five minutes had passed. "*We're ready down here. All ten missiles have accepted the new programming and are staged at the rear cargo hatch. Crews are in pressure suits and we've sealed off the corridors. We can evacuate the atmosphere from the area and blow the rear hatch whenever you're ready*."

"Excellent work, Commander," Jackson said enthusiastically. "You are clear to proceed. Tell the crews in that cargo bay to be careful."

"*Aye aye, sir*."

****

"Aye aye, sir," Celesta said before releasing the intercom switch. "We're a go! Police this area! I don't want any debris in here when we pump the air out."

At her command it was all assholes and elbows as nineteen spacers scrambled around the cordoned-off area picking up even the smallest piece of loose debris they could find, while another five packed up and inventoried all the tools they'd had with them. It was another twenty minutes before Celesta and Daya Singh were inspecting the area and doing a final check on the weapons.

"You're confident in this explosive mixture?" she asked as they went down the line checking statuses.

"As confident as you likely are about the software loaded into these missiles," he responded without looking up.

"Touché."

When they'd verified everything they went and gave last minute instructions to the team of specialists wearing EVA vacuum suits before exiting the area and locking down the makeshift hatch they'd installed in the bulkhead.

"Start pumping out the atmosphere," Singh said to the spacer standing next to him with a tile in her hand. She keyed in a few commands and the pumps could be heard in the next compartment over evacuating the chamber. They'd had to expand the cargo bay to include the area around the queued-up missiles in their mobile cradles.

"We're going to have some leaks, of course, but we'll be well within the limits for the environmental systems to handle," Singh said. "We shouldn't even feel any change in pressure."

"It'll be a drop in the bucket compared to all the leaks we already have," Celesta said. "We probably look like a lopsided comet with all the air we're streaming out of the starboard side." Singh winced and she regretted her flippant comment. While she'd only just arrived on the *Blue Jacket,* the chief engineer had served on her for years. He had been watching his baby take a beating that he knew she wouldn't be coming back from.

"Sorry," she said.

"Eh," he waved her off. "I'm too sentimental anyway. She'll hold together long enough for us to finish our mission."

"Chamber pressure is now low enough to safely blow the aft hatch," the spacer said after thirty minutes of silence, reading the vacuum pressure off her tile.

"We're clear to blow the outer hatch," Singh said.

"Let the team in there know to stand by and then blow it in ten seconds," Celesta said.

Thirteen seconds later a sharp *bang* was felt through the deck as the enormous armored external hatch was explosively jettisoned from the *Blue Jacket's* stern. Celesta waited a tense few seconds more to give the crew inside the makeshift airlock a chance to check things over and report back.

"Deployment team reports chamber is clear, no damage to the weapons," the spacer holding the tile said. "They're ready to begin operations when you are, Commander."

"Tell them to keep their safety tethers on and stand by," Celesta said. "We'll begin our last course correction soon and then it'll be their turn."

****

"*Team is in place, launch chamber is holding, we're ready down here, Captain*," Celesta said over the intercom.

"Acknowledged," Jackson said. "Turn over the operation to Singh and his people and head back up. I'm going to need you up here during this last charge."

"*Yes, sir.*"

"Nav, put a countdown for our last gravity assist on the main display," he said. "Helm, you're to continue coordinating with OPS and Nav ... no waiting on orders from me."

The gas giant loomed large on the main display as the *Blue Jacket* roared in for a close pass. They were already carrying so much velocity that this maneuver wouldn't gain them much speed, but it would allow them to drastically alter their trajectory without losing any speed, the only thing Jackson was really concerned about. Much more velocity and the mag-cannon turrets wouldn't be able to track the target on their pass.

"Cutting thrust and changing attitude now," the helmsman reported as he responded to a prompt on his own displays. The rumble from the three remaining main engines died away and the view on the main display shifted as he keyed the thrusters to put the ship's nose towards the planet. The small attitude thrusters weren't powerful enough to compete with their inertia so they were turning the ship so the main engines would push them through the turn, otherwise the gas giant would only alter their course slightly before they continued to shoot further away from Nuovo Patria.

"How long until we thrust back up?" Jackson asked.

"One hour and forty minutes, sir," the spacer at Nav answered. "The turn will take another thirty-five minutes."

"Very good," Jackson said, standing up and pacing, unable to contain his nervous energy any longer.

"Missile teams are good to go," Celesta said as she walked back onto the bridge. "Lieutenant Commander Singh says the atmospheric leakage is within acceptable limits and he has a tech monitoring it."

"The missiles didn't give you any trouble uploading the new software?" Jackson asked.

"They're old," she shrugged. "Probably a little older than the ship herself. But that may have worked in our favor. Once we used the bypass codes you gave us we were able to see there really wasn't much sophistication in the operating system. I'm confident our changes will work without any trouble. If anything, we've simplified it even further."

"Maybe," Jackson said. "It's still a huge unknown in our plan."

"We don't have much to work with at this point," she said. "I'm confident it will work."

"That's good enough for me," Jackson said. "OPS, tell all the department heads I want everyone in restraints once we come out of our last course correction. It could be a rough pass depending on what the enemy has in store for us."

"Yes, sir."

The bridge was quiet when the engines were throttled back up and the ship began to shake, already pulling against the planet's gravity. Jackson watched on the stylized plot Lieutenant Davis had put up on the main display to show their progress in two dimensions, looking down on the planet. He could see their projected course and the blinking green dot that represented the *Blue Jacket* as her course began to arc into the system.

Harsh vibrations began, causing everyone to hold onto something for stability as the engines ran all the way up to full power and played their part in the titanic fight taking place to determine the destroyer's course. Her inertia wanted her to keep flying straight, while the planet's gravity and the engines wanted her to swing around in a wide arc. One-third of the way through the turn Jackson became concerned the ship wouldn't be able to handle the course change, much less another pass with the enemy.

"We're through," the helmsman reported even as the shaking began to subside. "Making final corrections and throttling up to full power on new course."

"This is it everyone! Look sharp!" Jackson said loudly. "Commander Wright, tell your missile teams they are clear to begin deployment."

"Aye aye, sir," Celesta said, grabbing her comlink.

****

"That's it! Tell the deployment team to begin," Singh shouted to the tech standing next to him with the tile. He was shouting over the noise of four welders working near him simultaneously since the stresses induced by their gravity-assisted course correction had popped a few seams in their makeshift missile bay. It wasn't critical enough for him to bother the bridge with the news, but he had evacuated all non-essential personnel from the area.

Inside the chamber two specialists in EVA suits walked up and shoved the first two missiles out of the hatch, the nose cones pointed in the opposite direction from which the *Blue Jacket* was traveling. They quickly moved the cradles to the side and aft before rolling the next two up and repeating the procedure. Soon all ten missiles had been pushed out the aft of the ship and could be seen floating just outside, the flare from the mains reflecting off the weapons' outer casings as the ship slowly accelerated from the now drifting objects. The two specialists walked to the aftmost part of the chamber before activating another pressure hatch and alerting the rest of their team they were sealed off from the main launch chamber. A moment later atmosphere began streaming in from vents in the ceiling and the pair watched the pressure climb on their internal HUDs.

"Bridge, this is the chief engineer," Singh said into the intercom. "All ten missiles successfully deployed. They're all yours."

"*Thank you, Lieutenant Commander.*"

Chapter 22

"Thank you, Lieutenant Commander," Jackson said before closing the intercom channel. "Commander Wright, you may begin the ignition sequence at your discretion. Tactical! Have you found my target yet?"

"I believe I have located it in low orbit over Nuovo Patria," Barrett said. "It keeps popping in and out and without the high-power array I'm having trouble verifying it. It'll be another ninety minutes before I can confirm target's location."

"You better be on your game then, Lieutenant," Jackson said. "You won't have a lot of time to calculate a firing solution and engage before we're already flying back out of the area."

"Yes, sir," Barrett agreed. "All the computer needs is a positive lock on the target and it can calculate the firing solution almost immediately based on our previous engagements."

"And your inputs take into account what Commander Wright's program will be looking for?"

"Yes, sir," Barrett said confidently.

While part of Jackson wanted to have someone double check his work, he left it alone.

"We've received the first confirmation signal from all ten missiles, Captain," Celesta said from her seat. "Initial burn was successful. All ten were stacked up behind the *Blue Jacket* so it should have been hidden by our own engine signature. Second burn will be in ten minutes and then they'll be out of contact for the remainder of the mission."

"Hopefully we'll still be around to see if this works," Jackson said quietly. He'd thought he had said it softly enough to not be overheard but he saw Lieutenant Davis twitch at his fatalistic comment. He mentally kicked himself for that sort of talk when they were so close to what promised to be the end of the battle ... either for them, the aliens, or both.

"Long-range optics have positively identified the target," Lieutenant Davis said after an hour of tense, silent flying had passed. "It is still in low orbit over Nuovo Patria. Damage from the previous kinetic strikes is significantly repaired, but still visible on the port flank."

"You have that, Lieutenant Barrett?" Jackson asked.

"Yes, sir," Barrett affirmed. "Primary target is still the enemy's port flank. Secondary target is the corresponding damage on the starboard flank where the shot exited."

"Here we go," Jackson said. "OPS, sound the alert and set condition 1SS ... I want all pressure hatches on the ship closed. Make sure damage control teams are standing by. Nav, how close are we?"

"Range is three hundred and sixty thousand kilometers and closing rapidly, Captain."

"Helm, come to port two degrees and hold velocity steady," Lieutenant Barrett ordered. "The computer has a lock. Targeting now."

Jackson looked out the at the view on the main display as the dorsal turret swung to starboard and both cannon barrels pitched down in preparation to fire.

"Thermal build up on the target's nose," Davis said. "Probable plasma burst weapon. This one is far more powerful than the others."

"At your discretion, Lieutenant Barrett," Jackson said tensely. They were committed. There was no way to avoid the close pass with the enemy even if he'd wanted to.

"Stand by," Barrett said, his face a mask of concentration as sweat beaded on his brow and ran down his face. "Five seconds ... Firing!" The flash of the upper cannons firing brightened the bridge as the *Blue Jacket* bore down on the target. The shells were flying at an angle tangential to the destroyer's course and would, ideally, all impact the flank of the enemy ship in a devastating wave of destruction.

"Target is moving! Fast!" Davis called out. "Nine impacts on the port, aft quadrant. Unknown damage." Jackson cursed bitterly. The target hadn't shown any ability or even inclination to maneuver quickly enough to avoid their weapons-fire before, but now it had essentially "hopped" out of the way of eleven of the high-explosive shells they'd sent to it. He'd thought and hoped that with it being parked so deep in Nuovo Patria's gravity well that it wouldn't be able to avoid the full brunt of their one and only salvo.

"Try and recharge the—"

"Target is firing! Brace for impact!" Davis' strident call was followed a few seconds later by an impact of such force that Jackson's head snapped forward and he was flung against his restraints. He felt something tear in his shoulder and his vision was clouded with red.

He looked up, straining to breathe and trying to gain some sort of bearing as the main display was completely dark and warning alarms blared in his ears. He felt the *Blue Jacket* shudder and buck under him and knew secondary explosions were ripping her apart.

Barrett was slumped over his console, blood running freely from his head, and Davis was slumped over in her restraints.

"Is anyone—" he had to break off and clear his airways of blood before he could continue. "Is anyone effective?"

"I'm good, Captain," the helmsman said, his voice shockingly strong and clear. The helm station had a wide, steeply reclined acceleration couch with much more robust restraints. Apparently they performed their job as the spacer first class didn't seem any worse for wear.

"I'll be okay in a minute," Celesta said next to him, groaning as she forced herself upright.

"Lieutenant Davis!" Jackson called out as he popped his restraints off. "Jillian!" She started to blink and come around as she heard her name. "Are you okay?" he asked.

"I ... I think so," she said in a shaky voice. "My back hurts."

"I need you to reset the bridge systems," Jackson said loudly with slow exaggeration. "I have to know what's happening outside of the ship."

"Y ... Yes," she said, shaking her head. "Yes, sir." He walked over to check on Barrett as the deck thumped hard with another internal explosion, at least he thought it was internal, and he knew the ship was done. She'd given all she could.

"I'm fine, sir," Barrett said as soon as Jackson put a hand on his shoulder.

"The hell you are," he said. "You've got a nasty gash in your head. I'm looking at your skull."

"Better than seeing what's inside of it," Barrett said.

"True enough, Lieutenant," Jackson said. "Davis!"

"Systems are resetting now, sir," Davis said, her voice stronger than before. A second later and the main display flickered and snapped back to life. Jackson ignored the warnings and alerts scrolling down the left side and stared at the view.

"My God," was all he said. The entire prow of the destroyer was gone. The hull was peeled back and deformed, the edges still glowing red where the plasma burst had liquefied the hardened alloy. The dorsal turret was still there, but the cannon barrels had been melted away and damage from the slag could be seen all the way up to the base of the superstructure.

"Davis ... get me a damage report and try to get the external sensors online," he said as he watched atmosphere billowing out of the front of the ship, escaping from a hundred different compartments that didn't survive the hit. "Helm, all astern. Stop this ship."

"Engines all astern full, aye," the helmsman said, struggling to keep his eyes off the carnage in front of him.

"Target has moved into high orbit," Lieutenant Davis said. "Aft optical feed coming up now." A large portion of the main display was devoted to a pane that showed the enemy ship lumbering up away from Nuovo Patria and turning towards them. The damage from their nine shots couldn't be seen from the angle they were at. But one thing could.

"Thermal buildup on the nose again," Davis said with dread.

"Is it maneuvering towards us?" Jackson asked

"Yes, sir," she confirmed. "Radar is offline so I can't give you an accurate range, but the computer estimates it at less than two hundred thousand kilometers."

"What's the damage report look like so far?" Jackson asked as he stared at the enemy, the hatred and impotent rage churning in his gut.

"From the prow back to section fifty-two is gone," Davis read off the list, her voice numb. "Sixty-six crew unaccounted for and presumed dead. No weapons available. Limited maneuverability. Engine one is showing signs of imminent failure and reactor one has gone into safe mode. There's a whole list here, Captain ... do you want me to continue reading?"

"No, Lieutenant," Jackson said. "I get the picture. Commander Wright, is it possible that you have some good news for me?"

"I don't have any additional bad news," Celesta said, "but I have no way to see if the missiles were successful or not. It's possible the enemy may have spotted them despite our precautions."

"Should we begin accelerating away, Captain?" the helmsman asked.

Jackson thought a moment before answering. What good would running around the system do when the enemy still had full flight capability? The *Blue Jacket* was on her last leg and it didn't seem he'd given the enemy anything more than a light sting on the—

An immense flash washed out the display, interrupting his ruminations. He blinked as the display automatically dimmed and then waited as the optical sensors reset and brought the feed back up. When it did reappear he wasn't prepared for the sight in front of him.

The enemy ship was rotating slowly in space, its entire aft, port quadrant mushroomed open and spewing some sort of mixture of gas and viscous fluid that froze instantly as it hit open space.

"I can't believe it worked," Celesta breathed. Jackson could only nod his agreement as he watched the ship slowly stop its spin. Despite the damage to the aft section it looked like it was trying to limp off away from them.

"Enemy appears to be retreating, Captain," Davis said.

"Noted," Jackson said. "I wonder what its plan is."

"It looks like it's making a run for it," Barrett said.

"Yes, it is," Jackson said, frowning as he tried to work the problem out in his head. He could see only one obvious solution despite what the outcome would cost.

"Captain?" Celesta said, having learned during her short tenure on the destroyer to be alarmed when Captain Wolfe was wearing that look. "There's not much we can do. The ship is so damaged she can barely fly."

"We have to abandon ship," Jackson said simply.

"Sir?"

"You heard me," he said. "Davis ... sound the alarm. All hands, abandon ship. The *Blue Jacket* is no longer viable. Get all hands to the lifepods and get off this tub."

"I don't see how this helps—"

"This is not a discussion, Commander!" Jackson cut her off. "Lieutenant ... make the call. Now!" He walked over to where Celesta was still strapped in her seat. "I'm trying to save as many of the crew as I can," he said softly. "This ship is no longer safe and I can't guarantee that the alien ship isn't just going to heal up some and come back to finish us off. This is the best bet everyone has. The pods can last a couple of weeks and in that time another Fleet ship is bound to fly into this system."

"Yes, sir," she said, popping her restraints as the alarms began blaring and the automated messages began directing crews to lifepods. "You're coming too, aren't you?"

"I'm not suicidal nor do I have any intention of going down with my ship," Jackson said. "But I want this done while we're not under fire. The pods can drift a bit and let the *Blue Jacket* clear the area before activating the beacons. I want you to go get Major Ortiz and make sure the prisoners get off as well. Go, now."

"Yes, sir," she said, standing up. "It was an honor flying with you, sir."

"The fight's not over yet, Commander," Jackson said. "I plan to be on another ship in the near future and finishing what we started."

"I hope I'm there for that, Captain Wolfe."

"As do I, Commander Wright. Now get your ass moving."

Once she was gone he turned to the rest of the bridge crew.

"That goes for the rest of you," he said. "Everyone ... off the bridge. Get to your designated lifepod and get out of here before the reactors decide to go." They all got up, their faces reflecting a sort of shocked numbness, and shuffled off the bridge, the Marine sentry following them out.

"Captain—"

"I'll be right behind you, Davis," Jackson said, turning to look at his operations officer. "I need to make sure everyone else gets off first and then I'll use the pod two decks down, but I want you out with the rest of the bridge crew." She didn't say anything, just walked up and put her arms around his neck, kissing him on the cheek and then, more hesitantly, on the lips before turning and hurrying off the bridge herself. He just stood in shock for a moment, trying to figure out what the hell just happened, when he heard the alert that the first lifepods were ejecting from the ship.

With a feeling of detached calm he walked over to the bridge entry and closed the hatch, sealing it from the inside. He strolled over to the operations station as if he had all the time in the world. Adjusting the seat height, he began to log in through a secure backdoor that would allow him to access ship functions not widely known about. Menu screens that nobody else had ever seen began to populate the terminals at Lieutenant Davis' former station.

He opened one pane that allowed him to keep a running tally on how many crew were left on the ship and how many lifepods had been launched. So far it looked like the remaining crew was disembarking at a steady clip. After moving that to the corner he began verifying the backup dump to the servers buried down in the belly just aft of reactor two. These servers, really more just data cores, were already built into a tough alloy shell and ready to be ejected in a moment's notice. He was about to transfer the ship's log and eject it when he realized the log itself needed updating. After a moment of thought he decided on a video update and activated the imager embedded in the OPS station.

"This is Captain Jackson Wolfe, commanding officer, *TCS Blue Jacket*, and this will be the final log entry for DS-701. I have ordered all hands to abandon ship as she is no longer safe nor capable of controlled flight. We have been battling an alien incursion that is made up of a single ship since arriving in the Xi'an system nearly three weeks ago. We have inflicted grave damage to the enemy, but they have persevered and delivered a killing blow to my ship.

"My hope is that the data cores that this log is attached to will help the Terran Confederacy understand what happened out here on the frontier and help them prepare for what must be coming. My observations of this alien ship lead me to believe its mission was to learn about us and our capabilities even while it was destroying industrial and agricultural capability along the way. Any of my crew that are recovered can vouch for the data contained within.

"This Captain Jackson Wolfe, signing off."

He appended the entry to the log, sent it to the backup system, and ejected it after he got the confirmation it had been uploaded. By the time he was done the last few crewmembers had made it off the ship and the number remaining on his display showed one. He verified that the one crewmember left was himself before getting up and walking over to the tactical station.

The alien ship was still trying to put some distance between themselves and the stricken destroyer. He could already see that the edges of the massive wound they inflicted were beginning to curl in and pull together in an attempt to heal the damage. It was as if the damn thing couldn't be stopped. The imagery cementing his decision, he quickly pulled up another set of screens, logged in with his credentials, and began inputting commands.

It was nearly eleven overrides later when he finally began receiving warnings that what he was doing was successful, and highly dangerous. He watched as reactor one came back out of safe mode and joined the other three as they began winding up to full power, then past it. All four were soon operating at one hundred and thirty percent of their accepted maximum output. He quickly sent information over to the helm before racing over to the reclined seat and strapping himself in.

****

"Is there any way to tell if we're all off?" Major Ortiz asked. Between the stress of the order to abandon the *Blue Jacket*, and being suddenly forced into a zero gravity environment, nobody in the lifepod was looking all that chipper.

"No," Celesta said. "Captain Wolfe wants us to remain silent for a few hours before turning on the radios and beacons."

"Is there anyone left on the *Blue Jacket*?" the major asked, peering out the small portal in the side of the pod.

"There shouldn't be by now, why?" Celesta asked.

"See for yourself," Ortiz said, floating out of the way so she could look out. It took her a moment to understand what she was seeing, but after a second there was no doubt as the three remaining engines on the *Blue Jacket* flared brightly and the ship began to accelerate away from the formation of lifepods with surprising speed. Celesta knew who must be still onboard and she also thought she knew why.

"Goddamn it, Captain," she said quietly. "There had to have been another way."

****

Jackson strapped himself into the helmsman's seat, noting how wonderfully comfortable it was, before taking inventory of what flight systems were left available. Three out of four main engines, no bow thrust, and limited attitude control in general ... should be an interesting few minutes. He advanced the throttles smoothly and felt the pull as the mains pushed the destroyer away from the lifepods at maximum acceleration.

It took a long, arcing turn to come onto his new course since he couldn't use the bow thrusters to point him in the right direction. Once he was on the proper track he reached over and flicked up four hoods, each safety wired down with a fine copper line, to expose four ordinary looking toggle switches. He flicked them up one at a time and watched on his main display for confirmation that four circular hatches had been blown clear from the stern of the ship.

EMERGENCY AUXILIARY THRUST AVAILABLE

The message flashed on his display twice before the red button to the left of the throttles lit up and began blinking. When he'd flicked up the secured switches the thrust nozzles of four massive solid rocket motors, which had been right under the hatches, had been exposed to space. The system was a last ditch failsafe in case the ship was in a decaying orbit with main propulsion failing. It would also give the *Blue Jacket* a tremendous burst of acceleration when the time came and he ignited the boosters.

Jackson pulled up the powerplant vitals on one of the station's displays and watched as his reactors began to heat up to their maximum allowable limits. He'd disabled all the emergency shutdown protocols and allowed them to cook. The coolant system was taxed beyond its limits as the steam pressure built and the power generating turbines that were within the closed system were also pushed to dangerous levels.

"I've got one last little surprise for you mother fuckers," Jackson said with a grim smile. "Neither of us is making it out of this system alive."

Within a few minutes he could see the alien ship on the thermal optics. He made a few more course corrections and let the computer lock onto the exact point he wanted to be at and turned over control. The thousands of fine corrections needed at the closure speed he was achieving meant it was impossible for him to manually steer the stricken ship. As the computer fully took over the helm he cinched his straps down and pulled up another menu on his right display. He began venting superheated steam from the reactor coolant system to alleviate the pressure on the turbines, still needing them functional for the next few minutes, and pulled up a precise range calculation between him and the target.

When he crossed the seventy thousand kilometer mark he closed his eyes and let out a cleansing breath. He quickly disabled the water jets that directly cooled the reactors, relying on the pressure already built up in the system to continue providing power even as the reactor temperatures began to climb again, now far past their redline. He smacked the flashing red button on his left and waited as the ship vibrated harshly with the ignition of the four mammoth rocket engines. With an explosive *whump* he was shoved violently back into his seat as the *Blue Jacket* leapt forward with renewed vigor.

The human visual cortex was still a relatively primitive processing center whose evolution had not kept pace with technology. It was never designed to interpret objects at the distances and speeds humans were now able to achieve with their machines. Jackson knew this on an intellectual level, but he was still surprised when the alien ship went from a relatively insignificant spec to suddenly filling the entire view. The closure was so fast that he didn't have time to swear or even brace himself, both useless actions, before the final impact.

****

He watched his sensor display with interest as lifepods began popping off the port and ventral surfaces of the badly damaged destroyer. He'd watched the entire battle unfold in the Nuovo Patria system and had thought Captain Wolfe might have actually been able to defeat the leviathan. It was with dismay that he watched the *Blue Jacket*, streaming atmosphere and missing an engine, disgorge her crew even as the alien ship began moving out of the system. The trick with the ten strategic missiles had been brilliant, but ultimately not enough.

Just before he was about to finalize his recordings and make a hasty retreat the engines on the *Blue Jacket* flared and the destroyer flew off towards the enemy. He watched with further interest as white hot gouts of flame burst from the ship's stern and she streaked like a missile towards the target. He held his breath until the inevitable and the destroyer slammed her ruined prow into the exposed interior of alien ship.

When his sensors were able to refocus on the pair of ships he could see the stern of the *Blue Jacket*, badly deformed, sticking out of the wound in the enemy ship, which was now spinning out of control. He was still considering if that would be enough to permanently disable the beast when one or more of the *Blue Jacket's* reactors went critical and his displays were washed out in a brilliant nuclear blast that made him blink even with the sensors attenuating themselves.

This time when the image resolved itself he knew the alien ship was not going anywhere. It was now in at least a dozen large pieces, each spiraling away from each other at high velocity.

It was over. For now.

"I can't believe you did it," he said. "You crazy son of a bitch." He finalized the data packet he'd been preparing and prepped a com drone, pausing a moment to add a final message.

"This is Pike," he said. "The enemy has been stopped in the Nuovo Patria system. I've uploaded all the data from the time the alien appeared to when the *Blue Jacket* was destroyed stopping it. I've tracked an object originating from the enemy ship moving away from the battle at high speed back towards the frontier. I have to assume it's delivering a message back to wherever it came from. I cannot intercept it from where I'm at.

"We have the remaining crew of the destroyer in lifepods within the system and we need rescue support immediately. I'm tracking the debris from the alien ship and will update when relief arrives."

Agent Pike added the message and fired off the newest generation of com drone towards the next system over. He knew there were two CIS Prowlers sitting less than ten hours' flight time away. He leaned back in his seat, the instruments of his Broadhead softly pinging as he considered what he'd just been witness to.

Chapter 23

"Where am I?" Jackson Wolfe asked. It had taken him over ten minutes to get his mouth working in order to speak the words. When he finally managed it, they rasped out of his throat like dry autumn leaves.

"Please just answer a few questions for us," a voice said from above him. He couldn't see anything but shifting shapes in the light. "Do you know who you are?"

"Jackson," he said. "Jackson Wolfe."

"What's the last thing you remember, Mr. Wolfe?" the voice asked. He paused, confused. It had been some years before anyone had addressed him as "mister."

"My crew," he croaked, ignoring the question. "What happened to my crew? And where am I?"

"Please relax for a moment."

He felt his body begin to incline upwards, only then realizing that he'd been lying down flat. After that the lights began to get brighter as he felt someone unwrapping something from around his head. Soon he was blinking, the brightness of the light torturously painful.

"Wait here," the middle-aged man standing next to the bed said to him, turning to leave. Squinting, Jackson was able to see he was firmly secured to the bed with straps, so he wasn't sure where the man thought he'd be going. It was another thirty minutes or so before anyone else came in. He had drifted in and out of sleep during the time so it was impossible to tell.

"Commander Wright," he said with a smile that hurt his cracked lips. "Civvies and long hair? You're out of uniform."

She favored him with a sad smile before sitting down beside the bed. "It's just Celesta right now," she said. "We've both been taken off active duty pending an investigation into events on the *Blue Jacket* and our eventual trials. You're to be first so I've been cooling my heels waiting to see if you would ever wake up."

"No good deed, eh?" he said with a mirthless laugh. "So how long was I out?"

"Nearly two weeks."

"More to the point, how the hell am I still alive?" Jackson asked, accepting the assistance from Celesta with the glass of water that seemed to weigh a ton.

"The short answer is that when you hit the alien ship the superstructure was sheared clean off the hull," she said. "The bridge was sealed and had a self-contained, emergency life support system so when the recovery team finally got around to tracking down the missing pieces of the ship they found you still secure in the helmsman's seat on the way out of the system at high velocity."

"Interesting," he said neutrally. "I would assume I didn't just need a bit of rest and fluids to survive that?"

"No," she said. "You were nearly dead. Collapsed lung, bruised heart, severe dehydration, severe concussion, skull fracture, blood sepsis from all the untreated wounds ... that's most of the more serious stuff."

"Which was the worst?"

"Are you sure you want to know this soon?" When he nodded she reached over him and pulled the blankets up and back so he could see that his left leg now ended about six inches below the knee.

"Well ... shit."

****

It was two agonizing months later when Jackson was finally discharged from the medical facility. He'd been given a cheap civilian suit to wear as he was not entitled to wear his uniform under his current status. If he was cleared of the charges, an unlikely event given that most of them were true, he would have his rank and status restored. From what he'd learned from the smarmy attorney the JAG had sent over, he'd be lucky if all that happened to him was a quiet discharge from service and a ride back to Earth. The more likely scenario was that he was staring down the barrel of a long prison sentence.

He had been isolated from the rest of the crew during his recovery, something that was just short of actual incarceration, and informed in no uncertain terms that his security clearance was revoked and any discussion of the previous mission would land him in a Fleet brig no matter how serious his injuries were.

It was only the fact that he was still heavily medicated that even allowed him to view those restrictions with a certain ambivalence. On one hand there was an almost overpowering sense of panic that so much time had passed without the Fleet fully mobilizing. On the other there was the relaxed feeling of being safe on Haven and under the influence of powerful narcotics. As they weaned him off the pain killers and his recuperation and rehabilitation period came to an end the concerns of what they'd found on the frontier came flooding back. For a while, when he first woke up and realized he wasn't dead, he was almost able to convince himself that it hadn't really happened. Something else must have happened to his ship and his subconscious had made up some fantastic story to explain away his obvious incompetence. One look at Celesta Wright's face, however, brought that illusion crashing down around him.

Now, as he walked with defiance toward the waiting Fleet vehicle—complete with armed Marine guards—he knew that he would have just one chance to try and rectify the situation.

****

"Mr. Wolfe, please be seated."

Jackson sat down next to his JAG-appointed attorney and looked over his inquiry board. Two senior captains, one fleet admiral who pulled considerable weight on Haven, and his nemesis: Admiral Alyson Winters. Of course.

"This board of inquiry is to determine if the formal charges against you will proceed and a full court martial convened," one of the captains was saying, reading off a tile in front of him. Jackson thought his name was Brabus, but he couldn't read the name tag from where he was seated. "The *only* things we will be discussing today are the specific charges. Any mitigating circumstances that may exist shall be left for the full court martial proceedings. Do you have any questions?"

"My client understands the nature of these proceedings, sir," the lawyer spoke up before Jackson could even open his mouth.

"Very well," the captain said. It was definitely Brabus. Jackson could remember meeting him during a conference on Jericho

Station. "Admiral Winters ... you initiated the charges against Mr. Wolfe. You may proceed."

"Thank you, Captain," Winters said, looking at Jackson the way a cobra might look at a rat. "Jackson Wolfe ... you are charged with disobeying a direct order from a superior officer, theft of Confederate property, namely the *TCS Blue Jacket*, dereliction of duty that resulted in the loss of life as well as the complete destruction of your ship, the aforementioned *TCS Blue Jacket*. Do you understand the charges against you?"

"My client—"

"Your client can speak for himself," Jackson said sharply, glaring at the lawyer. "Now sit there and shut up unless I request your counsel."

"Mr. Wolfe!" Brabus said sharply. "A little decorum, if you please."

"Captain Brabus ... I'm from Earth. Apparently I have no decorum, just ask Admiral Winters," Jackson said. "Furthermore, I'm technically a civilian right now and feel little need to adhere to military etiquette and protocol."

"Very well, Mr. Wolfe," Winters said in a voice that was so brittle it crackled. "How do you plead?"

"Before I answer, I have a question," Jackson said, looking her in the eye. "How the hell is it that I'm sitting here and you're up there without a care in the world? You and I both know that you should be sitting in a brig somewhere awaiting—"

"That's enough!" Fleet Admiral Jessop boomed. "Mr. Wolfe, you will answer the question. Guilty or not guilty. Those are the only two options you have in what comes out of your mouth next. We are well aware of the situation on the frontier—"

"I highly doubt that," Jackson interrupted.

"—but none of that is germane to your situation," Jessop finished. "Try to muster what little dignity you have left and let's get this over with. I think we both know this is going to a full court martial."

Before Jackson could answer, the double doors at the back of the chamber opened with a crash and he could hear multiple pairs of footsteps coming up the aisle. Thanks to the injuries to his neck he couldn't even attempt to turn and see who it was.

"Now what the hell is going on?" Brabus said irritably, rising out of his seat.

"Admiral Alyson Winters," a voice called loudly from behind him. "You are under arrest. Please stand and surrender yourself to the Marines behind me."

"What is the meaning of this?" Jessop nearly shouted, his face turning red. "What's the charge?"

"Treason," another voice said, this one much more familiar. "There are a few others that will be filed later, but that's the only one she needs to know for now."

"And just who the hell are you?" Jessop asked, trying to reassert control on the proceedings as they spiraled into chaos.

"My name is Aston Lynch, aide to Senator Augustus Wellington," Pike said as he walked around the table. Jackson just stared as the arrogant prick that was Aston Lynch walked up to the bench with a self-satisfied smirk. "But I'm just the messenger. Winters is being arrested under the authority of CENTCOM Chief of Staff Marcum. Here's the paperwork." Lynch/Pike handed Jessop a sheaf of hardcopy documents and waited as he shuffled through them, his jaw dropping lower and lower as he read.

"Take her," Jessop said quietly, leaning back in his seat as the Marines walked up and grabbed a gibbering Alyson Winters roughly and slapped restraints on her.

"Thank you for the permission, Admiral," Pike said sardonically, "but we weren't exactly asking."

Jessop cleared his throat, looking at Jackson with obvious distaste, "*Captain* Jackson Wolfe, under the authority of CENTCOM Chief of Staff Joseph Marcum and President Caleb McKellar all charges against you are dropped and your rank within the Confederate Starfleet is reinstated, effective immediately. You are ordered to appear before the Chief of Staff at eleven hundred hours tomorrow."

"Thank you, Admiral," Jackson said, not bothering to stand while not in uniform. He watched as Pike leaned in and whispered something into Winters' ear. Whatever it was, it scared the hell out of her. Her expression transformed from one of anger and confusion to one of genuine fear. She looked at Jackson with a haunted expression. He smiled largely and waved to her, much to the disgust of Fleet Admiral Jessop.

After the chaos had died down and people were filing out, Jackson hauled himself out of the chair and turned to leave. He was still not fully mobile and he had to be careful how quickly he turned. As he was leaving, intent on making sure that the charges against Celesta were also nullified, he passed a smirking Agent Pike standing just outside the chamber door.

"Interesting timing, Mr. Lynch," Jackson said.

"Oh, you have no idea, Captain," Pike answered, breaking character. "I've had to sit on that for a few weeks waiting for this exact moment ... and it was every bit as glorious as I'd dreamed it would be. Did you see her face? Anyway, our analysts were going through the com platform logs and figured out pretty quickly what she'd done with your status reports. Normally that sort of thing would be overlooked, but when we have nearly two billion people dead, powerful people demand answers. Winters was stupid enough to assume just because she deleted her local copies that the evidence of her tampering was erased."

"I have to say I'm a bit concerned at the leisurely pace things seem to be moving," Jackson said, walking slowly beside the CIS spook. "I've been in medical for months. What the hell are we doing about this new threat?"

"*Seems to be moving* is the key phrase there, Captain," Pike said. "We're moving on things, and quickly. But it's going to take some effort to change the culture at CENTCOM and in Starfleet. Right now CIS is spearheading operations until Fleet is back on war-fighting footing ... if it even ever was. I'll let the Chief of Staff fill you in. It's a bit above my paygrade, to be honest."

"I doubt that prevents you from learning about it though," Jackson said sourly.

"We all have our unsavory habits," Pike smiled before his face morphed into the most serious expression he'd ever seen on the man. "Thank you, Captain, for not giving up. A lesser commander would have taken any excuse to turn tail and run when facing an enemy like that. There's no telling how many lives you saved."

"Yeah ... all we'll know for sure is how many I didn't," Jackson said, the full implications of the alien attack beginning to sink in.

"Don't lose heart. We're going to need you," Pike said, looking around as if suddenly bored with the conversation. "I left a little gift in your room. Think of it as returning the favor. I gotta run, take care of yourself."

Even with Jackson observing him directly it seemed the agent just sort of dissolved into the background, blending into the sparse crowd and disappearing.

When he got back to his room in billeting he saw there was more than one gift waiting for him. The first thing he noticed was a brand new set of dress blacks decked out with his rank, name, and awards. Sure enough, a full issue of dress uniforms and utilities were hanging in the closet. There was also a wooden box on the desk with a note on it.

This was floating around on the bridge when I found you spinning out of the Nuovo Patria system. Figured you'd want it back. Do you think Singh would make me one?

Pike

Inside the box was his 1911 pistol. He'd had it in his utility pocket when he'd taken the *Blue Jacket* and rammed her into the alien ship. He picked up the weapon and ran his hand down a long gouge in the slide, apparently the only damage it had suffered, and thought back on everything that had happened.

With the head trauma he'd suffered he actually had no real memory of the event that finally eliminated the enemy threat. The last thing he remembered was ordering the crew to abandon ship. He'd get strange glimpses of things when his mind hovered in that state between fully aware and dreaming, but they were so bizarre at times he had difficulty believing they were actually memories. In one of them he even kissed Lieutenant Davis, something that would never have happened in reality.

He placed the weapon back in the box, his right foot jarring something that had been stuffed up under the desk as he did. When he bent down a wide smile creased his face. A case of genuine Kentucky bourbon was nestled down next to the trash can. He pulled one of the bottles out and saw it was from the area's most legendary distiller, far better than the stuff Singh had been able to get him. He set the square bottle on the desk, admiring the black label that hadn't changed in centuries, and scrounged around for a glass.

Sitting heavily in the chair, he raised his glass in silent salute to the hundreds of spacers who hadn't come back from the *Blue Jacket's* final voyage, and then went about trying to forget everything that had happened since the destroyer had departed Jericho Station nearly five months ago.

****

"How's the leg, son?"

"Strangely enough, it itches, sir," Jackson said.

"I've heard of that," Chief of Staff Marcum said. "Phantom itch, I believe they call it. You still reach down to scratch the prosthetic when it happens?"

"Yes, sir," Jackson said. "Highly unsatisfying, sir."

Marcum laughed genuinely at that and gestured for him to sit down in one of the overstuffed chairs that were in the office.

"I'm sorry you had to go through that ridiculous puppet theater with Fleet Admiral Jessop," Marcum said, pouring three drinks and handing two of the glasses out without even asking if either of his guests wanted a drink before noon on a Tuesday.

"That was partially my fault," Senator Wellington said, sipping at the obscenely expensive Scotch and nodding in appreciation. "Well ... more specifically my aide, Aston Lynch. You've had the pleasure of meeting the man, haven't you, Captain?"

"Yes, sir, I have," Jackson said carefully.

"Don't worry," Wellington said. "I know who he really is. CIS administrator thought he was being sneaky putting Pike in my office, but once I figured out who he was the benefit has far outweighed the risks of having a spy walking around within my staff. Pike may be an enormous pain in the ass, but he can dig up information like nobody's business."

"To the *Blue Jacket*, and to her lost crew," Marcum said, raising his glass. "May they rest in peace." The other two also raised their glass and saluted. "Now ... to business. I've authorized the bump in your security clearance, Captain, and I want you working with CIS for the time being while we figure out what, exactly, we're going to do about this new threat. There are many considerations, mostly political, that may necessarily delay our response, but I want you working with the analysts and reviewing all the sensor logs you managed to save from your ship.

"I know that's not an appealing prospect, reliving all of it again, but it's vital to our efforts. You've not only defeated the enemy, albeit at great cost, but you're now the de facto expert in tactics and battle planning."

"That's somewhat distressing, sir," Jackson said. "Much of what we did was simply because our primary response wouldn't work by virtue of the ship's weaponry being in such bad repair. If I had working laser banks I can't say I'd have ever thought to employ the mag-cannons."

"What about that trick with the Mark VIIIs you were carrying?" Wellington asked. "I never did fully understand that."

"That?" Jackson asked. "That was a desperate move which, shockingly, paid off. We knew from our last few engagements that the cannons were effective, but simply weren't inflicting enough damage given the enemy's size and ability to heal. I had Chief Engineer Singh load up the payload bay of each missile with a powerful binary explosive we were able to synthesize with the chemicals we had on hand.

"When we made our final turn we lobbed them out behind the ship facing the opposite way we were flying. While the *Blue Jacket's* engines were providing enough thermal interference to hide it, each missile burned two complete stages, decelerating them along our same course. Once we fired the cannons and passed the target, all its attention was on us. The missiles slowly drifted into the area behind us, completely unnoticed since they were flying cold. Commander Wright had programmed them to turn and seek out any hull breaches in the enemy and aim for that spot, burning their final stage.

"We actually didn't think it had worked. It turns out the first two stages had decelerated them more than we anticipated and they simply arrived late to the party." Jackson looked up and saw the two men were actually leaning forward in their seats, hanging on his every word.

"As I said," he shrugged, "a desperate gamble. It came at a high cost since we flew right into the enemy's trap. They'd baited us to approach the planet and the plasma blast we were hit with was on an order of magnitude more powerful than any of the shots they had taken up to that point. It literally vaporized the *Blue Jacket's* prow and forward compartments. They meant to take us out, but the old *Raptor*-class was too tough for them to manage it with one shot."

"Stunning," Marcum said quietly. "Whether you know it or not ... like it or not ... you're vital to this effort, Captain. Just the experience of true combat ... I would never make light of the losses by saying I wished I was there, but your account of the experience is ... intoxicating. Fleet has forgotten what it is to be warriors first and foremost. CENTCOM is infested with administrative lackeys like Winters and Jessop, and neither of them has ever even stepped foot on the bridge of a starship while underway. That will all have to change if we're going to stand a chance against this sort of enemy."

"We'll also need to bring the other numbered fleets into the fold, sir," Jackson said, speaking before his brain could stop his mouth.

"Oh?"

"Black Fleet simply isn't equipped to mount any sort of defense against aliens who can wipe out planets and fire directed plasma bursts like the one we encountered, sir."

"That's about to change as well, Captain," Marcum said with a grim smile.

"Indeed," Wellington said. "Everything is about to change. After hundreds of years, humanity is going back to war."

Epilogue:

"You're absolutely sure about this man?"

"Quite sure, Mr. President," Joseph Marcum said, leaning back in the chair and waiting patiently while President McKellar read through the brief.

"I mean, I appreciate what he's been through and what he managed to accomplish—" McKellar hesitated.

"But?" Marcum prompted.

"But I could have a hard time selling this to the Senate," McKellar said. "A captain with a long record of disciplinary actions against him ... a suspected alcoholic. Let's be honest, Joseph, he's the poster boy for those who want to eliminate the Fleet's Earth Commissioning Program."

"Sir," Marcum said, his face darkening, "we could very well be in a fight for the survival of the species if what the analysts are saying is even half true. The bigotry of certain politicians aside, I need Captain Wolfe at the forefront of this. He has more combat experience than every other officer in Fleet combined, which isn't saying much, and despite his self-deprecating nature he's a gifted tactician and a born leader. The fact that he was able to defeat this alien ship with an antique *Raptor*-class destroyer and a crew I wouldn't trust to fly a garbage scow speaks volumes."

"Nobody here is saying he isn't qualified *because* he's from Earth," McKellar said, far too quickly and in a voice pitched up an octave. "I'm just letting you know what obstacles might be ahead."

"With all due respect, Mr. President," Marcum said, choosing his words carefully, "the Terran fleet has been a political institution for far too long. The actions of Winters and Jessop prove that. Winters alone cost us millions of lives with her game playing. This needs to change, and quickly, if we're to have a chance."

"I'll do what I can, of course," McKellar said lamely, shrinking away from even the perception of prejudice, like any politician.

"Of course," Marcum repeated. "If you'll excuse me, sir, I have work to do. We all have work to do."

****

"Are you feeling well, Senator?"

"Space travel disagrees with me and this is the fifth stop we've made on this sightseeing tour," Augustus Wellington said brusquely. "Just show us what you have, Doctor."

"Right this way, sir," Dr. Eugene Allrest said, gesturing towards the open doors at the end of the corridor. "We've been keeping the samples submerged in liquid helium for the time being. Whenever they come within ten meters of each other they begin to react and try to move towards each other. We lost one researcher before we understood what was happening."

"My condolences," Wellington said in a tone of voice that indicated he could care less.

"Here it is," Allrest said as they walked into a large chamber dominated by an enormous cylindrical tank that was filled with fluid. In the center of that floated something that looked like a discolored mass of medical waste. "From what we've been able to tell so far, this seems to be the central processing unit."

"It doesn't look like any processor I've ever seen," Wellington said, crossing his arms against the chill in the room.

"Well, no," Allrest said. "The samples we've been given would indicate that they are from a biologically constructed machine."

"You mean a life form?" Wellington asked sarcastically.

"I'm not willing to make that determination at this time," Allrest said stiffly. "While some of my colleagues may—"

"I don't give a shit what you eggheads are arguing about amongst yourselves," Wellington waved him off. "This is the same damn argument I've heard about four times already. What can you tell me about what happened on the surface of the planets this thing was visiting? That's you guys, right? I keep getting all the individual labs mixed up."

"Ah, yes ... of course," Allrest said, now flustered. "Upon arriving over a planet it appears the main construct would deploy smaller landers to the surface that contained segmented burrowers. The people of Podere were calling them 'worms.' These burrowers would ingest raw material, organic and inorganic both, and secrete a substance that Captain Wolfe referred to as a 'slick' in his reports.

"It is the same material that was routed via ducts to all parts of the main construct itself. From what we've been able to determine, this substance is the base building block for the technology used in its construction. The cells of the substances can be manipulated to create anything it would need. It's how the construct was able to repair itself so rapidly."

"I see," Wellington said neutrally. "This substance ... it shows no signs of intelligence when left on its own?"

"None that we're aware of," Allrest said with a frown. "Has there been new information from the colony worlds the construct has been to?"

"That's above your paygrade, Doctor," Wellington said. "Just concentrate on the specific tasks you've been given and try to refrain from wild speculation. The project managers will compile the results so that personal biases don't influence the overall findings on this effort."

"It was just an idle curiosity—"

"We'll be heading back to our ship now," Wellington said, walking past the scientist without so much as a head nod.

"I guess I've been dismissed," Allrest said sullenly.

"The Senator has a lot on his mind," the other man remaining in the room said. "He's been very impressed with your work here."

"Thank you," Allrest said. "I didn't quite catch your name."

"Aston Lynch. Here's my contact information ... I'll be in touch to stay abreast of your results. Good day, Doctor."

Pike hurried out of the room after handing the insufferable scientist a card with a few different methods of contact printed on it. He hastened down the long corridor in time to see Senator Wellington waiting impatiently by a lift car that would take them down to the secure docking arm. They'd been there for less than three hours, hardly worth the expense of the flight. But Wellington had been losing interest with each successive stop. The recovered pieces of the alien ship had been sent to different parts of the Confederacy to maintain objectivity, but Pike was beginning to wonder if their best scientific minds would be able to glean anything of actual use by this method.

Pure research was all well and good, but they were going to need practical applications sooner than later. Specifically: How do we kill them.

The pair rode in silence and continued to not speak as they strode through the security checkpoints and back out to the gangway that led up to the ship the dock crew had been gawking at since their arrival: a CIS Broadhead.

"It seems that these geeks are too indoctrinated to see past their own noses," Wellington said, flopping down on one of the plush seats in the lounge area once Pike had sealed the hatch. "No crew onboard, almost entirely constructed of biological materials ... how is it that I'm able to reach the obvious conclusion here and they're all bickering among themselves about if it is or isn't a life form?"

"We are keeping them fairly isolated right now. Once all the information is looked at in its entirety they'll come to some more useful conclusions," Pike said as he initiated the ship's prestart sequence.

"How did the operation on Xi'an go?"

"Like clockwork," Pike said, sitting across from the Senator. "The Prowlers flew in and nuked all four anomalies from orbit."

"*Anomalies,*" Wellington snorted. "These sons of bitches had four ships being constructed on the surface of that planet. Used our own people and cities as building material. We had better get our shit together and fast if we want to have any chance of stopping these bastards. How many planets were wiped out?"

"Four were a complete loss, but Wolfe arrived in time to save Podere from being the fifth," Pike said.

"Who else knows about the two planets that were eliminated before Xi'an?"

"Practically nobody," Pike shrugged. "That level of clearance is only held by a few people. The only reason I know about it is because I'm the one who found them. The Alliance had colonized them in secret and without approval from the Confederacy. It's plausible that they alerted these aliens to our presence."

"Maybe," Wellington grunted. "It won't matter if they did. We can't afford to alienate the Alliance right now and they're a touchy bunch. If we accuse them of causing this it wouldn't surprise me if they withdrew support."

"I'd hope this new threat would set aside the old animosities and the pointless posturing," Pike said.

"Look at you ... spook philosopher," Wellington said sardonically. "I hope you're right, Agent Pike. I hope this new threat doesn't just bring back our worst traits. Speaking of which, how are those idiots Winters and Jessop liking their new accommodations?"

"It didn't seem they were liking them at all when last I checked," Pike said, climbing out of his seat when the computer chimed to let him know they were ready to depart. "Winters especially seemed to be taking to life in a penal colony rather badly."

"Good, good," Wellington said with a self-satisfied smile. "Alright, Mr. Lynch. Let's get this thing moving and get back to Haven. We've got a lot of work to do and very little time to do it in."

"At once, Senator," Pike said, tossing Wellington a mocking salute before walking up to the flight deck and slipping into the pilot's seat.

****

"This is truly remarkable, Dr. Tanaka," Jackson said as he and the diminutive scientist walked along the corridor. "I had no idea this facility even existed."

"Very few people do," Tanaka said. "For obvious reasons. We've moved most of our heavy R&D off Haven and to this facility, mostly over security concerns, but given recent events being hidden may not be such a bad thing."

"No argument there," Jackson said. "Tsuyo Corporation must have started on this facility decades ago. A full shipyard inside an asteroid along with the labs? Amazing."

"I'm glad you appreciate the difficulty of the endeavor," Tanaka said, sounding genuinely pleased. "Tell me, Captain, what do you know of the Tsuyo Corporation ... other than the fact we seem to make everything?" The last line was delivered with a short, startling laugh.

"Not much," Jackson admitted. "I know you're quite secretive and seem to control much more than just the sale of your own tech. I suppose it's only natural that you wield so much influence given the fact you developed the warp drive."

"My predecessors, centuries ago, had tried to coin the phrase 'T-Drive' when it was first implemented," Tanaka said with a smile. "But 'warp drive' was so embedded in the culture that it stuck. I think you'd be surprised at that term's origin. One of the little known truths, however, is that Tsuyo did not develop the *warp* drive, as you say. We simply adapted it."

"Adapted it?"

"Yes. The original Tsuyo prototype was developed by reverse engineering a crashed alien vessel that had been found on Jupiter's moon, Europa, early in the twenty-first century," Tanaka explained. "Tsuyo funded the expedition to harvest the vessel and was thus granted exclusive rights to the technology. We've improved the design over the centuries, but all warp drives can still trace their lineage back to that wrecked craft."

"I had no idea about that," Jackson said, slightly awed. "Do we know whose ship it was?"

"No," Tanaka said. "The original recordings of that mission show that the ship had apparently been abandoned for some time before the robotic probes found it. No remains to speak of, either. We can make certain assumptions about the nature of the beings by examining the ship itself, but we have not encountered that species since we ourselves left the Solar System."

"Not all of us left," Jackson said absently.

"Of course, Captain," Tanaka said with a slight bow. "I meant no disrespect. My point is that even from the very beginning we knew we were not alone. In our arrogance we allowed the myth that the miracle of faster than light travel was a human invention and that we were the masters of all we surveyed. I believe the Universe just gave us a costly lesson in humility."

"That's as elegant a way to say it as I've heard yet," Jackson said. "As much as I've enjoyed the tour and the history lesson, Doctor, I have to believe there's another reason I've been brought to an ultra-secret Tsuyo testing facility."

"We're almost there, Captain," Tanaka said, gesturing up ahead where the corridor changed from alloy bulkheads to a transparent tunnel.

As they crossed the point where Jackson could gaze out of the acrylic tunnel he let out a gasp. Lying below him in a sealed-off, pressurized bay was the hull of a starship, but unlike any he had ever seen. Human ships all seemed to follow generally the same design methodology in that they were long, tubular, and bristling with antennas, weapons, and engines.

This ship, however, was sleek. She was also much wider than she was tall, her lines roughly arrowhead shaped in the front, tapering in at the middle, and flaring out again at the stern. Two enormous main engine nacelles were mounted on pylons that were tucked in much closer to the hull than any other ship he'd seen.

"Impressive, is she not?"

"Beautiful," Jackson breathed. "This is a real starship? Not just a mockup?

"Fully operational, the first of her kind," Tanaka nodded. "We began laying the hull as soon as we were alerted to the threat on the frontier. All of the technology that Tsuyo has been developing here has culminated in her design."

"She isn't as big as my old ship," Jackson observed.

"Yet she is still a destroyer, not a light cruiser or a frigate," Tanaka said. "Your *Raptor*-class vessel was in service for nearly half a century. This ship is half the tonnage yet three times as fast and boasting nearly ten times the firepower."

"What have you called her?"

"She'll be the first of a new generation of human starships," Tanaka said as he looked down upon the sleek vessel. "Built for one purpose: War. While this ship hasn't been named yet, in honor of your victory in the opening battle we've named this line of destroyers the *Starwolf*-class. Fast, deadly, and overpowering in a pack. The reason we asked you here, Captain, was to show you this so that you know steps are already being taken. We will be ready when the enemy returns."

"I truly hope so, Dr. Tanaka," Jackson said as he looked down at the warship. Even with all its advancements, he knew they were in for a long, hard fight with no guarantee of victory. If they were to win, it would take more than new gadgets and flashy technology. Did humanity even have the will to fight anymore, even if it was for their own survival? Only time would tell.

Thank you for reading *Warship.*

If you enjoyed the book the story will continue with:

Call to Arms, Book Two of the Black Fleet Trilogy.

Connect with me on Facebook and Twitter:

www.facebook.com/Joshua.Dalzelle

@JoshuaDalzelle

Also, check out my Amazon page to see other works including the bestselling
Omega Force Series:

www.amazon.com/author/joshuadalzelle

From the author:

Some of you likely bought this book after reading my other science fiction series: Omega Force. For those of you who haven't, thank you for taking a chance on a new author and welcome aboard. I thought it would be useful to give a little bit of background on this story as it is a bit of a departure from what I've done up to this point.

This trilogy is actually based on a story I wrote in my early 20's while living in the dorms at Ellsworth AFB. That original novel was extremely long, convoluted, and not as cohesive a story as I would have liked. Black Fleet is a series of three books that distills that original story down to its bare essence and refines the scope and focus of the tale. The result is, I hope, a hard military scifi story that has a bit more grit than Omega Force without being "dark."

The technology represented in this book is based on research, and in many cases existing prototypes, of tech that we have today. Borrowing heavily from the work of Miguel Alcubierre and his "warp" drive, the VASIMR engines developed by Ad Astra Rocket, and a host of technologies we have available now I wanted to keep this story free of any fantastical elements. I also stripped down a lot of existing military traditions and rank structure to create what I envisioned a fleet of the future would use. It's not supposed to be an exact copy of the U.S. Navy, but I wanted the similarities to be there. So ... thank you again for reading and I hope you'll continue on to the next Black Fleet story. For those of you wondering about the future of the Omega Force Series, I'm writing book seven even as this book is being released.

Cheers!

Josh

Made in the USA
San Bernardino, CA
21 March 2015